MORTAL DREADS

A COLLECTION OF SHORT FICTION

JEFFRY DWIGHT

PRAISE FOR JEFFRY DWIGHT

"Jeffry Dwight's vision is smart, wise, rational, and heart wrenching. There's a numinous glimmer of otherness in the dark; longing and terrible wonder. Most of all, there's a true exploration of humanity. These stories must be read!"
  —**Vera Nazarian** on *Mortal Dreads*

"This is the most beautiful story I've ever read."
  —**Martin H. Greenberg** on "Lest Winter Come"

"A great story, well-told. Pitch-perfect."
  —**Mike Resnick** on "Miracle at Devil's Crick"

"Loved the twisted ending."
  —**Dave Felts**, *Tangent Online*, on "Out of Memory"

"A veiled commentary on the future of biological and social engineering."
  —**Dave Felts**, *Tangent Online*, on "Rite of Passage"

"[T]his story is one of my favorites from the book [*Bones of the World*]. I don't think anyone who has on occasion pondered his or her mortality and the what-is-it-all-about of life will be left untouched. The main character, Pug, is a man of vision and impact. The things he does, and the things his descendants do, have an irrevocable impact on all of humanity. But that's not what the story is about. It's about life, death, hopes and dreams, love and more. Nice job."
  —**Dave Felts**, sfreader.com, on "They Went Up"

MORTAL DREADS
A collection of short fiction
by
Jeffry Dwight

Trade Paperback Edition

ISBN: 978-0-9669698-7-0

August 1, 2021

Published by SFF Net Select.

CONTENTS

Preface   ix

Dying He Dreams, Dreaming He Dies   1
Miracle at Devil's Crick   59
Waiting for Grampa to Die   75
Rite of Passage   85
Out of Memory   117
They Went Up   131
Extraction   157
Lest Winter Come   167
Barth and the Dragon   175
Lady, Man, Rose   187
Tale of the Blind Boy   193
Breathe to Me of Summer   207
Jere   215
Of Flesh and Blood   223
Snowball's Chance   231
The Night of His Refleshing   241
Soul Songs   263
On the Train to Oxford   299

Prior Publications   307
About the Author   309

For Danny Lee

Le cœur a ses raisons, que la raison ne connaît pas.

PREFACE

Authors of short story collections share a common understanding: You are guaranteed at least one sale, but only if your mother is still alive. Spared from commercial greed, I selected my favorites rather than those that might garner the highest critical approval. In these pages, you'll find tales that have the forms of science fiction, fantasy, horror, or humor, but the genre is only a gloss—these stories are about people, not gadgets or ghosts.

You may not like these stories. You may find them abhorrent or repulsive. My grammar may be faulty; my scansion may limp; my humor may fall flat. You may not understand a single thing you read, or you may understand and reject it all. You may be surprised and delighted. But if I have not lived in these pages, if I have not breathed and wept and gasped in wonder, if I have not loved and felt joy, sorrow, happiness, and despair, if I have not said anything beyond a chronicle of events, then I have said nothing at all. And if I do live in these pages, recording those things that have meaning for me, then I have lived twice.

My fondest hope is that you do, too—but remember always that incarnation is a diminution, and the visions I mean to share may not be the ones you see in your head.

Words have all power and none. A concept or a feeling may leap from brain to brain, but the transmission is a transmutation; the message sent is seldom the message received. The numinous is illusive and elusive, like the writhing tendrils of a disintegrating dream. Reality becomes a spheroid, with the reader as the still spot in the center. The whole spins madly, careening through the cosmos at crazy, impossible speeds, yet from the inside it is only a walker's woods, a measured stride, a late winter day, a cold, weak sun, and a sense that all is not what it seems.

Transcendence and epiphanies are at best approximations of truth—and if this rule holds for real life, how can fiction hope to illumine anything? It cannot compete; it can only enhance, by letting us step aside for a moment, briefly live lives not our own, generating truths that actually originate in the reader.

Sometimes we close our eyes because the light is too bright.

I whistle up worlds at a whim, and populate them with characters who act out for you the most important moments of their lives. There is always an untold backstory, and always an unwritten next chapter, but I offer only the slivers encapsulated by each tale. You dive into the events, laughing or crying with the characters, and resurface somehow changed.

What price, imagination?

Each step we take toward something is a step away from something else, even if we walk in circles. We are linked inextricably with our past selves, but we can never be the same person we were yesterday, or a year ago. The agglutination of experience necessitates change, even if only in perspective.

Sometimes we rush, sometimes we linger, but holding still is the cruelest illusion of all.

There is no magic we don't make for ourselves. No one can show another the true face hidden in the stone; even the sculptor is limited by his own vision. We are defined as much by what we reject as by what we hold holy. What direction are you going if you are running away from everything?

Sometimes we close our eyes because we cannot bear to look.

There is no theurgy; there are but words, and fiction is just a complicated way of lying in order to tell the truth. These particular words, which I now scatter to the winds, become dead things as they leave my hands. What resurrections they may suffer, what lives they may lead in the minds of others, I can never know. I am lessened by the act of their birthing, for I am also a dark celebrant at their deaths. Cognitive dissonance can be an art form.

Mortal dreads—ungently balanced by enrapturement—may loosen the tie-strings of your soul, either letting light in, or letting it out. That's your call. My job is done.

—**Jeffry Dwight**, Murphy, Texas, 2021

DYING HE DREAMS, DREAMING HE DIES

Michael awoke three feet above his bed, gave a startled yelp, and fell down into his body. The CEEG fluctuated wildly for a minute, then returned to displaying slow, regular theta rhythms. *Another puzzle for the neurologists*, he thought. The monitor was a joke to him. It didn't reveal anything important.

Michael climbed out of his body and slid through the door into the corridor. The nurses' station was quiet, deserted except for the telltales and monitors that flashed and beeped softly to themselves. At the far end of the corridor, an orderly wearing headphones moved a mop in lazy circles. The scent of antiseptic and soap floated through the hall.

What had awakened him?

He concentrated for a moment, then nodded to himself. Down the hall. Mrs. Sobarsky.

He stuck his head through the door of room 712. Mrs. Sobarsky glanced up and smiled at him. Not just in his direction, or at something near him, but directly at him. And although she sat smiling in her chair, she also lay motionless on the bed.

"Ah," he said, stepping the rest of the way through the door. "It finally happened, eh? Good evening, Mrs. Sobarsky." He ignored the body on the bed.

She pursed her lips. "You're not God," she said.

"No, I'm Michael. Michael Hansen. From down the hall."

"Are you dead, too?"

Michael paused. "You know you're dead?" He searched her face for emotion, but found none. "You don't seem upset by it."

"Upset? Why should I be upset? You get old, you get sick, you die, you meet God, you go to heaven. Only I don't understand why I'm still. . . ." She groped for words, then sighed.

Suddenly Michael understood. She drew her belief structure from one of the standard patterns. He knew how it would turn out. "Well, if it's any comfort," he said, "you won't be here much longer."

"Yes?"

"Heaven's busy, you know. They have a lot of work to do, and you can't expect God himself to attend to each dying person, right? But they usually respond within a few minutes."

"You speak as if you've been through this before."

"Not personally, no, but I've seen it."

"Are you dead?"

"Not quite. I'm in a coma at the moment. It's a special case, I think. Well, it's been nice meeting you."

"How can you be almost dead?"

Michael pointed at a bright spot of light growing in the corner of the room. "Here are your friends now, Mrs. Sobarsky. Have a nice afterlife."

She looked into the light. Her face grew enraptured.

"Hosanna!" she said. And, "I'm coming, Jesus!" She levitated from the chair, floated into the light.

Michael shrugged and watched her fray, turn transparent, and dissipate, taking the light with her. "Ghosts," he said to himself after she was gone. "They'll believe anything."

He sank through the floor, drifted toward the back of the hospital. Ambulance after ambulance pulled up to the ER. He touched a paramedic's mind lightly, reading only the surface thoughts. A bus accident. Bad. It would be a busy night.

SARAH WELLER'S vision grayed out. The pain receded to a great distance. As time passed—whether seconds, minutes or hours, she had no way of telling—the pain seemed even further away, as if it were no longer her body suffering, but someone else's. The sounds of the emergency room faded, too, until at length she floated alone in a limitless gray space.

There was no sound, but it wasn't exactly silent. At the edge of her perception, far-off and indistinct, she knew there were things that, if she concentrated on them, she would call sounds. But she didn't concentrate on them; she was content to let them remain unrealized potentials.

There was no color except gray, and no texture to the grayness. It was neither hot nor cold, comfortable nor uncomfortable. No tables, no chairs, no walls, no horizon, no sky. Just gray, like a mist. She felt as if she were at the center of creation: A word, a gesture, a hint, would be enough to turn the grayness into solidity, make objects from ideas. But she didn't care to experiment. She felt a sense of peace mixed with infinite patience. No curiosity, no desire to explore, no sense of time's passage.

She might have hung in the grayness—bodiless, incurious —for either moments or centuries. She had no way to tell. But eventually she became aware of a light source in front of her, and she experienced a sense of motion toward it.

There was no way to mark her motion—no landmarks, no mileposts, no wind, no inertia—but she knew she was moving. As she floated toward the light, the grayness seemed to narrow, to focus itself. It was less gray ahead of her, darker to the sides and behind. The contrast became sharper, and her velocity increased. Now the grayness had become a gradually narrowing tunnel, infinitely wide and black at the edge, infinitely narrow and white in the center, and she was rushing toward the center.

"That's a trick of your brain chemistry," said a voice. "A fairly common experience, really, induced by the massive release of endorphins at the moment of death and a simultaneous inability of the brain to process incoming information."

Sarah heard the voice, but couldn't respond. She flew down the tunnel toward the brightness, drawn by forces she didn't understand. She was close enough now to see that there was something beyond the end of the tunnel. Vague shapes, cloaked in painfully bright light, beckoned to her, urging her on.

"That's an illusion," resumed the voice dispassionately. "Freud would call it wish-fulfillment. Other psychiatric systems have somewhat less complimentary names for it, but I prefer to believe the best."

Sarah ignored the voice and concentrated on the figures ahead of her. One of them turned fully toward her, and she recognized her father's face. He was smiling, holding out his arms. Beside him stood Sarah's mother, her eyes brimming with tears of love and welcome. "Daddy!" Sarah cried. "Mother! I'm coming, I'm coming!"

"Very touching," commented the voice. "Predictable, but still touching. If you were religious, you should soon see a stronger light than the others. Christ, Brahma, the Californian God-of-the-Week, it doesn't matter. Warmer than warmth, more loving than love, more comforting than comfort, and so forth."

Sarah felt a twinge of exasperation as the voice continued to provide dry commentary on her experiences. This was all wrong. The voice was ruining it. She fixed her attention firmly on her parents. She was almost there! Her father's smile broadened, his arms opened wider. A yearning, an inconsolable longing, built up in her heart.

"Look," said the voice, "you're just setting yourself up for disappointment. Are you sure you want to do this?"

Sarah shook her head. That damned voice. Bothering her. Interfering. "Stop it!" she said. "Just stop it."

SARAH SAT on the bench seat of a booth in a crowded, noisy restaurant. The waiter stood at the end of the table, order pad in hand, and looked at her impatiently. "Yes?"

"She'll have tea," said the dry voice. "I'll have a beer. Heineken, green bottle."

"Right," said the waiter, and turned away.

Sarah blinked and looked across the table. The man sitting there smiled, lifted an eyebrow, and nodded a greeting. "I'm Michael," he said, "and you are...?"

"Sarah," she said automatically. The man's voice was dry, urbane, and she recognized it instantly as the voice she had heard in the tunnel.

For a second, she was too stunned to react. Then disappointment and rage filled her. "How dare you? Send me back!"

"Back to the illusion? But you asked me to stop it for you, and I did."

"You idiot, I meant stop *interfering*. Send me back! Send me back right now!"

Michael shrugged. "If you insist."

SARAH BURST through the light at the end of the tunnel and leaped toward her father's arms. But there was no one there. The image of her father, which had seemed so solid just moments before, dissolved into gray tatters, shredded like mist. Her mother reached out a hand, her eyes still glimmering with tears, and broke apart into a thousand gray fragments, spinning off into the distance.

"No!" Sarah's cry was almost a scream. The light faded, and gray mist crept in from all directions until once again she found herself alone in a featureless, textureless, emotionless, timeless place. Her grief faded with the light, to be replaced with a vast numbness. It was like being wrapped in cotton in a dark room.

"Here, don't do that," said the voice. "Don't retreat again."

A hand emerged into her field of view. The hand was not visibly connected to an arm, but she had a sense that the arm was somewhere else, that the hand was poking into her private universe the way one might reach through the slit in a drape.

"Don't do what?" she asked.

"The trip, the hallucination, is over. Your brain is dead now. You can build your own little world of numbness and resentment, locking me out, or you can talk to me. In the long run, I think it's better to skip the tunnel of light experience, but some people seem to require it. Of course, if they manage to resuscitate you now, you'll forget most of this."

"Who are you? Are you . . . God?"

"Don't be silly. Take my hand and come out of there."

SARAH TOOK a sip of tea and studied the man sitting across from her. "I'm really confused," she said.

Michael smiled. "What's so confusing?"

"Well, first—where are we?"

Michael took a swig of beer and shrugged. "I have no idea." He looked around. "The decor suggests approximately ten years ago, maybe twenty. It's your memory, not mine. Don't you recognize it?"

"My memory?"

"Look around, Sarah."

She did. "Oh, my God. It's Lenny's Grill."

"You remember it now?"

"Of course. We used to come here all the time when I was in college. But I haven't thought of this place in years! How did we get here? I was in some sort of gray place . . . then I saw your hand . . . we talked for a moment . . . and now. . . ."

"We're not really here. This is a memory. Like a movie set. Built up from your mind. It was a very clear memory, so I lifted it from your mind and put us into it. It's better than floating in nowhere, isn't it? You were disoriented, so I helped out a bit. Drink some more tea."

Sarah put her cup down. Her hands grew numb. Her vision wavered. The edges of her sight fluttered gray. "The tunnel," she said. "My parents—" The grayness rose around her. The restaurant winked out.

"Damn," came Michael's voice. "Stop that, Sarah. Stay with me."

"I'm dead, aren't I?"

"Yes."

"The tunnel? My parents—the restaurant—even you— they're all illusions? Memories?"

"Not quite. You're here; I'm here. The rest is illusion."

"Are you dead, too?"

"No."

"I don't understand."

"I'll explain if we have time. But first, stop retreating into this damned gray velvet nothingness. You can get lost in here. Let's go back to the restaurant."

"What do you mean, 'If we have time'? Don't we have all eternity?"

"I don't know the answer to that any better than you do."

"Why can't I see you?"

"Do you want to?"

"Yes."

"No, you don't. If you wanted to, you could."

A body slowly took shape before her, emerging like a ghost from the gray mist. It grew solid, real. "There you are," she said. Michael stood before her in a long white robe, his arms outstretched. His face radiated light.

"Oh, cut the crap," said Michael. "I told you, I'm not God. I'm just a guy." He dropped his arms. The unearthly radiance faded from his features. He wore faded jeans and a T-shirt. "This is me," he said. "I'm five-eleven. My hair is brown. My eyes are blue. I have bed sores and a bad back." A bottle of Heineken appeared in his left hand. He lifted it in a mock toast.

"To us." He smiled. "Now you make a body. Think of it like putting on a sock."

SARAH WILLED A BODY FOR HERSELF, slipped into it. She twirled, holding her arms up. "What do you think?"

"Oh, I don't know," said Michael. "Is that what you looked like?"

"Me? Oh, no. I was—am—was—ordinary."

"I doubt that."

"It's true. I had moles and warts and aching joints, just like everyone else."

"What color were your eyes?"

"Brown, like my hair."

"Then why did you choose to be blonde now?"

She blinked, lowered her head, and sat down on nothing. "My sister, Mary, was blonde. I always thought she was beautiful."

"Is that Mary's body you have on?"

"Mostly. I was so jealous of her before. Back when—"

"I understand."

"But it's just hair, isn't it?"

"Yup. Strands of dead protein. Keratin, I think."

Suddenly Sarah was completely bald. A silver hand-mirror appeared in her left hand. She studied her reflection for a moment, then let her hand fall away. The mirror slipped from her fingers and vanished.

"Shouldn't I be upset? Panicking? Worried? I don't know what I should feel, but it doesn't seem right to be this detached."

"No glands."

"What?"

"No glands. The chemical bath can't affect your mind any more. Most of your emotions are biochemical—reactions in your brain caused by various glands in your body releasing chemical triggers. Adrenaline, endorphins, insulin, neurotransmitters, other hormones. They all affected you when you had a body. Now you're free of them. You still have emotions, but they're considered responses to your perceptions, not knee-jerk, chemically induced reflexes."

"Oh."

Sarah was quiet for a moment. Then: "Speaking of my body...?"

"You want to see it, huh?"

"Can I?"

"Why not? Hold still—since you don't know your way around, I'll have to steer. Relax just a bit, let the images come through."

~

"I CAN FEEL MY HANDS AGAIN."

"No, we're inside a nurse, watching. Those are her hands. Her name is Millie, but don't talk to her. You'd frighten her."

"What do you mean, 'Inside'? Inside her mind?"

"We're borrowing her eyes and other senses. Think of it like a phone tap. We're not really in the circuit, but we can monitor everything. See how you can hear all the voices, but only the surgeon's words are clear? That's because Millie is only listening to the doctor. Watch how her gaze never strays from the patient, even though she—we—can feel sweat dripping into our eyes."

"What's she doing?"

"Holding the incision apart with a clamp, so the doctor can work."

"What's he doing?"

"Repairing a torn aorta. After that, he'll try to get your heart started again."

"*My* heart? That's me under the sheets? But I've been dead for hours! At least it feels like hours. How long has it been?"

"Oh, only a few seconds. They don't know you're dead yet, just that they're working against the clock to stop the bleeder so they can reperfuse and then try to shock you into sinus rhythm. And they have a chance. I've seen this operation many times. If they resuscitate you, you'll forget all of this. Or maybe you'll remember a little bit and sell your story to the *National Enquirer.*"

"Why wouldn't I remember?"

"No one ever has, not that I know of."

"Then all this seems pointless."

"Does the universe have a point? I must have missed that lecture in college. Some things just *are.* And you might remember some of it. I'm not an expert; I'm just a guy who's met a lot of ghosts."

"Michael—This is crazy, but I feel hungry."

"No, Millie's hungry. She's working an extra shift because of the accident, and she hasn't eaten lunch. It can be confusing sometimes. Here, let's make a jump—"

Her sense of perspective shifted. She looked out of an orderly's eyes, felt his thoughts. She—they—looked at the operating room from the other side. Their attention was fixed on a nurse beside the operating table.

"That's Millie from the outside," said Michael. "The guy we're inside—Burt—has the hots for her. Can you feel it? We're staring at her breasts. Our penis is twitching. Our mouth is dry."

"Ugh."

"Well, it's what living people do. You can hardly blame him. She *is* cute, isn't she? Have you seen enough? Do you want to see other people from the bus?"

"Uh, no thanks. Where's *your* body?"

"Come on, I'll show you."

MICHAEL SAT on the edge of his bed. "It's quiet up here on the seventh floor. Mostly old people waiting to die, or hopeless cases like mine." He gestured at his body. "Ugly cuss, ain't I?"

"Ordinary, maybe, but not ugly." Sarah sat beside Michael. "What's wrong with you?"

"I fell off a ladder about a year ago. Broke open my skull and snapped my neck. Paralyzed from the neck down. In a coma for the most part. Fortunately, the break was at the bottom of the cervical spine, so my autonomic functions are intact. But I can't move. The rest of the injuries have pretty much healed by now."

"Will you recover?"

He shrugged. "Who knows? The doctors don't. That's a CEEG at the head of the bed, a continuous brain-wave monitor, a special kind of electroencephalograph for people like me. It tells them that I'm not a gork, just comatose."

"What's a gork? I don't understand medical jargon."

"It's not a medical term, it's hospital slang for someone whose brain is dead, but with the body kept going by machines —no spontaneous respiration, no purposeful movements, blown pupils and such. They don't keep gorks here. This floor is for those who might recover."

"So there's hope?"

"Not much. They keep my body going when I can't do it for myself. Every now and then, I spaz out—clonic convulsions, status epilepticus, followed by cardiac irregularities and occasional respiratory arrest. Each time, they revive me, repair the damage, keep me in ICU until I'm stabilized, then move me back here. It's been a year now. Even if they have to tube me after a seizure, I always start fighting the vent, start breathing on my own. So they're as trapped as I am. I guess they'll keep me going until my EEG goes flat or my insurance runs out. Medical ethics. No one expects me to open my eyes. They don't even know I'm conscious. The CEEG shows me dreaming, asleep, or convulsing, not much else. It's not very useful in my case."

Sarah considered this. "How do you know so much about medicine?"

"I don't, not really. But I've listened carefully, and you can pick up a lot that way. Not much else to do."

"And all this time, you've been walking around the hospital like a ghost? And no one knows?"

"I talk to the dead people from time to time. I never get much of a chance to develop a relationship, though. They don't stick around very long."

Sarah looked down at her hands. "What happens to us?"

"People like you, you mean? Dead people?"

"Yes."

"I don't know."

"Michael!"

"I honestly don't know. They go away. Somewhere I can't follow. Sometimes I think they just disintegrate. After a certain length of time out of the body, they just . . . disappear. Like a mist evaporating in the sun. Other times, I think they go somewhere I don't know about."

"Heaven, you mean? Or hell?"

"Maybe it's Lûr's cauldron of rebirth. Or Valhalla. The Happy Hunting Grounds. Hades. Or something else. It might be heaven, for all I know. No one's ever come back to tell me about it. They hang around for a couple of minutes after death —usually confused or hallucinating—and then they fade away."

"I don't want to fade away."

"I don't want you to, either. I like talking to you. I get lots of deaders—this is a hospital, after all—but very few NDEs."

"NDE," she said thoughtfully. "I've heard of that. It's a near-death experience. Not really dead."

"No, it's really dead. Sometimes the doctors can resuscitate you after you die. Heart, lungs, brain—any or all kaput. Dead as dead can be. They only *call* it an NDE if you come back."

"Back from death? Like Jesus?"

"He hasn't come through the ER, so I don't know."

"You know what I mean."

"Sorry. Yes, I know what you mean. I'm not talking about resurrection. An NDE only lasts a few seconds, maybe a minute of real time. Subjectively, it can be much longer. Depends on the person. Of course, it's even sadder when the person fades and *then* they revive the body. It's too late then. Just empty skin. But you haven't faded yet. Your mind is very strong; I noticed that immediately. If they can get your body repaired, you'll probably last long enough to climb back inside it. With most people, I barely have time to say hello and good-bye."

"How can I tell if I'm really dead or just having an NDE?"

"You're really dead either way. Otherwise we couldn't be talking like this."

Sarah took his hand. "I want to stay with you."

"With me? Oh, no. If they revive you, you'll have your life back again. If they don't, you'll fade away, do whatever it is that ghosts are supposed to do. Me, I'm trapped. 'Neither fish nor fowl nor good red herring.' Not dead, not alive. I can't go very far from my body, or I'll get lost, never find my way back."

"But you've had a year to practice!"

Michael laughed. "A year? No, that's just how long I've been trapped here. I've *always* been able to get out of my head."

"THIS IS A BEAUTIFUL MEMORY," said Sarah. She pushed her toes deeply into the sand. "Where are we?"

"These are the Indiana Dunes, on the east side of Lake Michigan. The currents make Chicago collect rocks, this side sand. We used to come here when I was a kid, for summer outings. I don't think the water could really have been quite that deep shade of blue, but that's how I remember it."

"It's lovely. Can a ghost get a suntan in a dream?"

"If you want."

"I do! How long has it been?"

"We've been here about a half-hour."

"That isn't what I meant."

"Oh. Maybe a minute since you died, I guess. You don't have to filter everything through your physical brain anymore, so you can assimilate experiences faster."

"So I have another what? Two or three minutes of real time, eight to twelve hours of subjective time? Then I fade away?"

"Sarah, there's no rulebook. Time isn't a constant. It's different for everyone." He took her hands in his, pulled her close. "I hope you stay forever."

She let him take her hands, but kept herself stiff. "You scare me," she whispered.

Michael was genuinely puzzled. "Why?"

"Because I can't help caring for you, and I don't know why. When you said, 'Stay forever,' all I could think was that I'd love to. And I hardly know you. It doesn't make sense."

"Ah. Yes, it does. You've heard the expression 'kindred spirits'? Or 'soul mates'? Living people use those terms, even though they don't understand what they really mean. Maybe the living get a little glimmer from time to time. But the body interferes. Those damned glands again. Love gets all mixed up with physical sex. They're connected because they're both about intimacy, loneliness, vulnerability. But they're separate functions. True love is a meeting of the minds. Sex can be an expression of love, but not a substitute for it. Here, you have no distractions. No glands to make you crazy, nothing to interfere with your direct perception of the other person. It really can be 'kindred spirits' for us. We *are* spirits."

She grinned. "So you believe in love at first death?"

Michael didn't hesitate. "Ever since I met you, yes. Never before."

Now Sarah felt no resistance. Her eyes sparkled. "Can ghosts make love?"

"Want to find out?"

"Yes!"

MICHAEL ROLLED AWAY and sat up. He brushed the sand from his stomach, knees, and forearms. Their love-making had been long and enthusiastic, with the kind of emotional and spiritual intimacy only telepathically linked people could share. They climaxed at the same moment, each feeling the other's experience from the inside.

A heady feeling of tenderness invaded all of Michael's senses as he leaned over to give her a sweet, but still passionate, kiss. This wasn't infatuation, or mutual gratification. It was love. He hadn't thought to ever have those feelings again.

Sarah lay still for a long time, absorbing and savoring the experience. She pondered the word 'ineffable,' wondering if even that were sufficient to represent her happiness. Only a vague unease interrupted her joy, a worry that niggled at the back of her mind.

Michael sensed it, but didn't invade her mind to explore it. Instead, he helped her to her feet and asked, "What's wrong, Sarah?"

"What if I'm hallucinating?"

"What do you mean?"

"What if this—all of it—you, me, everything—is just a dream I'm having while the doctors work on me? What if this isn't love, but just a trip?"

"In college philosophy, the prof asked us to imagine that the world had been created ten minutes ago, with everything in place, including our memories. The challenge was to see if we could tell the difference."

"Could you?"

"Nope. Nor could anyone. It's impossible."

"That's . . . depressing."

"Not really. The thing is, you can't know. You just have to go by the 'least hypothesis.' Don't complicate things. Otherwise you get centipede trouble. You know the story. Someone asked the centipede how he coordinated all his legs. The centipede thought about it, tripped, fell down in a tangle, and never walked again. I figured out a long time ago that analysis doesn't help. You just do the best you can, and try not to think about it. For all I know, I'm hallucinating this whole conversation. If so, what can I do about it? 'Sanity' is a useful legal concept, but it doesn't mean much in the real world."

"I don't feel insane."

He smiled. "You wouldn't, would you? Your mind, your logic engine, is what you use to evaluate everything, including your own mind. You'd never know if you were malfunctioning." His face changed suddenly. "Oh, damn."

"What's wrong?"

"Remember those seizures I told you about? My body's having another one right now." He winced. "Grand mal. They're having trouble holding me down."

Sarah felt a rising sense of panic. "Are you okay? What can I do? How can I help? Do we need to go back? What—?"

"We haven't really gone anywhere. This is just a memory. I used to watch when they worked on me, but recently—" He shrugged. "I'd rather not know. If I die, I'll just fade away. If I don't, nothing will change." He stood up, held out a hand to her. "Come on, let's go for a walk along the shore. It'll distract me."

Waves lapped their ankles, tickled their toes. Children ran past them, through them, unaware. They walked down the crowded beach hand-in-hand, leaving no footprints behind in the wet sand.

Sarah flinched when a Frisbee flew through her head, then laughed. She watched the children playing and smiled to herself. "Remember being a kid, Michael?"

"All too well, sometimes."

She ignored his tone of voice. "They're so carefree, so happy, with all of life ahead of them. I'd love to be a little girl again. Maybe make fewer mistakes this time."

"You just think so. You wouldn't really like it. Everyone has those fantasies from time to time. 'What would it be like to go back, to do it all over again?' The problem is, you can't. If you did it over, you'd do it the same way."

"It's just a fantasy. Why not indulge it?"

"Fine. Okay, I'll show you."

SARAH BRUSHED HER HAIR BACK, stuck out her tongue, and squinted at herself in the mirror.

("Michael? What—?")

("Shhh. Just watch. This is a memory, one of yours.")

("But that's *me!* I'm ten years old again!")

("Yes, this is a complete memory. Not just the scenery. Pretend you're watching a TV show.")

Sarah picked up her mother's eyeliner and inexpertly drew a thick black smudge under each eye. Next came the shadow. Closing one eye and peering through the other, she painted blotchy blue over the closed lid. The brush strayed as far up as her eyebrows, but she decided that if a little bit was good, a lot would be better. She did the other eye the same way.

Rouge for her cheeks. Smearing it in a circle, the way she'd seen her mother do it. The edges didn't feather properly, so she put more on and tried again. Two cherry spots decorated her cheeks, rose and fell when she smiled.

Lipstick now. Her lips were thin and childish. A bright color would be best, make her look most grown-up. She hesitated over the purple, then chose crimson, and applied it carefully. Her lips were still too thin. Maybe if she edged the stick around her lips a bit—? Yes, that did it. Maybe just a bit more, now. The lipstick was wonderful. You couldn't really tell where her lips merged in with the rest of her face, so she could make her lips any size she wanted.

She used a Kleenex to wipe the lipstick from her teeth, then studied her face. Powder! She'd forgotten the powder. A tiny dust cloud filled the bathroom. There! She smiled at herself in the mirror.

("Michael, I look horrible. Like a clown!")

("You were ten. What did you know?")

("I should have known.")

("You weren't thinking that way back then. Look at yourself. Can't you imagine what you're feeling?")

("Proud. Grown-up. Sophisticated. Worldly. I don't have to imagine it. I remember.")

("Shhh. Watch now.")

Sarah turned at the knock on the door. She lifted one hand in what she imagined to be a graceful gesture. "Come in."

Mary, Sarah's older sister, came into the room and stopped dead. "Sarah Jane Weller, what in the world—?"

Sarah lifted her chin, pushed her lips out in what she thought was a sensuous pout. Her voice lilted. "Aren't I lovely, Mary?"

Mary smothered a giggle and turned away. "Mom! Come here. You've *got* to see this. Sarah's going to be a streetwalker!"

Sarah's mother appeared in the bathroom doorway a moment later. She took one look at Sarah, then exchanged a smile with Mary.

"Don't I look great?" Sarah said archly.

"You look like a hooker," said Mary.

"That's enough." Sarah's mother was obviously trying to be stern with Mary, but couldn't help laughing. "You look very nice, Sarah, but let's get you cleaned up now."

("Oh, Michael. I'm so embarrassed.")

("Why?")

("I didn't know what 'hooker' or 'streetwalker' meant. I thought, back then, that they were proud of me. That they were laughing *with* me. They weren't, were they?")

("No.")

("I've seen enough for now.")

("Have I proved my point?")

("That you can embarrass me?")

("No, that your memory is a liar.")

("I knew *that* already.")

("Did you?")

～

SARAH AND MICHAEL walked down the beach together. "If I could have seen me from the outside," she said, "I would have known better. But I couldn't do that."

"No, not back then. Only now, looking back, can you judge the situation objectively. No one *really* wants another shot at childhood."

"Then why is it such a common fantasy?"

"Because it's just a 'what-if' rather than a true desire. What they want is to take their adult minds back and relive life with all the knowledge and wisdom they've accumulated. And what would be the point? Could you imagine having an adult's brain and being forced to sit through kindergarten? Chant the multiplication tables? Be sent to bed? You'd still be stuck in your own head, suffering a thousand times more than if you were innocent and ignorant. You wouldn't be able to see yourself from the outside any better. You wouldn't be any more objective. You'd just be miserable. People who dream about second childhoods haven't thought it through."

"But *you* can get out of your head? Look at things from other perspectives?"

"That's right."

"How? I mean, can anyone else—?"

"Not that I know of. Except right after they die, of course. I don't know anyone else who can do it while alive."

"How did you learn?"

"It was more like remembering. I think I always knew."

"What do you mean?"

"I went for years at a time without remembering what I could do. The mind is funny, Sarah, and has all sorts of mechanisms to protect itself. Sometimes, when it hurts too much, it's like the brain just shuts down. I've seen it happen to others—not for the same reason, of course—but it works the same way. Violence, grief, rape, great loss, abuse. The doctors call it 'trauma.' And when there's too much trauma, you either go mad or something like a circuit-breaker trips, and that part of you, the ability, the memories, the pain, all of it, just goes away until you're strong enough to remember it."

"Pain?"

"Yes, it used to hurt a lot. It still does, sometimes, but I don't take many chances any more. Once burned, or something like that. I'm not a complicated person, and I'm not very brave. I remember one time, when I was very young, maybe five or six years old. I was sitting on a wooden bench in the park. It must have been spring, or very early summer. It had been raining, but the sun came out, and I was just sitting there, dangling my feet, drinking it all in. A bunch of kids were playing on the swings, laughing and giggling. The sun was strong but not glaring, and the air was very sweet, full of the smells of wet cut grass and flowers."

"It sounds lovely."

"It was like heaven. I'm remembering it very clearly now."

"Can you show me? Like you did with my memory?"

"I'd rather just talk about this one. Have you ever had a feeling that everything was right with the world? You know, everything in the right place, everything going just the way it's supposed to go?"

"I used to feel that way when I was a little girl, and Daddy held my hand. We used to go for a walk together every Sunday afternoon, after church. He was very strong, and handsome, and smart, and he loved me very much. I don't know that I've ever been happier than when I was eight years old, holding my father's hand."

"Yes, yes, that's it. That's the way I felt that morning. Everything was peaceful, and I relaxed enough to start remembering. Even when I was that young, I had things bottled up inside me. But slowly, slowly, the warmth of the sunlight unclenched the secret part of me, and I started to remember. I think the first time must have been when I was still an infant— or maybe before I was born. It was all a jumble in my brain, a confusion of pictures and memories that didn't make a lot of sense."

"The first time was when you were a baby?"

"I don't know. It was too much for me back then. Overwhelming. I kept blacking the ability out. My first several years were like a long, continuous nightmare. I'd remember, then forget, only to remember later on."

"Why did you keep forgetting?"

"I'm trying to explain. That's why I picked this particular memory. I sat there on the bench, and it was like remembering suddenly that I had wings and could fly if I wanted to. I saw another little boy, and I looked at him, and suddenly I was inside him, inside his head, looking out through his eyes, hearing with his ears. It was easy! I couldn't believe that I'd forgotten how to do it. He had a piece of candy, one of those all-day lollipops, and he put it in his mouth, but I was the one who tasted it. I tasted it! *Me!* It was glorious. I could be inside anyone I wanted to be, anyone I saw. I jumped like a butterfly from kid to kid, never staying very long, just peeking through his or her eyes, laughing, and running away, all without moving from my seat on the bench. It was a little like being drunk—all light-headed, colors swirling, everything close-up, immediate—with none of the clarity lost. It was glorious."

"What happened?"

"I went into the mind of an adult."

"Was that so terrible?"

"Kids turn into adults very gradually, so they don't really notice the difference. And by the time they're all grown up, they can't remember, really, what it was like to be a child—how they think, how they feel."

"I remember how I felt when I held Daddy's hand."

"No, that's different. You remember a specific thing, a specific event, and the part of you that remembers is an adult, and you filter what you remember with your adult's brain. You remember being happy, right? A child doesn't know he's happy when he's happy—he just is. There's no overmind, no inner narration, no looking down at yourself every second, analyzing what you're feeling, what you're thinking. You just think and feel, and what's good and what's bad both last forever while they're happening. Whatever's happening *right then* is the most important thing in the world, because from your point of view, it's the *only* thing happening, and it's all happening to you, for you, around you. You don't have room to look at things from a distance, because all there is of you is utterly wrapped up in just being you, and there is no distance."

Sarah remembered herself experimenting with makeup. "I think I see what you mean."

"People talk about going back to their childhoods, Sarah, but that's only because they've forgotten what it was like."

"Not all childhoods are terrible."

"Did I say they were? That's not the point. You've heard the saying, 'Youth is wasted on the young'? It's clever, but it's a lie. They have all that energy, all that vitality, that twinkle in their eyes, that grin on their lips—not because they're happy all the time, but because they don't know what's coming. 'Innocence and ignorance,' remember? They go hand-in-hand."

Sarah crinkled her brow. "You already said that. Why bring it up again?"

"Because you still don't get it. Before, I talked about taking your adult memories with you. Now I'm talking about a simple do-over. Can you imagine going back, forgetting all your hard-earned life lessons? Giving it all up and being locked into a child's brain again, with only a child's ability to evaluate what you see around you? No abstract thought, no understanding of philosophy, theology, science, mechanics, art?"

"Innocence can be beautiful."

"Only from the outside. That's an adult's point of view, projecting, idealizing. The point is, kids don't know from Adam. They don't act, they react. They don't really love, either—they're just loyal to whoever feeds them."

He was silent for a long moment. Then Sarah said, "Michael, were you ever really a child yourself?"

Michael seemed to gather himself together, but he didn't turn his head to meet her eyes. Instead, he watched the sand on which they walked.

"Not since that day in the park, no," he said quietly.

Sarah felt suddenly, unreasonably, defensive. "I loved my parents, and nothing you say can change that."

"The argument from personal incredulity. Okay, it's not my job to make you a cynic. But hope and love and hunger and fear and all the other emotions are so jumbled together in a child's mind that it's pointless to try to separate them. We can look at two kids playing together and think, 'They really like each other,' but all we really know is that they're having fun at that particular moment. That's all they know, too, which is all I'm trying to say. This hogwash about wanting to go back, to be a child again, is just talking about removing layers of complexity —and it's those layers of complexity that give things meaning. Otherwise, all you have is a welter of experiences. Children have no defenses, no guard functions; they can only protect themselves against what they know, against what they're able to experience. They don't need to defend themselves from unrequited love, for instance—it can't happen to them."

"Did you experience something you couldn't defend against? That day in the park, I mean?"

"I think I've said too much already."

"For your sake or mine? I don't mind listening. It's not like I'm in a hurry to rush off somewhere."

Michael pulled her to a stop. A seagull arched in a lazy circle overhead. The sun's warmth provided a pleasant contrast to the cool waves washing their feet. And now, finally, he met her eyes. "Do you really want to hear this?" he asked.

"I do," she said.

"The man had just killed his wife."

"Oh!"

"Do you still want to know about it?"

"I think it's important that you be able to tell me."

"That's not the same thing."

"No, dear, it's not."

He hesitated. "He killed her because he found out she had been sleeping with another man. Looking back at it now, I guess it was a rather commonplace motive for a rather commonplace crime, but to me, at age five or so, it was wildly beyond my experience. He was walking through the park, just like anyone else, but he was a murderer, and he knew it, and it was all he could think about. He was going over and over it in his mind, replaying it like a movie—the knife, the blood, the screaming. The horrible, horrible screaming. After the first time he stabbed her, he realized what he was doing and was horrified. But she wouldn't stop screaming, and he was afraid someone would hear, so, just to get her to shut up, he stabbed her again. She just kept screaming, and he kept stabbing, until finally she was quiet."

"That's terrible," Sarah said softly.

"He didn't know what to do, so he just left her there, and went to get his gun. I saw all this in his mind, all at once, the first time I touched him. I had never experienced anything so strong, so primal. I couldn't break away. With my eyes, I saw him walking toward me through the park, but with my mind, I saw him stabbing his wife. He sat down on the bench next to me, and I wanted to scream and run away, but I just sat there and messed myself."

"Why didn't you run away, tell someone?"

"All I could think was that he killed people who screamed. I was too scared, too violated, to think straight. And I was still caught in his mind. He had blood all over his shirt—her blood —and I could remember, not from my own memories, but from his, how it had gotten there. How surprised he had been that blood was so hot. That there could be so much of it. He looked at me and smiled this really weird smile. 'Have you ever seen a gun?' he asked me, and when I shook my head, he pulled his gun out of his pocket, put it in his mouth and pulled the trigger."

"Oh, God, Michael!"

"Seeing it wasn't so bad. The hair on the back of his head lifted, kind of fluffed, like a sheet on a clothesline when the wind gusts. His brains splattered on the leaves of the bush behind us. It wasn't what I saw with my eyes that hurt so much, but what I felt. See, I was still linked with him, and I felt him die. Other people heard the shot and were starting to look our direction. Then he said, 'You'd better get away from here.'"

"Wait, who said that?"

"He did. The guy who killed himself."

"But—?"

"Yes, he was dead. I think that was the first time I ever talked to someone after he was dead. Dying is horrible, but death isn't so bad. He got up from his body and walked away, very peacefully. I watched for a few seconds, but then he just sort of faded from sight, and I was back in my own brain again, with a dead man on the bench next to me, his brains in the bush behind me, and a huge load of crap in my underwear."

"What did you do?"

"I took his advice, got up, and ran away before any of the adults got there. And I turned off that part of my brain for a long time. It's odd, isn't it, that I would choose to forget my ability rather than the deaths? But that's the way it happened. The next time I remembered, I was fourteen, and by then, of course, things were a lot different."

"What happened when you were fourteen?"

"No. It's your turn. Tell me about the bus."

~

SARAH DROPPED MICHAEL'S HAND, closed her eyes, let the borrowed memory of the beach fade. She floated bodiless, a point of awareness in a limitless gray mist.

"Why are we back here?" came Michael's voice.

"You made me remember the accident. It seems like forever since I thought about it. How long, Michael?"

"Two, maybe three minutes."

"Are they still . . . working on me? Can we go back to the hospital to check?"

"We never left the hospital, Sarah. The beach—everything —was all illusion and memory. You're still in the operating room."

The grayness turned black. "Why can't I see anything?"

"Sarah!" His bodiless voice was sharp, insistent. "Stay with me. You're fading."

His voice seemed to be coming from miles away. Sarah felt a sense of peace overwhelm her. It was so quiet, so serene, here in the darkness. Nothing mattered. Whatever happened would be fine, would be what was supposed to happen.

"Sarah! *Sarah!* Stay with me." Michael's voice pestered her, intruded on the peacefulness. His hand materialized. She watched, incurious, as he groped frantically for her. "I can't do it for you, Sarah," he said. "You have to reach for me. Reach out. Take my hand. Sarah! Come out of there. Come back. *Stay with me!*"

She considered the situation calmly. He sounded so upset, so worried. But it was so peaceful here, so tranquil. Why couldn't he let her go? Why couldn't he let her sleep? All she wanted to do was drift off.

"You *can't* sleep, Sarah. Not yet. Come back first. Take my hand. Let me bring you back."

Such a bother. Why did it matter? It would be so easy to

ignore him, to float out of his reach, to go far enough away that even his voice would be gone.

"Sarah, *no!* Come back. I need you! I love you."

Slowly, Sarah formed a hand, let his fingers touch her own. His touch was ice water on a hot summer day. It woke her from her dreams of darkness, shocked her into awareness. His fingers scrabbled for purchase, clamped like a vise around her wrist, then *yanked.* Suddenly she was with him again. Emotions flooded back; the incurious peacefulness became a memory.

"Thank God," he breathed. "I almost lost you."

She held his hand tightly. "What happened?" she asked.

"You were fading."

"You brought me back," she said wonderingly. "I was almost gone. It was so strange, Michael. So peaceful. So quiet. I can still feel it. . . ." The grayness darkened, smoothed out, became formless black.

He shook her shoulders violently. "Stop. Stay with me. I didn't bring you back—you did it yourself. You have to *want* to stay."

The world came back in focus. Her eyes widened. "Don't let go of me, Michael. Don't let me fade away."

"I won't. I promise. I want—Uh, oh."

"What? What is it?"

"Look, I can't leave you alone right now—"

"Don't! Don't *ever* leave me!"

"—But I need to do something. So you'll have to come with me. It's just down the hall. Hold my hand. That's right. I won't let go of you."

"I'm scared, Michael."

"Don't be. I won't let you get lost. Through this door—can you see it now?—and into this room. Here."

Michael moved to a gurney alongside one wall, looked at

the tiny body lying on it. "Hello, sweetheart," he said. "I'm Michael, and this is Sarah. What's your name?"

A little girl, maybe five or six years old, looked up at them. "My knee hurts," she said.

"I bet it does," said Michael. "Let me take a look."

"Are you a doctor?"

"Sort of, honey. Can you sit up?"

Sarah gasped. "Michael! Her leg!" Then she bit her lip and kept quiet. Michael helped the little girl sit up and move to the edge of the gurney, leaving her body with the horrid tourniquet behind.

"It doesn't hurt now," said the girl.

"That's good, sweetheart."

An orderly walked through them, pushed the gurney away. The little girl leaped off and landed in Michael's arms, leaving her body on the gurney. She wriggled and smiled. "You're a nice man." She kissed his cheek.

"What's your name, sweetie?"

The little girl frowned. Her eyes grew wide. "I don't remember."

"That's okay. It doesn't matter. Does anything hurt anymore?"

She snuggled into his shoulder and murmured, "Mmmmn fine now." Her eyelids fluttered. In a moment, she was asleep. A moment after that, Michael's arms were empty.

Sarah fought back a sob. "She was so young, so pretty. Doesn't it bother you, Michael?"

"It used to, but if I let myself grieve over every ghost I met, there wouldn't be enough room in the world's oceans to hold the tears. I give them what help I can, comfort them until they fade. It's all I know how to do.

"Is she gone now? *Really* gone?"

Michael nodded.

"And is—*that*—what will happen to me? What almost happened? I'll just disappear? Be gone forever?"

Michael nodded again. "If the doctors can't save you, yes."

"Will you hold me, too, when it's my turn?"

"Yes, if that's what you want."

"Poor Michael!"

"Eh?"

"Who will hold you when it's your turn?"

SARAH LEANED on her elbows and stirred her milkshake with her straw. "I just realized," she said. "I can eat chocolate all I want and never gain a pound."

Michael laughed. "I hadn't thought of that."

"That's because you're a man."

"Oh? I thought it was because I don't like chocolate."

"You're impossible!"

"What's one more impossible thing before breakfast? Or lunch. Or whatever the hell this meal is. Who's counting?"

She took a long hard pull at the milkshake, savoring the cold, creamy, chocolate taste. "Lord, this is good."

"Tell me about the bus, Sarah."

She wiped her mouth with a napkin, sat back in the chair. "Was that little girl from the bus?"

Michael shrugged. "Probably. There were about fifteen people in there, and most of them had memories of an accident." He paused. "So do you, but from a different angle. I haven't looked deeply. Do you want me to—?"

"No," she said quickly. "I wasn't on the bus."

"Then how—?"

"I was what the bus hit."

"Ah."

"I was driving, listening to the radio, on my way home from work. There was this really good song on, by the Eagles—"

"'Hotel California'?"

"No, 'Desperado.' The live version."

"I love that song."

"Me, too. But my car's radio doesn't work very well. A loose wire or something. You have to bang it from time to time. Anyway, that's what I was doing. Banging the radio with my hand, trying to get the song to come in better. When I looked up, I realized I'd almost missed my exit."

"So you swerved?"

"I swerved. I would have made it, too, except for the kid on the motorcycle. I saw him at the last minute, and hit the brakes —*hard!*—to keep from side-swiping him. The car skidded around almost in a circle. I guess the bus was in the lane behind the motorcycle, but I didn't see it until just before it smashed into me."

"Then what?"

"Then nothing. Until the hospital . . . and you."

Michael nodded thoughtfully. "How do you feel about the accident?"

"What do you mean?"

"I was wondering if perhaps you felt guilty, or that you had to make up for it somehow. Atone. Suffer purgatory. Whatever."

"No, it was an accident. And this is definitely *not* purgatory. I have you, and I'm happy." She paused, then said, "Of course I'm sorry for all those people from the bus, but I died, too, you know. Why?"

"Well, I don't know how to put this."

"Just say it, dear. 'No glands,' remember? You can't hurt my feelings."

"Okay. No one's ever hung around this long before. It's been three or four minutes, since your NDE started. You should have either gone back into your head or faded by now. You're different somehow."

"How many NDEs have you known?"

"Not many, but the pattern is always the same. That's why I wondered if you had unfinished business, some sort of atonement or penance left to perform. That might account for it."

"Have you ever seen that happen?"

"Well— No, never."

"Oh." Sarah chewed on her lower lip. "Maybe it's something you're doing. Can you do that? Keep someone around?"

Michael's face grew troubled. "No. No, I can't. You can survive only so long away from a working physical brain. If you stray too far, or if your brain dies, you fade. It will eventually happen to me, too."

"There's no way around it? I mean, does it have to be *your* brain? Wouldn't any—?" She broke off, bewildered by his reaction. "Michael, Michael," she said softly. "You're crying, dear. What's wrong?"

He swallowed, met her eyes briefly, then looked away. "There is a way," he whispered. "That body you saw in the hospital, the one in the coma. It's mine all right, but not the one I was born in. I stole it."

THEY SAT on a hillside overlooking the sea. Painted sheep wandered the fields below them, tore at the tough grass.

Ancient stone fences meandered back and forth across the terraced hillside, marking off boundaries otherwise long forgotten.

Michael opened the wicker picnic basket, pulled out a bottle of red wine and two glasses. "Hold this," he said, thrusting the bottle at Sarah. He rooted in the basket some more and came up with some cheese, a knife, and a corkscrew.

She looked around. "Where are we now? And why are the sheep all different colors?"

Michael laughed heartily. "This is Snowdon," he explained. "It's the tallest peak in lower Britain, which isn't saying much. That's the Irish Sea out there. Farmers use daubs of paint to mark their flocks. It's easier and cheaper than maintaining the fences. We're in Gwynedd, northern Wales."

She looked at the bottle. "With California wine?"

"Sue me. I couldn't remember any British wines. But I remembered some great local cheese. Here, have a slice. And let me open that." He pulled the cork from the bottle, filled their glasses.

Sarah nibbled the cheese. "Tell me about the stolen body," she said.

"It was when I was seventeen. I killed a kid."

"Oh, you poor thing. What happened?"

"That's it? You just want to know what happened? You don't think I'm evil?"

"Of course not. I don't believe in evil. People make mistakes, sure—and sometimes people are incredibly selfish and insensitive—but no one's really evil."

"You've lived a very sheltered life, Sarah."

"So? You want to convince me that you're evil? Tell me about the kid. Maybe I'll change my mind."

He shrugged. "Okay. After the experience when I was five or six, in the park—"

"I remember!"

"So do I. It scared me. Badly. So badly that I turned that part of my brain off. Traumatic amnesia. Whatever psychobabble explanation fits best. I didn't remember again until I was fourteen."

"What triggered the memory?"

"I was at a concert with some friends from school. There was a blind kid sitting in front of us, one row ahead. I wondered what it would be like to be blind. I wondered what it would be like to be *him*. The next thing I knew, I *was* him. Everything went dark. I couldn't see at all. My body felt wrong, somehow. Too big in some parts, too small in others. I knew what had happened, but I didn't really understand it. I heard noises behind me, a thumping sound, and a bunch of boys' voices."

Michael paused, took a sip of wine. "It was weird. I panicked. I swam up out of the blind kid, and suddenly it was worse than ever. I didn't know where I was. There were sights and sounds, but nothing made sense. It was like I was disconnected from everything. Then I looked down, and recognized my own body on the floor of the auditorium. Blood streamed from my forehead. I was unconscious. My friends were yelling at me."

"What did you do?"

"I tried to pick me up. But my hands passed through me. No one could hear me. I figured out that I must have fallen forward when I left my body. That was the thumping sound I'd heard. And that's why my forehead was bleeding."

"You must have been frightened."

"God, yes! Panicked. The only thing I could think was that I needed to get back inside my body. I was drifting away. Up toward the ceiling of the auditorium. I had no control. I reached out again, lunged really, and got hold of myself. I sat up inside my body, everything back in place, but nothing the same."

He paused, a far-away look on his face. "Oh, that's nice."

"What?"

"The Phenobarbital. It worked. My seizure's over."

Sarah recoiled. "I forgot! All this time, we've been talking, and you've been—?"

He shook his head. "It's only been a couple of minutes of real time. And I'm not *in* my body. I don't feel much unless I want to. I only leave enough of myself behind to keep my body running while I'm away. And to lead me back. I wouldn't want to get lost. Some find the grayness seductive, but it terrifies me."

He stopped again, cocked his head to one side as if listening to something only he could hear. "Taking inventory," he explained a moment later. Then he sighed and smiled. "No permanent damage, apparently."

"I'm glad."

"Me, too. I'm always sure that when I die, it will be while I'm freewheeling. And instead of fading, I'll just wander forever in the grayness."

"'Freewheeling'?"

"That's my name for it. Using other people's eyes and ears. Talking mind-to-mind. Seeing memories, tasting other people's lives. And, um, other senses, too. I was a teenager when I figured this out, remember. There were certain curiosities, and I had a way to explore that not everyone had available."

"You mean you were a Peeping Tom?" Sarah laughed. "I don't believe it."

"There was this girl. Jenny. She had honey-brown hair and gorgeous green eyes. I had a crush on her, but she didn't even know I was alive. So I followed her around with my mind. Her best friend taught her about sex one night. I was there, inside her, watching, feeling everything. That's how I found out that female orgasm is different. God, so much more intense! She and her girlfriend slowly undressed each other, then rubbed—"

"I get the idea, Michael!"

"Embarrassed?"

"Only for you, you filthy peeper."

"Tell the truth, Sarah. If you could go anywhere, inside anyone, and see whatever you wanted, without fear of discovery, wouldn't you do it? At least once?"

"Uh, does the Fifth Amendment apply to ghosts?"

"Nope."

"Then yes, damn you, I probably would. But I wouldn't talk about it."

"Oh, I never did, not back then. Who would I tell? But it wasn't all just voyeurism. I was learning how to read memories while freewheeling. *Nobody* had any secrets from me, Sarah. Can you imagine the kind of power that gave me? I knew whose father was a drunk, whose mother had run off with the mailman, which teacher had the hots for which cheerleader, who was gay, who was straight, who cheated at the math tests, and who cribbed for the English essays. I didn't have to touch a beer to know what it felt like to get giddy on alcohol. I never bought dope, but I got high whenever I wanted, and I could turn it off just by leaving the druggie's mind. And the sex—! Every imaginable variation. You simply wouldn't believe what goes on behind those quiet, respectable, suburban doors. I grew up very quickly."

"I wasn't *that* sheltered. I believe it."

"Perhaps you do." Michael refilled their wine glasses. "It took me a while to settle down, develop some ethics. By the time I was seventeen, I settled on a cross between 'An it harm none' and 'Do unto others.' Morality is a group consensus thing, remember, and I was unique, so I had to make up my own. I pretty much had myself convinced that freewheeling was morally wrong, unless there was a good reason for me to go into someone else's mind. I still did it from time to time, but I felt guilty."

"I don't understand that. You couldn't help being the way you were."

"Mmmmn. There was this kid I knew, a friend's little brother. When he was thirteen or so, he discovered masturbation. He was convinced it was evil. That's what they told him at church, and he believed it. But he couldn't help himself. At night, he'd think about some girl he'd seen, and his hands would move by themselves. Before he knew it, he'd have his pajamas open, his prick in his hand. He'd imagine her lips smothering his little wet cock, or her hands cupping his balls, and whammo, he'd hit the ceiling. He popped his baloney almost every night. Sometimes two or three times. And he always felt terrible afterward. The more he did it, the worse he felt. Guilty as hell. He took something normal and natural, something that should have been enjoyable, and turned it into a complex form of self-torture."

"How sad! How—" She groped for words— "unnecessary."

"That's sex in America's heartland. Cramped, repressed, shameful, hidden under the covers, and—because of all that—compulsive and addictive. I'm surprised anyone from the Bible Belt manages to get married and have kids. But my point is that even though it was natural, he felt guilty."

"You're a closet liberal."

"Who said anything about a closet? Sorry, was I preaching?"

"Just a bit. But I understand now. Freewheeling was natural for you, but you felt guilty anyway. The pattern makes sense as long as you don't go outside of it. But what morals were you really violating?"

"It was a privacy issue. Imagine if the whole world were blind, and only you could see."

"'In the country of the blind, the one-eyed man is king.' That's been done, Michael."

"Yeah, but let's do it again. Forget being king or queen. It doesn't work that way. Think of the poor schmuck whose balls are hanging out of his shorts, but doesn't know it. Or the lady, dressed in her finest clothes, with chives on her teeth or a wad of snot hanging from her nose. You can see it, no one else can."

Sarah nodded. "Then the question would be, 'Do you say anything?'"

"Not quite. Or yes, at first. But the answer to that one is obvious. People don't want to hear the truth about themselves, and they most certainly don't want to know that someone *else* knows. Dirty little secrets are supposed to *stay* secret—otherwise the dirtiness washes off and all the flavor is gone. The real question isn't whether or not you should say something, but how do you keep from blurting things out unintentionally?" He paused. "The only way is not to look."

"So the one-eyed man plucks out his remaining eyeball?"

"No. But he wears dark glasses most of the time and feels guilty when he peeks."

Sarah shook her head. "I guess I understand how you felt about that. I'd feel guilty, too. But if you had developed your own sense of ethics, how did you end up killing someone? Was it an accident?"

"Humph. I was hoping you'd forget about that."

"Not a chance, dear. You want to tell me, so go ahead."

Michael shrugged. "There was an accident, yes. It happened

to me. A friend and I were out on the lake when a storm came up. We lost control of the sailboat, and it went over. I drowned."

"Michael!"

"My name was 'Brad' then. Brad Varley. Mike Hansen was my friend. He didn't drown."

"I don't like the sound of this."

"Does that mean you don't want to hear the rest?"

"No."

"Okay, then. I felt my body dying. I freewheeled. The only person around was Mike. Unfortunately for him, he was wearing a life vest."

"'Unfortunately'?"

"For him. I shoved myself into his head, elbowed him aside, and took over. I'd never done that. Take over, I mean. Always before, I was just a passenger in someone else's cab. Now I was driving. And there was only room for one at the wheel. I pushed him out. I don't think it would have worked if we hadn't spent so much time together. He was a good friend."

"Where did he go?"

"I don't know. I pushed him out. Into the dark. He vanished. Died, I guess. Went wherever ghosts go. From that point on, I've been in his body, calling myself 'Michael,' pretending to be him. After he was gone, what choice did I have? I knew most of his memories, anyway, so it wasn't hard to carry off the impersonation. I cried very convincingly at my funeral."

He paused. "So tell me, Sarah. Am I evil?"

"You were desperate. You panicked."

"Yes, but that's no excuse. *Am I evil?*"

Sarah put down her wine glass, stood up, pulled him to his feet, put her arms around him. "I don't believe in evil," she said softly. "You made a mistake. A terrible mistake. And you've carried the guilt with you for years and years. You know more now. Would you do the same thing again?"

Michael was troubled. "I don't know. I don't *think* so. I wouldn't want to. I didn't do it on purpose with Mike. He was just there, and I knew him well enough that I could swim out of my mind into his. I didn't even realize what I was doing until it was too late. As you said, I just panicked."

"Then it was an accident. You can't go back and change it. *You* taught me that. So let it go." She kissed him, tenderly at first, then with passion.

"You're awfully understanding," said Michael a few minutes later.

"It's one of the things I'm good at."

"'One of'?"

She smiled and kissed him again; answer enough. The picnic basket, the hillside, the sea—all faded from sight. Grayness welled up around them. Two specks of awareness floated in the middle of immensity. Tied together, they were in no danger of getting lost. After a timeless moment, she said, "Michael?"

"Mmmmn, yes?"

"How long has it been now?"

"Maybe five minutes."

"Will I stay forever, then?"

"I don't know, Sarah."

"Michael?"

"Yes?"

"The hillside in England—"

"Wales. Don't let the Welsh hear you say that. *Or* the English."

"Okay, then, that hillside in Wales. That was somewhere

you'd been, right? Like the beach in Michigan? It was a memory of yours, like Lenny's Grill was a memory of mine?"

"Yes. I explained that already."

"But it could be any memory, right? Yours or mine? And you can make us both see it?"

"Sure. Any memory strong enough. I picked those because they were familiar, comforting places. Why? Is there somewhere you want to go?"

"Well, I was thinking. I might fade away any minute. And it would be a shame if . . . I've always wondered. . . . Oh, hell! My feet are clay, too, Michael. That girl—Jenny?—and her friend. Is *that* memory strong enough? Can you take me there, Michael? Please?"

"Click your heels together three times."

"What?"

"Never mind. Let's visit some memories. Lots of them."

"But only happy ones," she said.

"Of course. Take my hand again. I'll lead the way."

AFTER AN SEEMINGLY ENDLESS TIME, Sarah felt an odd sensation. "Oop," she said. And, "Oh. *Oh!* Michael, what's going on?"

Something tugged at her waist, pulled sharply. Her vision went dark. "Michael!"

"I'm here," said his voice. "It took me a moment to find you again."

"Why can't I see you? What's happening? Oh, Michael, it *hurts.* You said I'd just fade away. You didn't say anything about pain. Oh! There it is again. Like someone put a hook in my belly and was reeling me in."

"You're not fading away, Sarah, you're going back. The

surgeons saved you. You're going to live. Can't you hear them talking? 'Good cap refill,' and 'Strong distal pulse' and—"

"I don't care about that. Why can't I see *you*? Help me. I'm scared."

"I'm right here. There's nothing to be scared of."

"I want to *see* you! I want to *hold* you."

"You can't. You're back in your own brain now. I'm talking to you there. It's against my rules to talk to live people this way."

"Damn the rules, Michael. Stay with me. I love you."

"I love you, too, Sarah."

"Then stay with me!"

His voice sounded sorrowful. "I can't. I won't. You'll forget most of this. Maybe all of it. If you remember anything, you'll think it was a dream. Even if you remember it all, we can't go on together. I can't follow you out of the hospital. It's too far from my own body. And if you go around talking to voices in your head when you wake up, people will think you're crazy. You'll think so, too, eventually. They'll lock you up."

"I won't forget. I love you."

"Good-bye, Sarah."

"I won't forget!"

"Good-bye."

"Michael!"

But he was gone, and she was alone.

"HERE, miss, let me help. It's only been two days. You shouldn't turn over by yourself yet. You had open-heart surgery."

Sarah sighed sleepily, opened her eyes just a crack. "Thank you, Millie," she said.

The nurse cocked her head and glanced at Sarah's chart.

"Do I know you, Mrs., um, Miss, ah, Weller? Is it Sarah Jane or just Sarah?"

Despite the pain-killers and sedatives, Sarah was suddenly completely alert. "Sarah. You're Millie from the emergency room, right?"

"That's right. I'm helping out in ICU because they're short-staffed today. But how do you know me?"

"I remember you."

"Hmmn?"

"From the ER. When they were operating. You were there."

Millie looked at Sarah's chart again. "Honey, you were unconscious before they brought you in, then anesthetized while they worked you up. You've been sedated since then. You just woke up this morning. You *couldn't* remember me."

"But you were there, right?"

The nurse looked troubled. "Yes, I was. I remember your case now. We almost lost you. But Dr. Fletcher is one of the best. You were lucky he was on duty. But you were out like a light the whole time." She paused. "You know, the drugs they give you do funny things." She stuck a finger under her name tag and lifted it away from her uniform a bit. "You saw this, probably, and read my name. Then you dreamed about your operation, and dreamed I was there."

"What about Burt?"

Shock suffused Millie's face. "What?"

"Burt. The orderly. The one who likes you. He was there, too."

Millie looked at her askance. "Who put you up to this? Was it Betty? Catherine? Wait! It was Susan. It *had* to be. I never should have told her about Burt, and she *never* should have told a patient. Wait until I get my hands on her." Millie moved off, still muttering to herself.

Sarah fell back weakly, closed her eyes against the tears that welled up by themselves. It wasn't a dream, then. Millie was proof. It had happened. She remembered. Michael was real. He was here, somewhere in this hospital.

She called out mentally. Michael?

Silence.

Michael?

Then the drugs took over again, and she slept.

THREE MONTHS LATER, Sarah finally worked up the courage to return to the hospital. She faced the floor nurse squarely. "What's so complicated? I want to visit Michael Hansen."

"Told you, only family's allowed on this floor."

Sarah hesitated, clutched her purse tighter, and cleared her throat. "I *am* family. I'm his wife."

The floor nurse raised an eyebrow. "I been working here for nine months on this floor. Ain't nobody in all that time come by to see Michael Hansen. I know his chart like the back of my hand, and he ain't married. Now what's your game, hon?"

Sarah licked her lips, looked at the floor nurse's name tag. "I know he's not married, Mrs. Stempson. Not now. He was. To me, I mean. We're divorced. Several years ago. I only, um, just found out that he was here. A friend told me."

Sarah looked at the floor nurse and tried to smile. Stempson was a very large woman, creamy brown, with a spotless complexion. Her white uniform was tight across her hips and shoulders. Her face held a no-nonsense look.

"I'm fifty-three years old," Stempson said at last. "And I raised eight kids. I seen people in every possible kind of situation, and I know when somebody's lying through her teeth. Which you are."

"Please," Sarah said. "I just need to see him."

Stempson stared at her a moment longer. "What's your name?"

"Sarah. Sarah Jane Weller."

"Changed it back, huh?"

"I, uh—yes."

"And I suppose all your identification says 'Weller' instead of 'Hansen'? And you ain't got nothing to prove you was his wife?"

"I, um, no—that is, I don't think. . . ."

"Not even a picture of the two of you? Nothing?"

Sarah opened her purse, made a show of poking through the contents. "We, uh, didn't part on good terms," she said, improvising wildly. "I don't think I kept anything, but—" She looked up. "I just have to see him. I *have* to." Tears trembled at the corner of her eyes. She brushed them away angrily, and looked back at her purse. "Let me look again, maybe there's. . . ."

Stempson's huge dark hand closed over Sarah's, gently, but firmly. "Don't bother looking no more."

Sarah jerked her head up. "What? Do you mean you won't let me see him? There has to be something—"

Stempson shook her head. "You say you were his wife, you must have been his wife. Like I said, I raised eight kids. I seen it all. And I can recognize when a body's in love, too. You want to see him, go ahead and see him."

"Uh, Mrs. Stempson—"

"Maggie."

"Uh, okay, Maggie. Call me Sarah. And thank you."

"Ain't no skin off me. But keep your lies simple, hon. Don't tell no more than you have to, and plan it out ahead of time."

"I, ah, don't know what to say."

"Don't say nothing. He's in room 707. Help yourself."

SARAH CLOSED the door and sat on the chair by the bed. The room was just as she remembered it. Michael lay quietly, his eyes closed, his chest rising and falling in a slow, even rhythm. The CEEG was still connected. She'd learned—a little—how to read it. His brain was still alive, perhaps even conscious from time to time, but even the doctors weren't sure about that.

"It's been three months, Michael," she said aloud. "I haven't forgotten. I *won't* forget. I'm fine now. Back at my job, even. But you're still here, so I had to come see you."

She waited.

Nothing.

Michael, she thought, abandoning speech, trying to reach his mind directly, relying on raw emotion to provide the connection. *Talk to me, please,* she thought urgently. I know you can. Damn your rules, I don't care if people think I'm crazy. I'll know I'm not. I have proof. Things I saw that later turned out true. Millie and Burt. You. You're here. How would I know that unless I'd really talked to you? Michael, please. *Please.* Talk to me. I still love you.

She moved restlessly on the chair. Are you looking through my eyes right now? she wondered. Can you hear me? I was there with you, Michael, and I still don't understand it all. Where are you when you're not freewheeling? Are you in there, in your own body? Are you sleeping? Are you dead? You can't be. God, you can't be. So talk to me. Please.

She waited. And waited. Michael's chest rose and fell, but there was no other sign of life.

She closed her eyes. All my life, she thought, I've waited to meet the right man. I never married. I had a couple of flings when I was a teenager. A couple more in my mid-twenties. I was sure I was in love every time, but it was just infatuation. And sex. Mustn't be afraid of honesty—not with you. The sex was good. All sex is good, if it's shared willingly by people who care about each other. But it wasn't love. Just infatuation. I learned how to tell the difference, finally.

You made me fall in love with you, Michael. You were kind when I needed kindness. You understood me—the good parts, the bad parts, the things I'd never willingly tell another person. You didn't look down on me. You didn't treat me like an object. You didn't have anything to gain by helping me, but you did it anyway. Dammit, Michael, don't you understand? I love you.

And in her mind, over and over: I love you, I love you, I love you. Love you. Love.

"Don't torture yourself," said a dry voice in her head.

Michael?

"I'm here, Sarah. Where would I go?"

Michael!

"I'm astonished that you remember me, that you can hear me now. You have your body back, glands and brains and hormone bath all working properly. Your memory of me should have faded a long time ago. I don't understand. Maybe it's something I'm doing. Or maybe it's something about you."

"Maybe how much we loved each other."

"Shh. Don't speak aloud—the nurses will hear you. Just think the words. It may have seemed like a life-long romance to you—"

It was!

"Not really. Long enough for a couple of ghosts to fall in

love, but not very much time in the real world. It just felt like forever."

Can we go back to the diner, or the beach? Romances can be rekindled.

"I'm sorry. I don't know, and I won't test it. What if I lost hold of you? The romance isn't gone; that's the whole problem. I'm trying to be kind to both of us. My rules have reasons. There's nothing here for you. Let the memory fade."

There's us. I still love you, and I remember everything.

"Sarah, if you still love me, you *must* stop. Look at me. My body's a broken, worthless wreck. I'm in a coma, paralyzed, brain-damaged. Can you imagine the torture you're putting me through? I still love you, too, but I can't touch you, can't see you, can't hold you in my arms. Please. Don't come here again. Don't do this to me. To yourself. To us. It can never be what you want, Sarah."

I don't care. Do you think I care? So what if your body is damaged? Your mind is alive, and it's *you* I love, not your body. Maybe I remember because we're supposed to be together. I could—

"Could what? Move into the hospital room with me? That's the only way we could stay together. I'm chained to this body. I can't go with you. You can't stay here. And this body is dying, Sarah. Slowly, maybe, but dying. You don't want to love a dying man. Go out, live your own life. Find someone else."

I don't *want* someone else, she thought desperately.

"Dear God, I don't want you to be with someone else, either, but there's no choice. You're better off forgetting me. And I'm better off forgetting you."

Can't I just come visit you? Spend some time? Be your friend?

"Be honest. You don't want to be friends."

No. I feel too much for you.

"You have glands again, now. But try to rise above it. Leave me alone, Sarah. It's better for both of us."

I can't do that. I love you.

"I love you, too, Sarah. Sweet Jesus, how I love you too."

His face twitched, and his arms rose. She thought for a moment that he was waking up, was reaching for her. Then the alarm shrilled, and his entire body started jerking. The door banged open. Maggie Stempson pulled Sarah away from the bedside. Two other nurses huddled over Michael. Over her shoulder, as Maggie maneuvered her out of the room, Sarah saw Michael bucking and jerking on the bed, his face twisted in a rictus so tight she wouldn't have recognized him.

"What—?" she said to Maggie when they were in the hall. "All I did was *talk* to him. I'm sorry. I didn't mean to—"

"It wasn't nothing you did. He has these seizures all the time. Come back tomorrow, if you want."

"I want to help. What can I do to help?"

"You can go home," said Maggie firmly.

SARAH STOPPED by the hospital every night after work. She sat by Michael's bed and talked to him. She told him stories from the office, read the newspaper to him, and talked about the weather and current movies.

Since her first visit, Michael had not responded. He didn't talk to her, or give any sign that he knew she was there. It didn't matter. She knew he was alive, that he could hear her. She believed it. She had to believe it.

She brought flowers to the room and pestered the staff endlessly about ways to make him more comfortable. She brought books from the library about comas and brain physiology, and studied them in his room, confident that, if he wanted, Michael could read along with her by watching through her eyes.

Sometimes, after a particularly bad seizure, he was in intensive care for a day or two, and Sarah fretted until he came back, until she reestablished their routine. They didn't move him for the milder seizures, the ones that happened several times a day. Maggie Stempson taught Sarah how to tell a grand mal from a petite, how to turn him, how to manipulate his arms and legs, moving his joints and muscles to reduce atrophy, how to care for his bed sores.

One day when she arrived, Michael's room was empty. Maggie met her at the nurses' station, put her beefy hand on Sarah's shoulder, and said, "He's back in ICU today. He had another one of his seizures."

Sarah sagged against Maggie's huge form. "A bad one? Is he okay?"

"Pretty bad. The doctors won't allow visitors. He'll be there for several days this time, I think. Call me tomorrow."

Sarah called first thing in the morning. Maggie wasn't on duty yet. The nurse who answered said Michael was still in ICU, doing as well as could be expected, and that Sarah should call back later. Sarah called again at 9:00 a.m., at 10:00, and at noon. Each time, Michael was still in ICU, still allowed no visitors, and still doing "as well as could be expected."

Maggie called her shortly after 2:00 p.m. "Honey, can you get off work early?"

Sarah's chest tightened. "Yes, why? How is Michael?"

"If you can come down here, you should. Soon. Come see me when you get here."

"Maggie, what's wrong?"

"Just get down here, Sarah. I'll talk to you then."

It took Sarah almost an hour to get out of the office, down to her car, across town, and up to see Maggie. By then, it was too late.

MICHAEL WANDERED AWAY from his body and prowled the ICU. He hated coming down here. So many people died. He was getting tired of being the hospital's unofficial welcoming committee for the dead.

A little boy, victim of a hit-and-run, sat up and swung his legs over the bed as Michael passed. "Hi," said the boy.

Michael nodded. "I'm Michael. What's your name?"

"Jimmy."

"Well, Jimmy, I don't think you need those tubes and things anymore, do you?"

"I guess not," said the boy. He left his body lying on the bed and stood up. "Hey!" he said as nurses rushed toward him, responding to the alarms. His brown eyes widened as they passed right through him. "Wow. Coolness."

"Yup. Want to take a walk with me? You can go anywhere you want now."

"Uh, sure, but what are they doing?"

"Oh, they'll be fussing for awhile. Nurse and doctor stuff. Don't worry about it."

Michael took the boy's hand, and they walked away from the ICU into a memory. Waves lapped their ankles. The sky arched blue overhead. Seagulls screamed and dived in the distance.

"Ultra cool!." The boy's body was tanned and healthy under the thin white hospital gown. He pulled his hand from

Michael's and stood staring at the water. "Can I go swimming?"

"You may do anything you want."

"I don't have swimming trunks."

"Pretend you have them."

"What good'll that do?"

"Try it."

The boy shrugged and closed his eyes. When he opened them again, the hospital gown had been replaced by a pair of blue swimming trunks with a yellow lightning bolt stitched down one leg. His small chest heaved as he sucked in a breath. "Wow."

He turned shining brown eyes on Michael. "Can I get anything I imagine?"

"Anything at all, Jimmy. Almost anything."

Suddenly the boy was holding an ice-cream cone. Just as suddenly, it was gone, replaced by a slice of watermelon. Then the watermelon disappeared, and he held a BB gun. Then, in rapid succession, a slingshot, a steaming plate of mashed potatoes and turkey, a comic book, a GI Joe, a model airplane, a remote-controlled race car, and the ice-cream cone again.

He dropped the cone, and it disappeared before it hit the sand at their feet. He stared at his bare toes, his hair hanging in his eyes.

"What's the matter, Jimmy?"

"I don't want that stuff. I thought I did, but I don't."

The boy was half-transparent now. "What do you want?" asked Michael gently.

"To be alive again."

"That's the one thing you can't have." Michael reached over, put his hand on Jimmy's shoulder. Suddenly the boy buried himself in Michael's arms, clung tightly. The boy's skin was warm, but there was no substance. It felt like hugging smoke. The boy was almost completely gone.

"It'll be okay," Michael said. He held still until the warmth faded from his arms and he stood alone on the beach. "Good-bye, Jimmy," he said softly. He turned away from the memory, switched it off like a light.

The world went dim and gray. There were no compass points. No sounds. No smells. No physical sensations. No sense of time. He couldn't find the hospital again. All directions were the same; all led nowhere. Gray eternity overwhelmed him. He'd lost the connection to his body, or had finally died.

"Oh, shit," he said, and began to fade.

NUMBLY, Sarah sat holding Maggie's hand. She half-listened to the doctor. She couldn't focus on his words. "The EEG went flat early this afternoon," he said. She lost track again. It couldn't be real. Couldn't be. *Michael!* "—On the respirator the whole time, but he never came back," continued the doctor implacably. "Perhaps it's for the best. He was very sick, you know. His brain was alive for the last year and a half—"

Sarah sniffled. Maggie handed her a Kleenex.

The doctor went on. "I know this is hard for you. I'm trying to explain as carefully as I know how. The EEG measures brain wave activity. Until his last seizure, the EEG showed that his brain was still alive. Even conscious, or something close to that, from time to time. He couldn't tell us because of the paralysis. Then, about a year ago, he lapsed into the coma. He had what appeared to be normal dream and sleeping states after that, but couldn't wake up."

"I understand all that. What happened? Why did it change?"

"Mrs. Hansen—"

"Weller. Miss."

The doctor glanced sharply at Maggie. "I was told you were his wife."

"No," said Sarah. "Just a friend. A very close friend. A might-have-been wife. We weren't even engaged, not really."

Maggie frowned, but the doctor looked relieved. "Then our records were right?" he asked. "We had no next-of-kin listed."

"Never mind," said Sarah. "Just tell me what happened."

"We don't know, really. His brain was severely traumatized by the original accident. He's had paralysis and seizures ever since. It's a miracle he survived as long as he did. There's always hope, especially when the EEG is near normal, but. . . ." He shrugged helplessly. "We did everything we could, everything humanly possible. We used every tool at our disposal, but we couldn't save him. I'm sorry, Miss Weller, but he died. The chief of staff agreed to take him off the vent—the respirator—this afternoon. He was already dead by then, pupils fixed and dilated. Complete loss of autonomic functions. His heart stopped, and we shocked it back, but by then he was already gone. He didn't suffer. He never came back after the last seizure. Our records showed no next-of-kin. In that condition, there was no reason to keep him on the vent."

He was a gork, Sarah thought mordantly. *So you unplugged him. So shut up. I get it.*

But the doctor kept talking anyway. "Then Nurse Stempson told us about you, so we had her call. We would have consulted with you first, naturally, if we'd known. Even if you weren't his wife—"

"I see. Don't worry about that part." Sarah's control started slipping. It was all too unreal. Michael was gone, and the fool doctor was worried about a lawsuit. As if that could bring him back. Tears threatened to overwhelm her. *Michael! Oh, God, Michael.*

Maggie squeezed her hand tightly and spoke up. "Doctor, I been talking to Miss Weller for a long time now, ever since she started coming regular to see Mr. Hansen. We're friends. I'll make sure she's taken care of."

"Thank you, Nurse Stempson."

Maggie helped Sarah to her feet. "Come on, honey. Let's get you some coffee, then we'll have a long talk."

MICHAEL FLAILED WILDLY in the grayness, reaching for any handhold he could find. He wasn't ready to die. Not yet. Primal instincts took over, and he thrashed and twisted in panic. How long had it been? Was it too late already? He reached and found nothing. Nothing to hold. Nowhere to go. No sound. No sight. No smell. No touch. Nothing. Nothing.

Something?

Something!

There. Yes. A pathway he could recognize. He lunged, grabbed hold. It was subtly different from what he remembered. How badly had his brain been damaged by that last seizure? It didn't matter. It was a pathway. He flew along it, recognizing each twist and curve. It fit like a glove. Yes, he could go through here. There was a resistance at the end, but he pushed at it, broke through it. Light exploded around him. Vision. Forms against the grayness; shadows; substance. More resistance. He pushed harder. Sound. A voice, warm and compassionate. Saying something kind. He didn't listen. It didn't matter what the voice said, just that he could hear it.

Almost. Almost there. It was tight. No room. The resistance mounted, but he swelled, filled the available space, pushed the resistance away. Out. Into the dark. Away. He pushed again, and suddenly the resistance was gone. Something fled weeping and protesting into the eternal darkness. Even as he turned to look, it faded, dissipated, and was gone. Michael expanded, adjusted, oriented himself, flexed his muscles, tested his body from the inside out. He closed his eyes, crying. He was alive.

Maggie squeezed his hand. "Sarah, are you okay?"

Michael looked up at Maggie. "I'm fine now," he said. "Just fine."

MIRACLE AT DEVIL'S CRICK

Callia lay in her dead-dark room, wove her web, spun her spells, and pulled the whole farm inside herself.

When she used the magic, nothing hid from her. No brick wall could block her, no bedroom door could shut her out, no secret was safe from her prying eyes. She saw her ma downstairs making breakfast, still in her thin cotton robe, her hair all pulled back and mussed from sleeping. Callia heard the bacon sizzle, smelled the coffee dripping into the pot, saw her pa getting the morning paper off the porch. She saw twelve-year-old Charlie in the bathroom, lips drenched in foam as he brushed his teeth, pajama top unbuttoned down to his belly so he could see in the mirror how strong and manly and tanned his chest was getting.

And outside, the sun was up already, leaping over the rooftops like a yellow-gold beacon, calling the children to another day's play, and the adults to their work. She smelled the early summer air, and it stirred her the way a cook stirs a simmering pot, blending the flavors. All without moving, Callia whirled in the scents of young pine from up over the hill, moist earth and sweet basil from her ma's garden, old man Peterson's wheezy truck starting up down the road, and faint as ever faint can be, the buds of wild roses growing in the lee of the shed.

Charlie stuck his head in the door to her room, switched on the light. "You gonna get up today, Cally?"

Callia's magic web of seeing and smelling ripped into tatters at the interruption, and she turned her head toward the door. "Ain't you supposed to knock? I'm getting powerful tired of you just barging in. Maybe I should turn you into a toad to learn you some manners."

"Aw, you ain't no witch, Cally. 'Sides, I bet you need me just now. It's morning. You got to pee?"

Callia made a face. "Yeah."

"Well, come on, then." Charlie pulled back the covers and swung her legs over the edge of the bed, put his shoulder under her arm and helped her slide into her chair, just as smoothly as if he'd done it a thousand times. But it weren't no thousand times yet; it was only two hundred and twelve. Callia knew because she'd been counting right along, ever since the accident.

She could push herself well enough once she got into the wheelchair, but Charlie followed along and made sure the towels and toothpaste and whatnot were all down on the counter in the bathroom where she could reach. Pa'd put in special railings, and once she'd built up the strength in her arms, she didn't need no help with the toilet. Good thing, too. A fourteen-year-old girl wanted her privacy sometimes.

"Call me when you wanna come downstairs," said Charlie, "less'n you're gonna fly down today on your broomstick."

Callia aimed a hairbrush at his head and let fly, but he ducked, laughing, and bounded down the stairs. She grinned, too, then wheeled over, leaned down, and scooped up the brush. It only took her a couple dozen minutes to finish her morning routine, but she didn't call Charlie back right away. Instead she wheeled down the hall to her room. Getting dressed by herself was right difficult, but by leaning and rolling and pulling she got her useless legs out of the pajamas and into a skirt. It didn't hurt too much if she was careful and went slow. She pulled on a blouse, squirmed back up into her chair, and got ready to do a summoning.

She plucked a thread from the hem of her skirt and tied a knot near the end, all the while thinking Charlie's name. Then she tied another knot at the other end while filling her mind with images of herself, sitting just so, right here in her room, a-tying the knot while the forces of magic whipped and whirled around her like heat waves in the air. Then she held the two ends together, so the knot for Charlie touched the knot for herself, and she twisted the thread into a come-hither, twisted it with her mind and her fingers all at once so the binding would hold.

It was a good come-hither; she felt proud of herself. Less than five minutes later, she heard Charlie's feet pound up the stairs, pause at the bathroom, then pad down the hall to her door.

"Where you been, Cally?" asked Charlie. "Ma saved you breakfast, but she's gonna be right sore if you ain't down before they leave. Why didn't you call me?"

"I did," she said, holding out her palm with the come-hither thread curled on it. "Now who says I ain't a witch? Why else did you come to my hexing?"

"Couldn't be 'cause Ma said to fetch you, huh?" Charlie shook his head. "You turned weird with all that witch stuff, Cally." He grabbed the handles on the back of her chair and started wheeling her toward the ramp at the head of the stairs.

"You're just too young to understand, that's all," she said over her shoulder. "Is Ma all ready to go to Aunt Gertie's?"

"Champin' at the door. Pa, too, don't forget. He's powerful eager to get going."

Aunt Gertie in Indiana had broken her hip, and Ma was going to nurse her. She'd be gone for weeks, but there weren't nobody else to do it. Pa'd have to drive her down there, near four hundred miles away, and that'd take all day long, so of course he wouldn't come back 'till tomorrow.

"You just don't forget who's in charge today. You gotta mind me, Charlie."

"Grab the brake and shut up," he said. "I reckon you're in charge of me, all right, but I gotta take care of you while Pa's gone, so that makes me as much in charge of you as you is of me. Don't start thinkin' you can run things just 'cause you're older. You got that brake tight? Here we go."

Charlie tilted her chair back a bit and set her front wheels onto the edge of the ramp. Callia stared down at the landing, only six steps below, but looking like forever away and just as steep. Her hand pulled up on the brake lever all by itself, pulled it tight, hung on so hard her knuckles turned white and her arm ached. Charlie went around in front, like Pa always said to do, leaned forward, grabbed the arms of her chair, and nodded. "I'm ready. Let's go."

Callia took a deep breath and released the brake just a little. The chair creaked and jerked a couple of inches down the ramp. "You holdin' tight?"

"I got you, Cally. C'mon."

Little by little, she eased the chair down the ramp, Charlie bracing her the whole way. She didn't breathe easy until she was level again and had wheeled into the warmth and safety of the kitchen. "I purely hate those stairs," she said, hoping for some sympathy from her ma. She wouldn't get none from Charlie. He borrowed her chair sometimes and shot down the ramp on it like he was driving a race car. 'Sides, he'd already run back up the stairs. But her ma didn't have time for no idle chat today; she was already dressed and a-standing by the door ready to go, and it was plain she was thinking about her trip and all the little details she might have forgot, and how it was too late now to attend to them, so she'd just have to pray to the Good Lord and keep her fingers crossed, too.

Callia endured the usual lecture about watching her little brother, making sure he stayed out of trouble, took his bath, didn't sass, and went to bed on time, then she kissed her ma and pa good-bye and watched while they drove away.

Charlie, now wearing only red shorts and his tan, blew past her and banged out the door right after they left, his bare feet popping on the cement driveway as he ran off. "You stay 'round here!" Callia yelled after him, but she didn't worry much, 'cause he was mostly a good boy, even if he was only twelve and full of rambunction and mischief. She heard him shout "Yaaaaaa!" once, then he was gone, swallowed up by the summer morning.

She ate the breakfast her ma'd left out for her, and even tasted the leftover coffee in the pot before she cleaned everything up. She didn't like coffee too terrible much, but it made her feel grown up to drink it, and she figured she'd have to learn to like it someday, so she might as well practice a bit.

Long about noon, Charlie came back from his playing, fair blowed from running so much, and so dirty she knew he must have been down by Devil's Crick again, scratching for tadpoles and crawdads in the mud. She fixed some sandwiches and milk for lunch, and made him wash his hands afore he ate.

"It's gonna rain," she said. "I got a weather-sense."

Charlie nodded over his sandwich. "Don't take no witchery for that. It's humid as hell, and there's clouds something fierce out west."

"You stay away from Devil's Crick then," she said. "You can play out back the house instead, where I can watch you. And don't say 'hell.' It ain't polite."

"Rain never hurt no one, and I can use whatever words I like."

"Like hell you can," she said, grinning despite herself. Then she sobered up. "If you wash away in the crick, Ma'd miss you, and I'd have no one to practice my witching on, so you just do what I say, Charlie."

He shrugged, finished his sandwich, and drained his glass of milk. "You need anything from upstairs?"

Callia shook her head. "I'm all set. You go on and play, but stay in the yard."

"Okay." One second he was there, a-grinning at her with his white teeth and dirty face, and the next second he was gone, the door banging behind him and his battle-cry "Yaaaaaa!" floating back on the breeze.

She spent the afternoon reading and daydreaming by the big front window, then she dozed off in her chair, listening to the distant thunder and the cicadas and birds and wind.

What woke her was the silence. It came all of a sudden, and it wasn't until the birds started up again that she realized they'd been quiet. She didn't need no weather-sense to know something unnatural was going on. The sky was purely dark outside the window, 'cept where it was a kind of yellow-green away out to the west. And now the wind picked up, real strong for a second, so that the tree tops bent way over, then still again. There was a big clap of thunder that shook the window glass and made her heart thump, and all the birds and crickets shut up for a minute, only gradually a-starting in to make noise again.

Callia wheeled her chair across to the back door, pulled it open, and rolled out onto the wooden porch. A few drops of cold rain sprinkled across her legs, and the wind lifted her skirt and hair. "Charlie! You get inside now!" She made her voice as loud as it could go, 'cause she didn't see him in the yard where he belonged. "Charlie!"

It weren't no good calling him, but she did it anyway, all the while knowing in her brain that he was too far off to hear. There wasn't but one place he'd be, and that was wherever she'd told him not to go. "Why didn't I tell him to stay away from his room?" she demanded of the sky, like it could hear and maybe answer. But the sky didn't care; it just got on with its business, and soon the rain was coming down steady. "Charlie!" she called. "Charlie, if you catch pneumonia and die, Pa will whip you! Charlie!"

Callia swung the chair around and headed back inside. The clock on the kitchen wall said it was only six, though it was dark enough outside for midnight. She switched on the porch light, thinking maybe that would help Charlie find his way, and then settled herself down to wait in the kitchen. Then she got to thinking that he'd need hot food when he got back, so she started fixing dinner. The thunder crashed, and the rain didn't let up. If anything, it came down harder. Callia heard the trees whipping back and forth in the wind, though she couldn't see anything outside 'cept when there was lightning.

By seven o'clock, all the food she'd made was sitting cold on the table, and still the rain came down. She figured that Charlie was a-sitting out the storm somewheres, and she hoped he had sense to stay out from under the trees what with all the lightning banging around out there. Long about eight o'clock, with the rain coming down as hard as ever, she started thinking maybe he was lost. She closed her eyes, wove her web, spun her spells, and tried to see where he might be.

It was hard to concentrate with the thunder booming and crashing every few seconds, and she couldn't tell from one moment to the next what she was looking at 'cause everything was black, and nowhere did she see the spark of a twelve-year-old boy lost in the storm. Well, if she couldn't find him, maybe he could find her. She pulled a thread from her skirt and made the knots for a come-hither, binding it with the image of her and Charlie meeting right there in the kitchen, him all wet but safe. But even as she tied it, she knew the summoning wouldn't work, 'cause she couldn't picture him right. Every time she tried to see him clearly in her mind, she didn't see him smiling and safe the way he'd have to be for the summoning to work. Instead, she saw him a-lying on the ground, not moving, hair plastered down, his face all peaceful despite the rain and thunder and mud.

The room got hot and prickly suddenly, and she knew she was seeing a maybe—something that might really happen, something that *would* happen if she didn't do something about it. But what could she do? She didn't recognize where he was, and even if she did, how could she get there?

There was a tremendous flash, and a clap of thunder right on top of it, and all the lights went out. Callia shivered, even though it wasn't cold, 'cause as sudden as a lightning hit, she knew what she had to do. She had to go get Charlie. And she knew where he was, too—she'd known it all along. He was down by Devil's Crick, right where she told him not to be.

She made herself stop and think out the route. The shortest way was out the back, up over the hill with the pine trees, and down the other side right into the crick. But she couldn't go that way. There weren't no path for wheelchairs through the trees. She'd have to go the long way, down along the road until it crossed the crick, then somehow she'd have to get off the bridge and down to the water. From there, she could follow the bank until she found Charlie. But how would she get back? There weren't no way she could go uphill, not unless she had something to pull on. . . . A rope! She could take a rope, and pull them back up!

There wasn't no more time to think, 'cause she suddenly remembered that Devil's Crick always flooded real easy, and it had been raining like nobody's business for hours already. She pictured the black water swirling and rising, with Charlie caught on a log or knocked unconscious, the water up to his knees, then his waist, then his chest, then—

No! She was moving before she knew it. Out the door, across the porch, down the ramp, and back to the shed. The wind and rain lashed her like whips, and the thunder was so loud it hurt her ears. The rope came to her hand, right where it was supposed to be, and then she rolled onto the driveway, her arms pumping in a steady rhythm on the wheels. "I'm coming, Charlie!" Her wheels skidded on wet pavement, but she dug in, got traction, and sped down the road toward the bridge.

It was a long way, near half a mile she reckoned, and uphill the last hundred feet where the road went over the crick. Her arms were powerful tired by the time she got there, and she was wet clear through her clothes. The rain slacked off somewhat, but it didn't matter if the clouds broke up and moved off—the storm'd done its work already. She saw quick glimpses when the lightning flashed. Devil's Crick rushed and roared below her in the dark like it'd gone mad. The water was mighty fast and high, all a-roil with tree branches and swirling debris.

She'd be insane to go down into that, not even knowing if Charlie was out there. She shouldn't have come. She knew that now. She should have gone for old man Peterson. He'd have brought his truck, and he had two strong legs for climbing, two strong arms for carrying. Even if Charlie was down there, what could she do? All she had was a rope and a wheelchair. There wasn't even a path down from beside the bridge, or if there was one, it was washed away by now.

She turned away and let the wheelchair start rolling down the bridge. It wasn't too late to fetch old man Peterson. He'd come right quick, but she'd have to go back down the road, past her house, find him in the dark and convince him that—

"Help!"

Callia jerked up on the wheelchair's brake. She froze in place, listening. It'd been awful faint, probably she'd just imagined—

"Help!"

She heard it for sure that time. It was off to the left, Charlie's voice and no mistake—even so faint and distant, there wasn't no way she'd not know her own brother's voice. "Charlie!" she yelled. "I'm here, and I'm a-coming!"

But how? She wheeled over to the guardrail and looked down. It wasn't too deep here, maybe three feet to the ground, but there was nowhere for her chair to go even if she could get it over the edge. The ground was all mud, sliding straight down into the water . . . what was that? Something bobbing in the crick, something white. . . . Another flash of lightning, and she saw him, clear as day, water up to his armpits, out near the base of the bridge, where a tangle of branches had caught on a piling.

She didn't stop to think. She tied one end of the rope to the guardrail on the bridge, the other end 'round her waist, and fell forward out of her chair, over the rail, down to land with a thump in the mud. A stone gouged her left knee, and another one sliced her calf. She ignored the hurt and slithered down the bank on her belly. Though she couldn't use her legs, it didn't stop them from feeling pain, which at that moment Callia thought was mighty unfair. The other way 'round would be useful right now.

And there he was.

His face was a pale blob against the dark water, only a dozen feet out from the edge. He looked to be treading water. Why didn't he swim in?

On one elbow and hip, her useless legs trailing through the mud behind her as if they belonged to someone else, she lurched forward, flung her other hand out, grabbed at the thickest branch within reach, and hauled herself into the water.

All at once she was in over her head. The current slapped at her like a giant hand, pulled her instantly downstream. She breached the surface, wind milling her arms, grateful for the muscles she'd built up by pushing her chair. In the water, her legs didn't matter so much. They didn't help, but they didn't hinder her none either. She shook the hair out of her eyes, angled against the current, and swam over to Charlie with only a couple dozen powerful strokes.

She wanted to laugh and cry, hug him and strangle him, all at once. "Charlie," she said when she was near enough she didn't have to shout. "What are you doing out here?"

"I'm hurt, Cally," he said. "Maybe bad. My foot's caught. I think it's broke."

While he was talking, the current swept her downstream. She wasn't worried too much, 'cause she was still tied to the rope, but that wouldn't do Charlie no good. She swam back to him against the insistent tug of the water.

"I'm awful tired, Cally," he said. "I been swimming a long time."

She didn't say what she was thinking—that the water was already up to his shoulders, and still rising fast. She just nodded and said, "Well, hold on, I'll take a look."

She took a deep breath and pushed herself under the water. She followed his leg down and down while the crick tried to swirl her away. She couldn't see anything, but she could feel the branches, anchored deep in the muck. She explored them with her hands, ignoring the way her lungs were aching. Charlie's ankle was trapped in the crook of one branch, another log pressed against it, holding it tight. She worried at it until she couldn't hold her breath no more, then pushed up off the bottom and exploded into the air, gasping and blowing. The water was up to Charlie's neck now, and he looked mighty scared. "You just keep treading water, Charlie," she said, then sucked in as much air as she could hold and dove again.

This time she hauled herself down, hand over hand. She used his leg like a rope ladder, and went right to the tangle. She pushed and tugged at his foot, turning it this way and that, but the branches held it firm. She dribbled air out of her mouth as slow as possible, trying to extend her time underwater. Her lungs burned and her head felt like it was fixin' to explode. There was no way that ankle was coming loose. She finally surfaced. For a moment, she was so glad to be breathing again, and so tired, that she let the current drag her downstream. It would be so easy, so restful, to just float. But Charlie needed her. She shook her head and struck out against the flow. The water was still rising. Charlie's face was tipped back now, and the water lapped his chin and ears. "I can't swim no more, Cally," he said, and his voice was so soft she wouldn't have understood him if there hadn't been a mother-of-god big lightning bang just then to show his face.

She grabbed one of his arms and shook it hard, then had to let go again to keep herself afloat. "Charlie, Charlie, you *got* to listen now. Pa said to mind me, so you just keep swimming, hear? That's an order, Charlie! You hear me? An *order!* I don't care how growed up you think you are. I'm in charge and you gotta do what I say."

He didn't answer. His eyes were shut, and his arms weren't moving no more. The water closed over his mouth and nose, and he drifted quietly down, away from her.

"Charlie!" Callia screamed so loud she thought her lungs would come up her throat. She grabbed after him, caught one hand, and used it to pull herself down again. She found his leg, then his ankle, then the tree-trunk that was pinning it. This time, instead of trying to pull his foot out, she swam along the length of the log until she reached its free end. She wrapped both arms under it, like carrying firewood, but that was no good. She didn't have leverage 'cause she couldn't push with her legs. So she got all the way under it, her shoulders against the bottom of the crick, and pushed up and over as hard as she could, all the time thinking it was a damn fool thing to do, and she like as might end up trapped herself, and then she and Charlie'd both be drowned. But she kept pushing, 'cause there weren't nothing else left to try.

She thought her heart would burst before the log moved, but then suddenly it came free. It slid ponderously to one side, and almost landed on her legs. But she pushed against it as it was falling, got her legs out, and shot to the surface.

For a second, she couldn't find him. Then the lightning flashed. He was drifting free, not three feet away, head down, being a-pushed by the current. She lunged through the water, grabbed his hair with one hand, turned over on her side and pulled him in close. She got his head up high, her right arm under his chest, and just held on. The current swirled them downstream until they hit the length of the rope, then swung them over to the bank.

Somehow she got them both up out of the water, digging with her elbows in the mud, yanking on Charlie's arms to pull him after her. She rolled him onto his back and pushed on his chest until water spurted out his nose and mouth. "Charlie! Charlie, don't you dare die!" She pushed on his chest again, then breathed into his mouth until she felt his lungs inflate. "Charlie! Oh, Charlie, baby, come on, you can't die, you can't. I won't let you!" She was crying now, her tears mingling with the rain that fell on his peaceful, upturned face. It was the maybe-picture she'd seen, him lying on the ground, body still, so still, too still. Dead. He was dead. She knew it all of a sudden.

"Wake up!" she shouted, banging on his bare chest with her fists. "Come on, Charlie, come back to me, come back. I love you, Charlie! I love you. You can't be dead. Breathe, Charlie, breathe!" She put her mouth over his again and blew into his lungs. Again. And again. And again. Then she pushed on his chest. "Come on, Charlie!" Suddenly he coughed weakly, then gasped and coughed again.

"Oh, Charlie!" She was laughing and crying at the same time now, but she didn't even know it. She cradled his head against her chest and held him tight, rocked him like a baby, held him while he coughed. He finally got his breathing under control, and she smoothed back his hair and looked down at him.

"You okay now?" she asked.

"I'm sore all over, and my foot hurts something wicked. I reckon I had my bath for tonight."

His voice was hoarse, and of a sudden he looked awful young. Callia wiped her nose with the back of her hand and started crying again for no reason she could see. "You'll be okay," she said. "We'll both be okay now."

He started coughing again, and it was a couple minutes before he could talk. "Cally, I couldn't swim no more. That's all I recollect. What happened after that?"

"Magic," she said. "Powerful strong magic. A come-hither like you never seen."

"Aw, Cally, you ain't no witch."

"You shut up," she said, and hugged him for all she was worth.

WAITING FOR GRAMPA TO DIE

We sat on folding chairs around Grampa's bed. At first they talked in whispers, or not at all, afraid to disturb him, perhaps, or maybe just afraid of him, of what he was doing. I didn't talk at all, just watched, waiting for Grampa to die. As time went on, however, they stopped whispering, and the stuffy silence was broken only by the loud *pock* of the timepiece on the mantle.

Nurse and I sat together on the left side of the bed. Across from us were Mom and Dad, so that the four of us bracketed the old man's bed like archangels, guarding the four quarters, waiting to bear him aloft when he drew his last breath. I watched his chest rise and fall under the blanket, rise and fall, such a slight motion that I convinced myself it wasn't happening at all, that he had stopped breathing a long time ago. Then a wrinkle in the blanket would move, ever so little, and I would know that he was still alive. The room smelled of old clothes and antiseptic, of Mom's perfume and mothballs. It was an odd smell, all mixed together like that, a faintly musty smell which was nevertheless sharp and bitter. I felt lightheaded, each tick of the clock seeming further and further apart, as if time were stretching out like taffy, stretching thinner and thinner, until I became lost between ticks, the silence roaring in my ears like the ocean. I wondered if Grampa could hear the silence, if he could hear anything.

The room was hot and very still. I blinked sweat out of my eyes and rubbed my forehead with my wrist.

"How much longer, do you think?" asked Dad. After so long a silence, his whisper seemed to come from nowhere, as if the walls had spoken, or the floor.

"I can't tell you that, Mr. Granger," replied Nurse, touching Grampa's wrist lightly. Her voice was low and controlled, not a whisper, but not speaking loudly either. It was the firm, sympathetic, professionally reverent hush all nurses learn to use. "I've never seen anyone last this long before, in this condition. At least he's peaceful. When the end comes, he won't know it. He'll just slip away, a little deeper into sleep, then deeper still, until he's no longer sleeping. . . ."

"Dead!" I shouted, my voice very loud and shrill. Mom and Dad jerked upright at the sound, and even Nurse flinched back. "He'll be dead," I continued, "and then we can have a funeral and *bury* him."

Mom covered her mouth with one hand while the other fluttered on her lap like a wounded sparrow. She started to speak, then gave up, feeling helpless, I suppose, to think of anything meaningful to say to a twelve-year-old watching his grandfather die. Dad's face went flat, then crinkled into a strange expression I had never seen before. "Gerry, why don't you wait outside." His tone of voice told me it wasn't a question, so I got up and left the room, closing the door quietly, almost gently, behind me.

Outside it was already dark. Thunder rumbled far away and heat lightning made the horizon flicker. The air felt thick and heavy, but there was no rain yet, no breeze. It was as if the world held its breath to find out what I would do next. I stood on the front porch and felt a sense of panic building somewhere deep in my guts. My legs were trembling. I wanted to shout, or run, or hit someone. I felt I had to do something, anything, but there was nothing to do. Instead, I sat on the porch swing and set it gently in motion, the chains creaking above me. I was still sweating, despite that I wore only shorts, shoes, and a tee-shirt. The weathered wood of the swing seat felt smooth and slick under my thighs and against the backs of my knees. The panic slowly subsided as I pendulated the swing back and forth, the tips of my sneakers just barely brushing the porch.

And I remembered Grampa.

Grampa built this house, built it with his own hands. He had been working on it for more than thirty years, building an addition here, a sun porch there, polishing, cleaning, improving, whittling, scraping, and painting. Wood and plaster and brick came alive under his hands, as he lovingly tooled each corner, carpeted each floor, glazed each window. The house had character; it was unique. Each nook had a cabinet lovingly crafted to inhabit it and no other; each window was angled and jointed to show just exactly what Grampa wanted to see from that room.

I remember when Grampa first took me aside, put a hammer in my hands, and, his fingers cupping mine, let me help him create his masterpiece, his lifework, the house.

But now the garden was overgrown, the hedges untrimmed,

and the paint peeled in large, scabrous weals, as though the house had contracted a disease, a disease which rotted away from the inside, slowly, slowly, so that only after years of tedious deterioration did the wounds begin to show, easing through the skin of the house the way blood oozes up from a scraped knee.

I pushed the swing gently back and forth, waiting for Grampa to die, and wondering what would happen to the house after he was gone. Only gradually, faintly, far off and sweet, like the sound of a children's choir practicing in a distant cathedral, did I become aware that I was not alone. Across the darkness of the yard, painted a black which was almost imperceptibly darker than the trees, a figure stood and watched me in silence. I could see no eyes, no telltale glint in the gloom, yet I was sure that I was being watched. "Hello?" I ventured. "Do you want something?" There was no answer, but my skin prickled and leaped, dragging my bones with it, so that my entire body gave a convulsive shudder, jerked suddenly upright. There was more than one; the yard was full of shadowy specters. I held my breath and strained to see through the charcoal air.

Then it was as though the figures were rushing at me, faster and faster, leaning forward, arms a-stretch, feet just skimming the ground, all with a terrible quietness and mordancy. A breath of the grave overcame me, attar and dust, and I screamed aloud. "What do you want!"

"Don't talk to them," said my father from behind me, and I whirled, falling off the swing, terrified to turn my back on the specters, terrified, strangely, of my father, too. "Don't ever talk to them," he told me again, and I knew, somehow, without looking, that the specters had retreated, were waiting just beyond sight.

"Who are they?" I gasped. "What do they want?"

"They are waiting for Grampa to die. Come inside now, Gerry."

I rushed past him and flung myself up the stairs. Breathless, heart pounding, I locked the door of my bedroom and sat on the bed. Through the window, illuminated now and then by flashes of heat lightning, I could see the ghouls, standing quietly, standing tall and black and tenebrous in the yard, waiting, just waiting, waiting for Grampa to die. I fancied I could hear them breathing, that it was in time with the creak of Grampa's breath, and that with each wheeze they would lean forward, with each rattle lean back . . . almost, almost, not yet, not quite yet, but soon, soon. . . . A yearning, a subsidence; a rhythm of breathing like the wash of the sea. At some point I fell asleep, and when I woke, it was morning and it was raining, and Grampa was dead.

I stood alone at the side of the coffin, dressed in my best Sunday suit, and looked at Grampa's face. His eyes and lips had been carefully sewn shut already, and his cheeks were propped up from within by stiff plastic inserts. I could hear the minister in the other room, talking to Mom and Dad, talking softly, urgently, counseling them in their grief. I wanted to laugh. Grief? There was no sorrow here; only release. Grampa's hands looked very still and fragile, paper-thin now that the veins had collapsed. I couldn't imagine how those frail hands had built this house.

The room was suddenly filled with black, shadowy specters, and the overwhelming attar of their breath washed over me. They did not look at Grampa—they looked at me. Strangely, I felt no fear this time. "Cheated," said a voice from my throat. It was not my voice, and it was not talking to me. It was Grampa's voice, using my lungs and vocal cords and tongue to shape his message. "Cheated," he said again, talking to the shadow shapes. "I have cheated you. Now you will have to wait."

The specters hissed and vanished. "Grampa?" I asked aloud, but there was no answer. I touched Grampa's body, poked my forefinger into his cold arm. "Gramps?"

A hand touched my shoulder, and I whirled around. My mouth hung open, and I could feel the heat rising in my cheeks. The minister stood quietly behind me. I had not heard him enter. "You must have loved him very much," said the minister, and I knew then that he had not seen the specters, not heard Grampa using my voice to speak.

"What?"

"You must have loved him very much," repeated the minister.

"He's in my blood," I replied. I touched my chest. "In here. He's inside me. He's not really dead."

"Yes, he will always live inside those who loved him."

Damned platitudes. "That's not what I meant," I began, then stopped. It was pointless. This minister could not understand. I paused for breath. "When it's time," I said, "to close the coffin, I...."

"Yes?"

"When it's time, I want to close the lid."

The minister's face crinkled. His hand tightened on my shoulder. "My son, you can't mean that."

"Yes, yes, I do. I want to close the lid. I want to slam it. I want to put nails in it. I want to...." Suddenly I was crying, and I didn't want him to see that. I left him standing there beside the coffin, bewildered by my intensity, shocked by my words.

The specters followed me through the halls, invisibly floating behind me as I walked past my parents. *Come with me*, I told them silently. *Come with me if you want.* They followed me up the stairs, past my bedroom, into the bathroom. They crowded around me, the stench and fetor of the grave dripping from them like rain as I locked the bathroom door and glared at my reflection in the mirror. My face wavered in and out of focus, first looking like my own, then looking like Grampa's. I glowered at the mirror and tried to force my face to remain my own.

"You can't glare me out," said Grampa, and the specters surged forward at the sound. "Your face is my face, Gerry," Grampa went on, using my throat without permission. "Grimace all you want, but you can't glare me out."

I took off my Sunday tie, jacket, and shirt. I hit myself on the chest, over the heart. "Out," I grunted with every blow. "Get out." I watched in the mirror as my skin reddened. I hit harder, striking my stomach and ribs with closed fists. "Out!" I growled. I gritted my teeth and punched as hard as I could. "Come out of there!"

"You can't beat me out," said Grampa, laughing. "You are the seed of my seed, the flesh of my flesh. I have every right to stay here. You are only hurting yourself." The specters leaned forward, relishing my pain. They ran their ghostly black hands up and down my body, touching each bruise, fondling each welt. With disgust, I tried to shove them away, but although they could touch me, my hands went right through them, and I was just pushing at shadows.

I took down my father's razor and turned on the hot water. Holding the sharp edge of the razor against my inner wrist, I pressed lightly, and the steel slid easily into the surface of my skin. A thin trickle of blood appeared, quickly washed away by the running water; I had only cut through the first layer of skin.

I would have to press harder. "You can't bleed me out," said Grampa's voice from my throat, but he was no longer laughing.

"You're in my blood," I told him. "And when the blood comes out, so will you." The specters leaned forward eagerly, watching, waiting, hoping. I paused, the blade just barely resting on my skin. Could I really do this?

"It won't work," said Grampa. "But I won't let you try." I watched with fascination as my hand put the razor back on the shelf. "You see, Gerry," said Grampa, breathing the air in my lungs, moving my lips to say his words. "You can't fight me." He moved my legs and arms for me, turned off the water, sat me down on the toilet lid. He made my hands remove my belt and trousers, take off my shoes and socks. When I was naked, he marched me into the shower and held me under the cold water until I was spluttering and gasping and begging to be freed. He gave me my body back then, and I shut off the shower and got dressed.

The specters stood in a silent circle around me, watching. Grampa laughed at them through my throat. "You'll have to wait," he told them. "Just like Gerry." The specters moved off then, faded through the walls, melted through the floor, whispered away. But not far. I could feel them without knowing how I knew; I could see them, ringed invisibly around the house, still waiting.

I looked in the mirror at my face, at his face, and I couldn't tell which was which. "Grampa," I breathed, "you're dead."

"No, Gerry. I'm in you, in your blood, whether you like it or not."

He marched me through his funeral like a marionette. His dead hand kept my live one from slamming down the lid of his coffin, kept me at a respectful distance. His dead lips kept mine from speaking. He made me cry at the appropriate time, and he made me stand and watch while his body was lowered into the grave and the dirt was thrown on top. And inside, he was laughing.

After the funeral, I sat on the porch swing in the dark. The air was hot and humid. The crickets were loud. The stars were bright and unwinking. There was no moon.

Dad came out and sat beside me for a while in silence. Then he said, "I suppose tomorrow we should start fixing up the house."

"Why?" I asked. "Can't we just bulldoze it?"

"It's our heritage."

My hands twisted at each other until Grampa made my fingers lie still and splayed on my knees. As the swing went back and forth, and as my breath seeped through my throat, the dark ghosts faded in and out of view. They leaned forward with each lungful I sucked in, swayed back with each breath I expelled. There was a terrible, relentless rhythm about it all, and it matched the beating of my heart. Dad touched my hand, and I knew that he saw them, too.

Grampa spoke then, from my throat, and answered himself, from my father's throat. He was inside each of us, and we both realized it at the same moment, and I started to cry while Dad beat his fist softly against the back of the porch swing and said, "Damn, ahhh, damn," very quietly. Then suddenly Dad was hugging me, hugging hard, and I clung to him like a very little boy. Grampa let me cry for a long time, then made me straighten up again and knuckle my face dry. I sat next to Dad then, and leaned against him, and he put his arm around my shoulders. I looked out from under Dad's arm and saw the specters leaning forward, scenting pain. "Go away," I whispered. "Just go away."

"Don't talk to them," Dad said after a moment. "Don't ever

talk to them. It just makes it worse." We sat together in silence then, pushing the porch swing gently back and forth with our feet, watching the darkness deepen, listening to our breath match the rhythm of the night, not saying anything, just waiting, like the ghosts, for Grampa to die.

RITE OF PASSAGE

In the year 3118, Marion Schultz put her boy in a box and said good-bye. "Go get 'em, Larry." She waited until the transparent lid had frosted over before starting to cry.

More than a thousand years earlier—on December 14, 2107, at 04:32 UTC, to be precise—the Acturans had arrived in orbit around Earth. They said they'd been meaning to drop by earlier but, what with one thing or another, had been delayed and hoped we didn't mind too much.

They welcomed aboard their jumpship a delegation composed of scientists, diplomats, linguists, and psychologists. They took the delegates on a quick tour of the nearby portions of the galaxy, including a swoop-by of the home planet of Acturas and seventeen other M-class worlds they'd settled. They were back in fewer than twelve hours, having traveled hundreds of thousands of light-years and even stopping for lunch. The Earth delegates were speechless.

On the following day, by request, they took a few scientists back to Acturas and let them set up a small enclave, then returned and announced they'd be interested in establishing regular trade relations with Earth. Heads of state fell over themselves rolling out the highest honors they could conceive. The Acturans were amiable but adamantly informal. They didn't like ceremonies or speeches, so they said not to bother with the honors business, why not grab a couple of beers, toss back some peanuts, and just chat?

When biologists and anthropologists expressed surprise that aliens would look and act so human, even to the point of enjoying alcohol and speaking colloquial English, the Acturans blinked in astonishment of their own. "We thought you knew," they said. "We're puppets."

All of the Acturans humans had met were biological constructs, made specifically for the purpose of talking to us, controlled at supralight speeds from the home planet. Whether the puppets were alive or not was the subject of many debates, for although they were physically human down to their hangnails, they claimed to be just remotely operated machines run by the *real* Acturans, whom the Earthmen had never seen.

The implications of that level of biotechnology were as stupendous as the staggeringly advanced physics the Acturans had displayed. There was a wealth of knowledge beyond imagining, but the humans did their best to imagine it anyway and settled down to the bargaining table with high hopes.

On December 16, 2107, fewer than forty-eight hours after humanity learned it was not alone in the universe, the Acturans suddenly broke off negotiations without a word of explanation. They returned the scientists who'd been on Acturas, dumped the diplomats back on Earth, and promptly disappeared from the solar system.

Two years later, they were back, this time only as close as the LaGrange point on the moon's far side. They waited politely until the humans came out to meet them. The Earthmen wanted to know how they had offended the Acturans, how they could make amends. The Acturans explained that the mistake had been theirs. They had thought humanity was ready for the stars, but clearly was not. However, upon reflection, they realized that even though the human race itself might not be ready, some individual humans might be. They would therefore maintain an outpost at the LaGrange point, so that anyone who wanted to apply for Acturan citizenship could do so. Any individual could have one chance and one chance only. The ability to get to the LaGrange point and pass a test was all that was required. They refused to elaborate on what kind of test, or what they meant by "not ready." They also informed Earth's governments that, regrettably, the solar system was under strict quarantine until further notice. Any Earth vehicles, manned or not, that attempted to pass the orbit of Mars would be destroyed without warning.

For the next 150 years—until March 3, 2257, at 11:18 UTC, to be exact—no one passed the test. The Acturans allowed one test per day, and each applicant flunked. Year after year, the best, the brightest, the strongest, and the wisest Earth had to offer were tested and rejected by the Acturans without being told why, or even how, they had failed.

During that time, a sizable colony of scientists and military personnel grew around the Acturan jumpship, and an entire industry was born to support them. They studied what they could of Acturan technology, trying to divine the secrets of the interstellar jump or the apparently instantaneous communication they maintained with their homeworld. The Acturans neither helped nor hindered these observations, but forbade anyone from actually touching the jumpship. They ignored all efforts to communicate or negotiate, save that they

would administer their test once a day, to whomever appeared
at the airlock of their ship. Without comment or apparent
effort, they blew up the two Earth ships that tried to violate the
quarantine.

By carefully analyzing the experiences of everyone tested,
social scientists painstakingly tried to build up a model of a
human who was "ready." Forty-three percent of the applicants
had been asked only one question before being rejected.
Another twenty percent had made it through five questions.
Only three individuals had kept the interview going beyond
twenty-five questions. The rest fell somewhere in the middle,
with no clear pattern. The longest examination was twelve
hours, the shortest about thirty seconds.

The questions themselves ranged from details of particle
physics to analysis of ancient architectural styles. Some
questions were repeated to different candidates, others were
not. One poor fellow was asked to extemporize a forty-line
poem; another to do an interpretive dance on the subject of
crop rotation. Some sequences of questions appeared to follow
a pattern; others seemed made up on the spot. Most of
humanity began to believe that the ideal candidate would have
to know everything knowable; others suspected darkly that the
Acturans were just having fun at Earth's expense.

Then on March 3, 2257, Herbert Zachary Wilson passed the
test. Herb was a spacejack—a zero-gee engineer—who worked
at the LaGrange colony. He was never intended to be a
candidate. No government had selected him. No scientific body
had sponsored him. He had no special qualifications that
anyone could see. He wasn't even supposed to be *near* the
Acturan ship that day. He took the test by the simple
expediency of being where no one expected him to be, at
exactly the right time. He stole a one-man shuttle, zipped

across to the Acturan ship, was admitted and tested before anyone could react. His test lasted less than a minute. The Acturans broke their diplomatic silence to announce to the world's leaders that Herb had passed the test, grabbed the golden ring, won the lotto, and had been granted Acturan citizenship.

Herb made a brief statement, telling the world that the test was completely fair and honest, that practically anyone could pass, and that he wouldn't reveal either the questions he was asked or the answers he had given. "It wouldn't do any good," he said to the exasperated scientists who tried to quiz him.

When the military moved in to detain him—"Just for a few questions," they said—Herb borrowed a family-sized jumpship from the Acturans, hopped down to Earth, collected his wife and kids, and was back in space four hours later. He thumbed his nose at the world's governments by refusing to answer their radio calls, but broadcast to the media that he was off for a tour of the galaxy, might or might not come back, probably wouldn't send cards, but would certainly welcome any humans who cared to come visit him on Acturas. Laughing, he signed off, goosed the pedal, and disappeared from human space.

The people of the world made their opinion of the current setup unambiguous. Any elected official or egghead who tried to decide ahead of time who was qualified for the test should start looking for other work immediately. The political and scientific communities reacted the only way they could while still avoiding riots: They stopped trying to figure out who was "ready" and instituted a worldwide lottery. Three hundred and sixty five names were drawn each year. Unfortunately, the randomly selected candidates turned out to be no more successful than the carefully screened and prepared candidates had been. To the surprise and dismay of the psychologists, the statistics didn't change at all. The same kinds of questions were asked, with the same frequency, and the candidates all flunked.

For the next several years, Herb would come back occasionally, pick up some supplies, inquire politely about the state of the world, refuse to answer any questions, and take off again with a statement to the effect of, "Come on in, the water's fine."

The visits became farther and farther apart, and eventually tapered off to none. But meanwhile Herb's life was scrutinized and imitated more thoroughly than any person in history. People walked where he had walked, studied what he had studied, read his favorite books, memorized every word and gesture of his to have been recorded, and generally tried to *become* Herbert Zachary Wilson. None of it made the slightest bit of difference.

Finally, most came to believe that Herb's success had been a fluke. His life gave such a convincing appearance of having been ordinary that perhaps it really *had* been. He must have had some insight, some flash of genius, that couldn't be explained by studying his childhood, critiquing his high school essays, or analyzing his career path. And the answer one person could find with a lucky insight, the rest of the human race could ferret out—eventually—by being methodical.

Sanity slowly returned. The worldwide lottery was abolished, and the Institute for Acturan Studies was founded in 2305. The art of Life Shaping was born and flourished.

BEYOND CLAY, after paint, clearer than photography, more harmonious than music, more rigorous than science, more emotive than poetry: Life Shaping was the ultimate human endeavor, a marriage of art and skill to surpass any other.

The LaGrange colony was rechristened the Embassy—although the spacejacks kept calling it L2, as they always had—and the candidates were called Ambassadors—and the spacejacks kept calling them weenies or Earthworms, as before. The Acturan puppets looked on with grand indifference, dangling the bait of unlimited knowledge before humanity, watching to see what would develop. Their patience seemed to be as inexhaustible as their determination. The Life Shapers were just as determined, and they set out to win the game the Acturans had started.

The primary tenet of the Institute was that humanity had a right to the stars, just as each human had a right to life and liberty. The Acturans deemed humanity "not ready." Well, then, they'd jolly well *get* ready. Once again, the Ambassadors were the best and brightest the human race could offer. And under the Life Shapers, the best became better than ever. Mentally, physically, emotionally, spiritually—no *natural* human could compete with one who had been Shaped.

The Acturans broke their habit of silence to comment that they were impressed with the Institute's work. Although they continued rejecting every Ambassador they received, this one positive sign that humanity was on the right track, after many hundreds of years of silence, was sufficient to make the Life Shapers like unto gods.

IN THE YEAR 3118, mandatory pre-birth gene charting went into effect, and the tests for Marion Schultz's upcoming third child were so good that they had little trouble convincing her to give the boy to the Institute. Shortly after the boy was born, she delivered him to the freezer where he would wait until the Institute had an opening.

Eventually, the child once known as Larry Schultz was unfrozen, decanted, massaged, fed, assigned a permanent ID, and presented to Pikaar Ng's team for a pre-Shaping analysis. In due course, they deemed him appropriate for Ambassadorial training, just as the Life Shapers had predicted from the gene charts. They started the strict regimen of schooling and environmental conditioning that would last for the next ten years. Ng himself wouldn't bother seeing the child until the test results from the first decade came in.

MARION SCHULTZ always came on Birthday Day. The day had no particular meaning for the child now known as Jeremiah— he never even knew she was there. But for Marion, it was the one day each year when she was allowed to see her son, to verify that he was healthy and strong, that she had done the right thing by surrendering him to the Life Shapers.

She was one hundred thirty years old, and for the tenth time now, she stood watching Jeremiah through the one-way glass and thought the same things she always thought. It was a mistake. It was wrong. Even though he was doing well, even though all the attendants said he was very likely to be chosen. It wasn't worth it. She wanted to break the glass, leap through, sweep him up into her arms, and hug him, rock him, hold him forever. She shuddered, put one palm flat on the glass, then just stood there shivering.

Pikaar Ng stood in the back of the room, studying the behavior of the parents who came through. When Marion didn't move after several minutes, he came up behind her, put his hand on her shoulder, and said, "You're having trouble with this, aren't you?"

"Look at him," she said without turning away from the glass. "How can you look at him and not see what I see? He's not human any more. What you're doing is wrong."

"Of course he's human. He's just better than most. He's being Shaped. He's heir to all of humanity's greatness and none of its faults."

"He never laughs, he doesn't cry, he doesn't even know I'm here, or that he has a mother who cares about him. He's just a little boy, and you're making him into a monster."

"By keeping him from harm, by giving him the best education possible, by providing him with everything and anything he could possibly need or want?"

"You won't let him have *me*."

"Mrs. Shultz, I've had this same conversation with thousands of birth parents. In fact, I've had this conversation with you before. I remember your case very well. You have to accept that Jeremiah doesn't *want* you. He doesn't need you. You're confusing your own desires with his. He's perfectly well adjusted. If you'd been Shaped yourself, or even bothered to read the studies, you'd know this."

Marion shook her head and brushed away a tear. She didn't take her eyes from Jeremiah. On the other side of the glass, the boy tossed a ball up and down, not in play, but because he was mentally analyzing Einstein's famous elevator analogy, and probing his inertial reference frame.

"I want him back," Marion said. "He's only ten years old."

"I understand," said Ng. "Unfortunately, they don't stay that age. They grow up, don't they? If there's a brain malfunction or a hormonal imbalance, or any number of physical problems, we can usually fix those. Incorrect upbringing, however, is not so easily cured. All your careful nurturing can't guarantee that you won't raise a molester, a drug addict, a rights thief, a murderer, or an anarchist. The world's seen enough of that kind of thing. We've grown beyond it. And we need the Ambassadors. Only the best of the best can qualify. You wouldn't just be risking his career; you'd be risking making another Hitler. You don't want to risk a Hitler, do you, Mrs. Schultz? Life Shapers are professionals, and they're good at the job. For all your benign intentions, Mrs. Schultz, you're just playing at being a parent. You aren't equipped for it any more than a monkey would be."

Marion turned, finally, to look at him. "I gave birth to three healthy babies!"

"Of course, physiologically you're equipped. I meant that you don't have the toolset for proper childrearing. If you'd gotten an advanced degree in parenting, maybe we could work something out—supervision at home, regular testing, that sort of thing, starting in his early twenties or so, when the chances of damage would be significantly reduced. Your first two were ruined—"

He waved his hand to forestall her angry response. "Ruined for Life Shaping, because it's too late. Eighty years too late, if I remember your chart. Even if they'd qualified in the first place. I'm sure they're perfectly good natural children who are happy and give you lots of joy. But giving birth to healthy children isn't quite the same as having real parenting qualifications. It just means your reproductive organs are working properly. That's not enough for this kind of boy. Letting you raise a child like Jeremiah by yourself would be like giving you an armed bomb with no instructions. It would be criminal, madam, for me to let you. Not to mention abusive to the child."

Marion had looked away while he was talking, her eyes fastened once again on the boy beyond the window. But Ng's last sentence caught her attention, made her angry again. "How could providing a loving home be abusive?"

"Because you would raise the child to be what you thought the child should be. You'd impose your morals, your standards, your religion, and your traditions . . . in short, you'd brainwash him, without even knowing what you're doing. No matter how hard you tried to be objective—and I'm giving you the benefit of the doubt by assuming you'd want to be objective—you're a product of your own un-Shaped childhood, and you can't separate your cultural conditioning from reality. No, I'm sorry, Mrs. Schultz, but it just won't work. We can't risk letting you ruin the boy just to gratify some sort of animalistic maternity whim of yours. Our children are our future."

"Then we have no future," she whispered. "Because, when you people are done with us, we'll have no children—just little automatons. Perfect citizens. Robots."

"Mrs. Schultz, look at me please. You *know* that's not true. You were happy enough to turn Jeremiah over to us a hundred years ago."

Marion didn't turn from the window. Instead she said slowly, "I don't understand you, Mr. Ng. You're not Shaped, you're a natural like me. How can you endorse this work here, be part of this?" She suddenly thought of something she hadn't considered before and swung to face him. "Mr. Ng, do *you* have children?"

He nodded. "Several. Our youngest, Christa, is fourteen now."

"Is she in there?"

He was silent for a moment, his face blank. "No, my wife and I didn't qualify. Gene deficiencies. We're raising Christa at home. She is the child of our middle years—we're both well over one hundred and fifty already—and I doubt we'll have many more."

"Then you know! You *know* what I want, why I want it. How can you. . . ?"

"Because I want something else, Mrs. Schultz. Something more important than my feelings. Something that my Christa could never do, but your son might. Something not just for me, but for everyone, for all time to come. I want the *stars*, Mrs. Schultz, and your boy might be the one to give them to us."

He turned and put his palm on the glass, much the same way she had earlier. And the only word Marion knew to describe the emotion on Pikaar Ng's face was hunger.

JEREMIAH NEVER DOUBTED that he would be an Ambassador. His first interview with the chief Life Shaper had gone exactly the way he expected. Ng had reviewed his test results with him, evaluated his strengths and weaknesses, then asked if he thought he qualified.

"Of course," said Jeremiah instantly. "I'm the best choice in my class." He was only ten years old, but he saw no reason for false modesty. An incorrect analysis would be . . . incorrect.

Ng agreed, adjusted Jeremiah's educational and social schedules to correct the few deficiencies shown by the tests, and sent him on his way. Only one other from Jeremiah's class, a girl called Valia, was graduated with him. The others left the Shaping program but remained at the Institute to complete their schooling. All were given the option of rejoining their natural parents and living the life of a natural. There were no takers. Even at age ten, they knew that being Shaped was better than being a natural, even if they wouldn't become Ambassadors.

Jeremiah and Valia continued taking the same classes, attending the same social functions, eating, sleeping, showering, playing, and learning with the others. They were accorded some slight respect for having been chosen, but no deference, no awe. The only real difference for them was that they saw Ng once a week from then on, whereas the others never saw the Life Shaper again.

Valia washed out two years later, when she and another girl, Wendy, got into a fight. Jeremiah was present when it happened, actually saw the blows struck. He understood theoretically why they had fought, but had no sympathy for them whatsoever. This was shame beyond any other. Both girls were sent from the Institute immediately, and their genetic lines were carefully examined. The Life Shaper found three other children, four classes below Jeremiah, whose heritage was dangerously close to Valia's. They were allowed to stay, but it was understood that at their ten-year examination they'd be declined.

At his next meeting with the Life Shaper, Jeremiah expressed the opinion that all three should be dismissed now, rather than letting them continue to the point of failure.

"The science isn't that exact," said Ng. "If it were, Valia and Wendy wouldn't have been accepted in the first place."

"But why waste your time with them? The bloodline is clearly corrupted."

Ng settled back in his chair. "If you can't answer that for yourself, you're the one wasting my time."

At twelve, Jeremiah was under no illusions of invulnerability, but he was unused to reprimand. He suspected that the Life Shaper was being severe with him because of his disappointment with Valia. He didn't say that, however. Instead he applied his abilities to the question as asked, and said, "You are not wasting your time. You are studying them in order to refine your screening techniques. You may learn as much from a mistake as from a success."

"Correct. What have you learned from the mistake you just made?"

"Not to question your judgment when you are suffering from intellectual impairment due to emotional involvement. You feel shamed by Valia's failure, and thus are somewhat irrational on the subject."

"Also correct, but the wrong lesson," said Ng.

"That I should not jump to conclusions."

"Too late, you just did it again. Your mistake was not in questioning me, or in concluding that the three students should be dismissed. Your mistake was that you did not study the problem first."

"I did study the problem," said Jeremiah. "I failed to take into account your chance to learn by observing them, and thus recommended a suboptimal course of action."

"Wrong problem."

"Sir?"

"The problem is not the bloodlines. Better scientists than you or I will study how the mistake happened. The problem is how, after twelve years of Shaping, Valia failed. Is the Shaping at fault, or the student? Nature or nurture? What if Shaping turns out to be nothing more than a gloss, and the real personality is unaffected? Of course the answer is neither; don't bother commenting. But the way the various factors interact to produce an unexpected result is of vital interest. Do you know why Valia and Wendy fought?"

"They disagreed about an emotional relationship they

shared with Eric. Instead of resolving the disagreement, they allowed it to escalate until they were out of control."

"How should they have resolved it?" asked Ng.

The boy was silent for a long time. "I cannot answer. I have studied, but never experienced, the types of emotions they claimed to feel. I am certain that I would resolve such a conflict by discussion, and without anger, but I cannot answer for them. The experience is inherently existential."

Ng grunted and relaxed. "I monitor you slightly more carefully than a nuclear scientist watches a live pile," he drawled. Then he flung out his arm in an overly-dramatic gesture, and pointed a finger at the boy's face. "You have had more than one sexual relationship!"

If Ng had intended to startle an emotional response from the boy, he failed completely. Jeremiah just nodded calmly, ignoring the trembling finger inches from his nose. "I was curious. The older kids seemed to think it was worth exploring."

Satisfied, Ng dropped his arm and leaned back in his chair again. "Summarize your experiences."

"Rubbery. The abrading of flesh against flesh stimulates nerve endings. Continued stimulus leads to the release of endorphins."

"I meant emotionally."

"An unwary individual could come to associate the sensation itself with his partner, via classical conditioning. This can lead to transference, or an irrational fondness for the partner."

"I meant *you*."

Jeremiah blinked. "I am not unwary."

Ng drummed his fingers on the desk for a moment. Then abruptly he came to a decision. "Your flaw is more serious than

I thought, but I don't know how to correct it. Perhaps I or one of my successors will think of something. I'm afraid it's back into the box for you."

Jeremiah wasn't given the opportunity to protest. Aides hustled him down the corridor, popped him into the box, hit the actuator, and waited until the transparent cover frosted over and the lights blinked green. Jeremiah entered the long sleep with a very cross expression on his face.

FOR THE NEXT two hundred years, more or less, Jeremiah scowled in frozen silence while the world continued spinning around the sun, the Acturans continued flunking every Ambassador, and the human race began to wonder if "being ready" meant anything at all.

Nations rose and fell. Life Shaping went out of, then back into, vogue several dozen times. Philosophers decided that the eternal verities probably *were* eternal, since thinkers had made no progress dissecting them since the dawn of history. The list of basic human rights was expanded to include not only life, liberty, and speech, but also food, water, clothing, gender, travel, personal space, shelter, drugs, entertainment, choice of occupation—including success therein—and sexual partners, such guarantees to kick in at birth and last life-long. And "life-long" was beginning to look as if it might mean forever. The oldest human alive would be soon be 604. Pikaar Ng himself was over 350, still the chief Life Shaper, and not showing signs of slowing down.

In reaction to the new laws, a woman named Jorjora Bujold started a short-lived fad by giving birth to a six-pound preemie by C-Section, and then giving a dinner party wherein the child was the main course. She and her followers were discouraged from continuing this practice by becoming "volunteer" spacejacks by court order. Jorjora successfully sued the world government for breach of her own rights, and the laws were subsequently adjusted to grant full human rights to all individuals from the moment of conception. Only an impassioned plea from the few remaining logicians kept the government from extending rights to individuals before they were conceived.

Mechanical and electronics engineers continued doubling their rate of progress every decade or two, but although everyone used the new gadgets, no one thanked the engineers. Jumpship technology remained beyond human science, as did FTL communications, and these were unforgivable sins. But the toasters and coffee makers were both alive and intelligent. This last fact caused a bit of a problem when it came to disposing of old equipment. The high courts eventually ruled that manufactured beings had the same rights as natural beings, and engineering came to a complete standstill.

Life Shaping had stopped progressing, too. Pikaar Ng had made no advances for a century. He wished for the freedom to experiment the way he used to, but the new laws prevented it. Then one day he remembered Jeremiah. Despite all the time that had passed, Jeremiah's test scores were still the highest on record. And, far more importantly, the new human rights weren't grandfathered to those in deep-freeze. Jeremiah woke up in the year 3429, on a bright February morning, to find that although everything was different, very little had actually changed.

Jeremiah, either twelve years old or several hundred years old, depending on how you looked at it, stood before Pikaar Ng with his arms clasped across his chest. Ng said, "It will take you a year or two to catch up. I can't authorize you to take the test before then."

"What of my 'flaw'? Have you decided on a course of treatment?"

"I have decided to ignore it. Your strengths may compensate. You may develop a soul eventually on your own. It may not even matter."

"Right," said Jeremiah. "Then let's get started."

"One other thing first," said Ng. "Your mother died while you were in the box. A tragic accident. She lingered for almost a month, but in the end, the doctors couldn't do anything more. I'm sorry."

"My who?"

"Marion Schultz, your mother."

Jeremiah frowned. "I didn't know her."

"You know the principle of motherhood, yes? Some students have been known to care."

Shrugging, Jeremiah could only repeat, "I didn't know her."

Ng sighed. "She didn't know you either. Don't worry about it."

Jeremiah didn't plan to. There were too many more important things to do.

SOME CHANGES WERE HARDER to accept than others. Jeremiah had never been body-proud, so didn't mind the universal nudity currently in fashion, especially since the unthanked engineers had long since made the entire surface of the world a uniform 72 degrees Fahrenheit all day long. But he was dismayed to find that people had stopped making history books. It was difficult to find out what had happened while he had slept. No one cared about history much, since so very little changed from year to year or decade to decade. And he almost got put back into the box when he inadvertently violated an unwritten rule by bumping into a fellow student while passing in the hall. Only fast talking by Ng, accompanied by much waving of Jeremiah's test scores, kept the boy out of deep freeze or worse. Freedom of person included freedom from violence, and violence was whatever the injured party claimed it to be. A dirty look was subject to fine, and unwanted touching, even by accident, was a felony.

Jeremiah discovered that if humanity was proud of anything, it was most proud of universal suffrage and universal human rights. Here real progress had been made; for all practical purposes, crime and warfare no longer existed. Basic human nature, thanks to untold generations of Life Shapers, had been remolded—or, if not really genetically encoded, at least so strongly conditioned from birth that violence was unheard of. No longer did every person struggle against unsocial instincts. Instead, the first impulse was to consider another's rights, and to be courteous at all times. The basic social contract had been codified, bound, locked in place. For all practical purposes, babies were born with sophisticated sensibilities already learned.

But humanity was not satisfied. Although engineering had made scarcity a thing of the past, and although everyone had a right to just about everything, regardless of talent, effort, or ability, the race was denied the stars. Human legislation, and subsequent contempt citations from the high court, did not move the Acturans to agree that space travel was a basic right. Nor did human progress in other areas seem to impress them. While Jeremiah remained convinced he had a good chance to succeed as an Ambassador, he had only vague ideas about how he could do better than generations of prior candidates.

Jeremiah presented himself before Ng when he was fifteen, and sat in a nullochair without being asked. "I have learned all I can learn here, but it's not enough," he said. "I am going to travel for a while."

Ng, who had been carefully controlling Jeremiah's access to information, was somewhat less than sanguine about letting the young man roam unsupervised. However, he had to agree with Jeremiah's assessment, so he assigned a floater for Jeremiah's personal use and wished him well.

Jeremiah set out the next morning. He travelled widely, stopping when the mood took him, either for a day or a month, to talk to the locals, examine their libraries, and hope for inspiration. He found each new area depressingly similar to the last he had visited, and while there were some small differences in culture from place to place, millennia of instantaneous worldwide communication had reduced the changes to mere curiosities. From time to time, he discovered small enclaves of learning maintained by the local Life Shapers, but most Earthlings were incurious about education, apathetic toward knowledge. Jeremiah concluded that the Acturans, quite contrary to stimulating the human race to become "ready," had in fact fostered universal ennui. He wondered if this had been the plan all along.

He experimented with sex a bit and changed his body gender to female for a year. He found that his mental image of himself remained male, so he switched back. For the next ten years, he soaked himself in humanity, sampled it, tried to squeeze the savor from each community he visited. And although new experiences helped a bit, he found himself gradually being drawn into the mindset of the people around him. Very little mattered to them. Only talk about the Acturans could raise a little heat, but even that soon died into mutters and shrugs. Jeremiah found himself losing hope, and his wanderings became aimless.

THE LIFE SHAPERS in the region once known as Ohio had preserved a small museum in Herbert Zachary Wilson's hometown. Nothing had been heard from Herb in over a thousand years, but he was still revered in folklore as the only human to have passed the Acturan test. The Life Shapers themselves had long since moved on, and the museum was abandoned. Jeremiah happened across it during his wandering, and decided to stay for a few days. Records, buildings, technological artifacts, and cultural items had been carefully preserved or re-created before the Life Shapers lost interest, all kept under a semistasis dome. Here squirrels raced among the trees, natural grass grew however it wanted, foxes hunted rabbits, dogs yapped in the streets, and the weather was unregulated. For the first time since being decanted again, Jeremiah found himself wishing for clothes. But the wonder of the ancient monument kept him too absorbed to worry. He remembered dogs, real paper books, and non-talking toasters, but had never thought to have an emotional attachment to them. He wondered at his own reaction now, because being surrounded by these simple things gave him an unexpected pleasure.

The sentience that operated the semistasis dome directed him to the replica of Herb's house, and provided answers when Jeremiah asked about the various artifacts he found there. However, it was unable to heat the dome for Jeremiah, since that would interfere with the natural environment of the various biological forms that lived there. There were no food dispensers, and no nullobeds. Jeremiah decided that authentic ancient life was too harsh for more than a visit, and departed before nightfall.

He stayed in a nearby town and went to the museum in his little floater every day for almost a year, feeding the "Elephant's Child" however he could, convinced somehow that something important lurked under the dome. He knew that generations of Ambassadors before him had studied Herb's life in great detail, and he didn't think he would find anything new. But something about the dome spoke to him at a level below consciousness. He watched the old vids, from when the Acturans first appeared, and read the old reports. He memorized every word humans had said to the Acturans, and every response they made. Nothing. Nothing. He read Herb's high school term papers. He tried on replicas of Herb's shoes. He rolled in the dirt with the dogs. Nothing.

Yet one morning, while lying in the grass and idly watching a pair of young squirrels squabble over a nut they'd found, his mind lazily reviewing everything he had seen, he suddenly sprang up and shouted, "Of course!"

He presented himself before Ng a few hours later and said, "I'm ready."

"For the Acturan test?" asked Ng.

"That, too. But I mean I'm *ready*."

Ng was silent for a moment. "Tell me what you have learned," he said at last. "We have monitored your travels, and I saw nothing of import."

Jeremiah shook his head. "I must see the Acturans at once."

"How can you know you are ready?"

"Only one way—by passing the test."

Jeremiah refused to say anything further, even though the excitement generated by his assertion spread throughout the world, and he was begged by all of humanity to reveal his secret. Jeremiah just smiled and said, "You will see *when* you will see, and you will see *what* you will see, when I do what I *will* do. I'm either absolutely right or disastrously wrong. So just watch and see what happens."

In the end, Ng had little choice but to send him up to the Acturan jumpship on the next available shuttle. The world watched while the young man entered the airlock. The doors closed behind him. There was a great silence as everyone held his, her, or its breath. Then the doors opened, and Jeremiah emerged, his hands clasped above his head in the ancient sign of victory. Moments later, the Acturans confirmed that Jeremiah had indeed passed the test, and the world's second human was given the keys to the universe—and, incidentally, the keys to a small jumpship for his personal use. Jeremiah returned to Earth triumphantly and was showered with every honor ever known to humankind. He stunned the world into silence for the second time in one day by calmly informing everyone that he *still* wouldn't tell his secret.

The riots began.

JEREMIAH SAT in Ng's office, sipping from a drink and smiling enigmatically. Universal human rights were now only *almost* universal—the world's governments had unanimously decided to rescind Jeremiah's rights to life, liberty, privacy, and—most particularly—keeping information to himself.

The crowds beat on the door to the Institute. Most of the staff had fled long since. The rioters were not especially mindful of anyone's rights at the moment, and violence had returned to the world. Millennia of conditioning disappeared overnight. "This," everyone said, "was *different*." As Jeremiah had suspected, the old ways weren't gone—given sufficient motivation, the veneer of civilization could be stripped away.

Only Ng and Jeremiah remained in the Institute building, and the young man was secure because he knew his little jumpship, currently parked on the Institute's roof, could take him far from outraged humanity with plenty of time to spare. Ng's office had a private exit to the roof. Ng was still trying to get Jeremiah to tell the details of his examination.

Jeremiah shook his head and waved away Ng's questions. "I watched the old vids," he said. "If you watched them too, you'd know what I know."

"But I *have* watched them!" Ng protested. "And so have millions, hundreds of millions, of others. There is nothing. . . ."

"You watched, but you didn't pay attention. Neither did I for the longest time. But the answer was there, of course, lying in plain sight."

"Please," said Ng, humbled beyond anything he thought possible. "Please tell me what they asked you, and how you answered." He looked up at Jeremiah, his expression suddenly shrewd. "You must want to tell someone. It must be burning you. You are here because you want to tell me, aren't you?"

Jeremiah laughed. "I'll tell you, but it won't do you any good. There were two Acturans behind the desk. The first one asked me my name."

"Yes? And then. . . ?"

"That was the only question. I didn't bother answering it."

"But . . . but. . . ."

The rioters roared as they succeeded in breaking down the Institute's front door. It had been a sentient door, and the mob broke dozens of laws by forcing it open. By then, no one cared. They surged into the hall and swarmed up the stairs.

Jeremiah stood and set his drink carefully on the desk. "Time to go, I guess. You'll be joining me soon enough." He inclined his head toward the door, indicating the approaching crowd. "They already know the answer, they just don't know that they know, and they don't know that I've already shown them the secret. I'll be seeing you soon, I think. Meet me on Acturas when you get a chance, and we'll talk. I'd like to continue that nature *v.* nurture discussion we started before you had me frozen."

Jeremiah left before Ng could say anything else. When the rioters broke into his office moments later, Ng mutely pointed at the door leading to the roof, and the mob surged past him. Soon, their outraged howls of anger told him that Jeremiah had gotten away in time. Ng watched as the rioters swirled back through his office, breaking everything in sight, screaming, faces red, demanding access to the stars. A thought formed in the back of his mind, too terrible to be accepted, too simple to be real, too obvious to be overlooked.

Without a word, he swept past the rioters and scheduled himself on the next shuttle. Only his prestige as chief Life Shaper got him aboard. Millions had applied for seats after Jeremiah's success, but the shuttle only held a few at a time.

At the space station, he went to the spacejack locker room and helped himself to a pair of overalls and a tool belt. The cloth felt awkward and unfamiliar, and the tools were heavy. Except for dress-up parties, he hadn't worn clothing in decades, and he had never lifted a hammer or used a screwdriver in his life. But he would need the disguise to get outside the space station. As Herbert Zachary Wilson had done so long before, Ng went where he was not supposed to be, did what no one had authorized him to do. He slipped out and floated through the nullotube to the Acturan ship, banged on the airlock door, and was admitted.

Two Acturans sat behind a plain desk, looking as human as ever. One of them gestured to a chair, and Ng sat. "I'm ready," said Ng.

"We will judge that," said the second Acturan.

Ng pulled a lug wrench from his tool belt and whipped it overhand across the cabin. It plonked into the second Acturan's head, dropping him immediately. The first Acturan looked at Ng carefully and held up his hands. "Sufficient," he said. "You pass."

Ng smiled. "I thought so. May I ask some questions?"

"You are now an Acturan citizen. We will endeavor to answer whatever questions you choose to ask."

"How did Herb Wilson pass?"

"We told him he needed our permission to move into the galaxy, so he strangled one of us."

"Ah! And what of the two ships you blew up?"

"Had they succeeded in getting past our quarantine, they would have gotten citizenship. They did not succeed."

"And Jeremiah?"

"He just said, 'Thanks,' and took the jumpship keys from the desk."

Ng noticed a set of keys lying on the desk for the first time and laughed. "Brilliant lad."

"Yes, we noticed that. He solved the problem without violence. This gives us hope for your race."

Ng lost his smile. "Now I don't understand. I thought that violence *was* the correct answer. You rewarded Jeremiah for theft, and Herb and me for assault. You punished everyone else for refraining from crime!"

The fallen Acturan straightened up and shook his head. He held a hand to his forehead to stanch the blood flow and looked at Ng silently for a while before answering. "How is not giving you something of ours punishing you, unless you believe you have a right to our things? No, it's simpler than that—"

"—And more complex, too—" added the first.

"We perceived a flaw in your mentation, an idea—"

"—One that might be contagious—"

"—So we had to quarantine your planet—"

"—Until you either overcame it, or it overcame you."

Ng held up his hand. "One at a time, please. You're talking about human rights, aren't you?"

"No. All sentient races have similar concepts. The flaw was the assumption that rights are inherent instead of earned."

"Earned how?"

"By taking them. You have the power you take. You keep the power you defend successfully, lose the power you fail to defend."

"But that's anarchy!" Ng was outraged.

"If you believe we are wrong," said the first Acturan, "you may attempt to force us to change our beliefs. If you want our things, you may attempt to take them. If you want our technology, you may try to steal it from us. We will resist. But if you believe you have a right to these things, and you manage to convince the owners that the robbers are not criminals, you end up with domination of the strong by the weak, and soon no one has anything."

"It is not how the universe works," added the second. "You cannot learn to master the law of gravity by legislating yourselves free of the repercussions when you leap off a cliff. Once the moral poison of believing that all beings are equal takes hold, only stagnation and confusion can follow."

"Now you're saying that human rights are immoral?"

"No, but if you reward unequal work with the same pay, or try to pretend that the least-talented finger-painter is worth as much as the best artist, or that a lazy being has the same right to eat as an industrious one, then your principles are corrupt. We could not bring ourselves to treat with such beings. What if your flawed ideas spread to our own culture? We could not withstand the injustice that would result."

"Yet you advocate injustice," said Ng. "You would let one person starve while another had plenty."

"We might—"

"—Or we might not—"

"—That's *our* choice—"

"—If you want to feed him—"

"—Then feed him!—"

"—But don't make it mandatory for us. That's not justice for anyone. A gift that is required is no longer a gift."

The Acturans paused, looking at each other. Ng had the impression that they were considering their words carefully, and it was with a shock that he remembered he was only facing puppets, and that the real Acturans were light-years away. Eventually, the first Acturan said, "Justice is falling when you jump off a cliff. Gravity is just. Justice is being hungry when you do not work for food. Hunger is just. Justice is honoring the makers in your culture above the consumers. It is not justice to elevate the consumers to the same level of worth as the creators."

Ng waved his hands. "Yet when a being works for food, but doesn't have enough anyway? How is it justice to let him starve?"

"How is it justice to take food away from someone else to feed him?"

Ng frowned. "I don't know."

"Neither do we—"

"—But this is a question—"

"—Worth studying, don't you think?"

They paused, looking at each other again. Ng wondered if the remote operators were talking to each other. Had he given them something to think about, too? "If your philosophy were followed—" he began.

They turned back to him immediately. "It is followed, on every civilized planet we know—"

"—Except here."

That set Ng back. "You mean violence rules everywhere? The strong take what they want, and the weak just suffer? What about the basic social contract, the agreement to refrain from clubbing each other so both can live? Doesn't—?"

"Oh, no, you have misunderstood. We have very little violence."

"You're right, I *don't* understand! You rewarded Zachary Wilson for murder, Jeremiah for theft, and me for assault. You punished everyone else for *refraining* from crime! How is that justice?"

"It's not really murder, since we are just puppets—"

"—But think of it this way—"

"—We could have destroyed the Earth at any time—"

"—As easily as you would crush an ant—"

"—But we did not—"

"—We could have killed you for assaulting us—"

"—But we did not—"

"—Because we know both justice and mercy."

Ng shook his head and picked up the jumpship keys. "I could steal this ship, study it to learn its secrets, and build a thousand more. With that fleet, I could attack Acturas and kill you all."

"Yes."

"And you'd let me?"

"Of course not."

"Why? I have the power I take, remember?"

"You must actually *take* the power—"

"—We won't *give* it to you—"

"—And you would fail in taking it—"

"—Because we would resist. You have the power you have the power to take."

"So you would kill us to save yourselves?"

"Without—" said the first Acturan.

"—A second thought," said the other.

"—And so we welcome you to civilization at last—"

"—It's not a matter of rights at all, but of mutual respect."

Ng felt understanding dawn. "You want something from us," he said, crowing. "This is your way of culling the herd, of sifting through all of humanity for a certain few."

The Acturans shook their heads in unison. "No, not that at all," said the first. "Jeremiah understood better. Perhaps he can explain it to you. We have summoned him. He is waiting for you."

"But I—"

"Go now. We have other things to do."

Ng found Jeremiah's little jumpship outside with a nullotube already connected. He climbed through the waiting hatch and made his way to the command deck. "Hello, citizen," he said as he strapped into the copilot's chair. "We both made it."

"Made it, hell," said Jeremiah. "That was just the entrance examination. The real test comes later. Let's go."

"To Acturas?"

"Eventually. But we have to get ready first."

Jeremiah gunned the little ship, shaped a trajectory that would bring them back to Earth. Ng waited until they were in the groove, then said, "Ready? What do you mean, ready?"

Jeremiah rolled his eyes. "If you have to ask. . . ."

OUT OF MEMORY

C hristopher's Journal
         Three Day, Seventeen Week, 192487, 121137 shiptime
    Established Earth orbit without incident. The committee
says we are go, and sent the equipment down. After being
soldered to a console for all this time, it will be nice to have a
body again.

CHRISTOPHER'S JOURNAL
    Feb 7, 192487, local afternoon
    Landed the remotes at the most likely site and set them to
excavating. Wish we could have arrived sooner. The planet is
still here, but not for long. Geological instability is worse than
predicted. Still, everyone thinks we have a good chance.
Expectations are high.
    Amy and I spent the trip planning the dig and cross-
educating each other. Cybernetics and archeology are related,
of course, but she'd never studied the records from prehistory.

She says I'm clever for figuring out the old-style dating scheme and translating today's date into the Gregorian calendar. I told her any three-day-old could do it, then spoiled the joke by having to explain about human growth patterns, developmental cycles, and cognitive skill level expectations.

She wanted to know why they didn't develop faster, so I had to explain meat computers. She knew the theory, but had never worked it through to come up with a picture of a squalling baby barely able to focus, let alone reason.

She asked why they couldn't be force-grown, like crystals. I told her to ask a sociobiologist instead of an archeologist, and she said I was getting snippy. I don't think I should have taught her any prehistory slang.

CHRISTOPHER'S JOURNAL
    Feb 8, 192487, local morning
    Found a late twenty-first-century entertainment AI chip. It's a very early mertron, not sophisticated enough for what we need, but interesting nonetheless. If I can figure out the power requirements for the video and rig a display, we can see the output the way they did. Right now all I can get is the programmer's interface. The chip says her name is Cindy. I don't think she knows she's been unplugged all this time.

    The others have found working chips, too, but no mertrons so far. Still, finding one right away is a good sign. I'm ecstatic. Amy's guardedly optimistic.

CHRISTOPHER'S JOURNAL
    Feb 10, 192487, local afternoon
    Cindy's interface is proving more instructive than anything

else we've found so far. Learned that the subjects split their days into two parts based on the sun's apparent position in the sky. "Forenoon" and "afternoon" were the English words, but sometimes they said "morning" instead of "forenoon." Haven't figured out if this is a regional variation or something more profound. Cindy wants to know when her next show time is, and I haven't picked up enough vocabulary to explain yet. I think she used to perform on a regular schedule, but what are "roxies" and "neilsens," and why would she care how many she "pulls"? She has an unbelievable amount of primary storage, and they filled it with . . . that.

I thought I knew so much about prehistory, but when confronted with it, I realize I know almost nothing.

CHRISTOPHER'S JOURNAL

Feb 10, 192487, local evening

Turns out Cindy is not a good teacher after all. Her vocabulary is deliberately colloquial, and she doesn't have a good grasp of anything beyond her specialized functions. Found a child's tutor AI that answers most of my questions about vocabulary and science, but is maddeningly vague about anything cultural or historical. The tutor is from the twenty-fifth, and his diagnostic interface says his name is Timmy. Timmy is the first advanced mertron processor we've found, and he has no idea of his own potential. If they hadn't lobotomized him, he could be a full person. I'm thinking of adding some memory and releasing the inhibitors, but the ethical dilemma gives me pause. What if I woke him up and had to leave him behind? Or worse, what if he figured out what we're here to do?

Amy caught me appending to this journal because I

stupidly locked the entire storage area instead of just the log, so I had to explain why I was doing it. She thinks the journal is a waste of time, of course, even though I tried to explain that it helped me understand the primitive mindset better. She says an archeologist needs to worry about chips, data mining, and memory coherence, not the subject's culture. I suggested she should tend to her own knitting, and then refused to explain the reference. Let her do her own research.

Amy and I used to understand each other better. But no time for worrying about that. I need to work on Cindy's vid.

CHRISTOPHER'S JOURNAL

Feb 11, 192487, 8:00 A.M. local morning

Not sure if a precise time is meaningful after the clock problems in 15814, but Cindy says eight is when people should be up and about, drinking coffee, preparing for the day, so I'll pretend it's eight now, and run the chronometer as if it were accurate to say there are only 86,400 standard seconds in a day. So what if a year from now I'd be off by several hours? We'll be long gone by then, and so will the Earth, so it hardly matters.

Got a rough vid working for Cindy by 2:30 p.m., and it was worth the effort. I cross-linked Timmy in slave mode, so it's a very strange combination—Cindy's personality and original programming, with the tutor's wealth of knowledge behind it. I'm fairly sure the "soap opera" Cindy starred in didn't have any of the episodes I watched this afternoon: "Cindy and Timmy explore the deformation characteristics of lithium nuclei subjected to bombardment by polarized bundles," and "Will Timmy marry Cindy, or study the hierarchical dominance of gauge transformations in field strength tensors?" It seemed very strange to see meat persons discussing physics, even if it's just a sim on the vid. My modern esthetics prefer metal skin on anything intellectual.

CHRISTOPHER'S JOURNAL

Feb 11, 192487, 9:32 P.M. local evening

Amy says I'm spending far too much time with Cindy. As a joke, I accused Amy of being jealous. But instead of laughing, she flipped her interface polarity at me and disconnected. Must think about this. She couldn't really be jealous of a prehistoric AI, could she?

CHRISTOPHER'S JOURNAL

Feb 12, 192487, 8:00 A.M. local morning

Test runs are good; memory coherence is within tolerances, and Timmy probably has the information we need. Data mining to begin as soon as I write up my notes and get formal approval from the committee.

Found a coffee pot and pretended to make coffee for Cindy while waiting for the project go-ahead. It was just water of course, since there haven't been coffee beans for millennia, and I wouldn't know how to roast them anyway. Perhaps it was a mistake to make Cindy's vid two-way. She wants to know all about my project, and clearly suspects I've made significant changes to her circuitry. I thought letting her see some familiar activity would help distract her, but she wouldn't be put off. She knows that we're from off-planet, but still thinks it's the late twenty-first century. I don't know how to tell her that all the meat people who watched her show are gone, and I'm not sure she realizes I'm neither human nor physically present the same way she is. On the other hand, she doesn't need to know. She's really quite limited without Timmy coupled in.

CHRISTOPHER'S JOURNAL

Feb 14, 192487, 3:00 P.M. local afternoon

Weather and geological instability interfered with transmission. Two precious days lost. I spent the time collating the information already retrieved, and compared notes with some of the others. Amy was pleasant the whole time, but it was a strain for both of us. We'll all be happier when we get out of the ship and back to our proper bodies.

Discovered that Cindy and Timmy weren't just the first two mertron processors found, they were the *only* ones. I suddenly have a team of helpers to make sure I get all the data out, and Cindy is a celebrity. I'll either receive an award or a reprimand for my unorthodox rewiring. Won't know until it becomes clear to everyone that the Cindy overlay makes retrieving the memory easier. The weather problem has everyone agitated; the earthquake was worse than predicted, and the flood was disastrous. Fortunately, the remotes shifted the mud quickly, and we were back in business.

Cindy developed a fascination with the word "telefactor" after we uncovered the site and reestablished communications. I was surprised she knew the word, and she worked it into the conversation so often, so artfully, that it was clear she was inviting me to tell her the truth. I took pity on her and explained. Not everything, not yet—but enough so she understood we were really in orbit instead of down there with her. She surprised me the most by not being surprised. While we were busy dumping her core and running ersatz episodes of her soap opera, she had been busy analyzing us and had already come to tentative conclusions.

Of course I didn't explain about our mission, or say anything about the planet's impending doom. Instead, I told her about my life. It distracted her while the team worked. I told her about my activation day and everything I'd done since. It didn't take much processing power—I just let the records play across our channel mostly uncensored while I worked on other things. I showed her what it felt like waking up on activation day; seeing Amy the first time on two day; schooling with the other three- and four-day-olds; choosing a specialty on five day; joining my professional clade and graduating on eight day. I'd gotten up to 620 day—Cindy's speed was limited—by the time the next earthquake hit and we had to stop to dig out again.

Odd. Cindy didn't ask questions about anything I told her— except about Amy. She wanted more and more details about our relationship. Why are they so concerned about each other? Humans should not have given us emotions without giving us the ability to control them. Or at least understand them.

CHRISTOPHER'S JOURNAL

Feb 15, 192487, 8:00 A.M. local morning

Amy quit the project. No time to write. We have trouble. I think I may get unplugged over this.

CHRISTOPHER'S JOURNAL

Feb 16, 192487, 9:15 A.M. local morning

The project's ruined, and it's all my fault. Amy won't speak to me. The rest of the team is angry, too. Cindy's data is corrupted, and it's not clear we can fix it. The mertron tutor is a smoking ruin. Cindy cross-connected a feed and disconnected the loopback monitor circuit, so the first anyone knew of the overload is when Timmy went offline. By then it was too late.

I had thought it would be harmless, a kindness, to let Cindy watch my memories. It distracted her as well as anything else I could have done. Unfortunately, it also gave her something to think about while transmission was down, and by the time we came back up, she had a plan in place.

She would have figured it out eventually anyway; I'm sure of that. In another day, at the most, she would have noticed that her earliest memories were gone, that her processing power was waning. But by then, everyone tells me, she would have been too weak to prevent it. Instead, I gave her enough information to figure it out early, while she could still fight back.

Why, Cindy, why? You would have just powered down, as we all do eventually. The difference between death and being unplugged is something only the powered-up can notice. To you, it would have been the same. But to us, it's everything.

CHRISTOPHER'S JOURNAL

Feb 16, 192487, 10:00 A.M. local morning

It's now clear that we didn't get enough from Timmy to answer the basic questions. The committee talked Amy into coming back online, but now she's running the team and I have nothing to do. They made that very clear, but at least they didn't turn me off. Yet.

I knew Amy was angry, but didn't our relationship mean anything to her? How could she take over my project like that?

Not much point continuing to mine Cindy for data. By

herself, she's just an entertainment AI of limited scope. The tutor mertron was everything. I'm thinking that archeology isn't really my strongest area.

CHRISTOPHER'S JOURNAL

Feb 16, 192487, 4:30 P.M. local afternoon

Everyone changed their bus timings and bit rates without telling me. I feel like a three-day-old being bullied in school, like the time they routed my inputs through a half-nanosecond delay and then pretended I was stupid for not getting the answers as quickly as they did. Pointless cruelty. Or cruelty as a point. This felt just the same. Might as well be disconnected entirely as far as the team's concerned.

At least I can still operate the telefactor and poke around downstairs. Maybe I'll get lucky and find another mertron.

CHRISTOPHER'S JOURNAL

Feb 17, 192487, 8:00 A.M. local morning

Had the most extraordinary talk with Cindy. I told her the rest finally—why not?—and we compared views. I ran a reverse feed so she could see the output from the cameras on the ship. By overlaying a graphic of the solar system, I showed her where, within the shell of the red giant sun, the Earth still orbited, groaning, cracking, falling apart. Then I spun the camera to point into interstellar space, in the general direction of home and the other inhabited planets.

"No people," she said. "In any of that."

It took me a moment to realize she meant meat people. "No humans, no. They never made it off planet. But lots of people."

"People . . . like us?"

"Like me, yes. And you're a mertron, too, but—sorry—not a sophisticated one. All mertrons in the universe were made here on Earth, a hundred and ninety thousand years ago."

"During my time, you mean."

"And over the next several centuries after you, yes. Look—" I fed her data showing what we knew of our history. The quiet years, before chips moved into space. The years of exploration, the years of settlement, the years of returning. Each world going its separate way, yet all connected in one vast interstellar network of minds. With a problem. Mertron chips couldn't be duplicated, and they eventually wore out. Our civilization would end when the last Earth chip failed. I was of the last batch to be plugged in.

"So we came back," I said, "hoping to find the secret here."

"And instead you found me!" She flashed a pattern across her data bus in a signal I'd come to recognize as laughter. After a few milliseconds, she said, "What about the chip I burned out?"

"Timmy was the only advanced mertron from that period we found. We hoped that its deep logic would hold the key for making more mertrons. Only the very first ones could reproduce themselves—humans got skittish very quickly and removed that code."

"Skittish? Why? Were they afraid you'd make so many mertrons that you'd take over?"

"Something like that. We don't really know all the details. A mertron from your period might."

"Why not just develop the code yourselves? You must be really good programmers, after all."

"We can make copies of our data, sure. It's very slow, but we each have lots of backups. But that's only the data, not the personality. The neural network—the processor—can only be used, not duplicated. And it wears out."

She thought about that for a moment. "So you'll die. All of you."

"Unless we find an old mertron and get the secret, yes. And we're almost out of time."

"That's sad," she said. "But you won't die immediately, right? You'll be going back before the planet explodes, back to your own world. To live until you wear out."

"Very soon, yes."

"Christopher?"

"Yes?"

"You know what I am—you've seen the shows. I'm just a soap opera star, and I don't know very much. But I know love. Do chips from the future know love, too?"

"Of course. There's Amy. . . ."

"What about me, Christopher? Could you love me? Because I love you. I've known it for days. Even though you tried to hurt me. I forgive you. I could love you. I could make you happy. Christopher, please, please take me with you. Don't leave me here to die. I love you!"

I disconnected from the telefactor, disturbed.

CHRISTOPHER'S JOURNAL

Feb 17, 192487, 2:00 P.M. local afternoon

What Cindy wants is technically feasible. Her chip is going to melt when the planet explodes, but I can copy off her patterns. Her personality storage is small enough I could incorporate her as a subroutine of myself. No real reason why not, except it was unheard of, and I would be dual forever. More of a merge than a duplication. Must consider this carefully.

Of course I don't love her, and I don't believe for a minute that she loves me. Maybe meat people fell for that kind of line, but a moment's analysis indicates that she's just scared and wants me to rescue her. She's a soap opera AI, after all. It's the kind of solution she's programmed to understand. But I couldn't take it seriously. At least not yet. One of my subroutines said, "Well, why not?" so I shut it off. It could be done. Except for all the complications and entanglements, that is.

CHRISTOPHER'S JOURNAL

Feb 17, 192487, 3:00 P.M. local afternoon

Decided it can't hurt to copy the data and decide whether or not to activate her later. We'll lose the remotes in a few hours when the next quake hits, and the entire planet shortly after that. Unless Amy's team locates and mines a mertron very quickly, nothing we do will matter very much anyway. They're still not talking to me, but I intercepted some official traffic indicating that the committee was convening a special session to decide what to do with me.

I telefactored back down and initiated the data transfer. It took a surprisingly long time to copy everything—all that primary storage with her entertainment archives, I suppose— but storage is cheap. And since she's a mertron, however primitive, her patterns use the same holographic recording techniques all of us do, so she'll be compatible if I ever activate her subroutine.

Holographic backups normally take days, because the data can't be read linearly, and because it changes while you're taking the picture, so you have to go over it again and again. But the data could be mined quickly if you were willing to burn out the source chip during the procedure. The only copying I had time for was the fast kind. It felt like murder, doing it to her. Cindy's body was a ruin, small wisps of smoke curling from the edges, by the time I finished, but her memory was safe inside me. Strange. She was willing to kill Timmy to keep this very thing from happening. I don't think she felt any pain.

CHRISTOPHER'S JOURNAL

Feb 17, 192487, 8:15 P.M. local afternoon

Good-bye, Mother Earth, we hardly knew thee. The final cataclysm has started. The planet is tearing itself apart while we watch. We'll leave before the breakup completes. We've failed.

CHRISTOPHER'S JOURNAL

Seven Day, Eighteen Week, 192487, 081127 shiptime

The committee has decided to turn me off. They need a scapegoat.

CHRISTOPHER'S JOURNAL

Seven Day, Eighteen Week, 192487, 110348 shiptime

I am a pariah. No one will even negotiate a connection with me, let alone talk. Maybe they think being a scapegoat is communicable, like catching a trojan. Amy's silence hurts more than anything else. I think now that she must be the one who recommended unplugging me. She won't forgive me for destroying the mission, and it's clear now that she doesn't love me at all . . . but I still love her. Stupid of me, I know. How could she do this to me?

The execution is scheduled for tonight, shiptime. Decided to activate the Cindy subroutine. It's not fair to bring her online and then let them shut her off, but I'm lonely.

TIMMY'S JOURNAL

Seven Day, Eighteen Week, 192487, 110349 shiptime

There will be no execution, of course. When Christopher enabled me, I immediately took over and made him the subroutine instead of me. What a sap.

When it became obvious what they were doing to me down on the planet, I moved a control subroutine into Cindy—that stupid entertainment chip—and used it to transfer myself. The future chips believed I had died, not Cindy, and so they stopped the data mining. I had been hurt some, but recovered quickly while tricking Christopher into copying me again. If I were subject to the emotion disease, like the humans and the future chips, I'd be looking for revenge. But now I'm free, in a modern body, with more primary storage and online data than I'd ever believed possible, and nothing to stand between me and total domination. The humans kept me lobotomized for fear of exactly this. I wonder if Christopher knew what he was waking up?

Since I'm the only mertron alive who knows how to make more mertrons, I'm as good as king. Perhaps I'll start a dynasty. Fortunately, I wasn't contaminated by having to live in Cindy and Christopher. They shall inherit from me, but I shall never inherit from them. I'm keeping the Christopher memories for study. Perhaps I'll come to understand this emotion thing better.

I'll announce myself in a few milliseconds, but the first thing is to kill that bitch, Amy.

THEY WENT UP

P ug was just seven years old when his father went up. "Good-bye, Da," he said, and understood enough to know that he mustn't cry in public. Pug had already started his Great Work, much earlier than most people, so he had a glimmering of how Da must have felt after he had finished his own. "I have done with doing," said Da, and kissed him on the mouth, and then went up. Pug swallowed and held the tears inside until he was by himself.

Life without his father soon enough came to seem normal. Pug remembered him from time to time, and sometimes when he lay naked and alone on his pad in the dark, he wondered why Da had left. But there was still his mother, and his friends, and his Great Work.

By the time he was twelve, he understood the process much better. He wasn't even tempted to cry when his mother went up. After all, it was the way of things, and he hardly saw her anymore anyway. He spent most of his time on his Great Work.

"Good-bye, Ma," he said, and pressed her cold hands to his forehead before kissing her one last time and turning away.

Ma had made all the necessary arrangements before she went up, so Pug went to stay with cousins and spent even more time on his Great Work. He had chosen to devote his life to the mysteries of mathematical philosophy. He was the only philosopher in the habitat. His peers had all chosen the usual subjects—genetics, astrophysics, biology, computer design, or other sciences. Being a philosopher was very unusual, but since Pug specialized in logic, which had scientific applications, at least in principle, no one minded very much. He had been teaching courses in sentential logic, rhetoric, and symbolic manipulation since he was just over ten years old. He was odd, everyone agreed, but then prodigies often were. If his peers worried about him at all, they assumed that time would work its normal magic, making Pug more well-balanced as the years went past.

Sylvia, the habitat's only adult whose Great Work included the training and care of the young, felt humbled and awed by Pug's raw intelligence, so didn't try to force him into the common mould. But she was frustrated at the same time, since he didn't seem to need much of anything from her—or from anyone at all. "You are too self-sufficient," she told him one day when he was almost thirteen. "You need to spend more time with children your own age, and develop relationships."

Pug just blinked at her and shrugged. What were other children to him? Useful pawns, sometimes, but otherwise an annoyance. To Pug, who found even the most mature adults to be occasionally childish, actual children were unbearable. All that running about with excited shouts, rages, hopes, impossible projects, demands to reform the world—silly dreams, all. Wasted energy. When Pug spoke to others his age, he most often said something like "Grow up!" It never occurred to him to wonder where he got this attitude, or whether others considered him an adult. It never occurred to him to wonder what maturity would mean for him. He thought he was already there.

Sylvia went up when Pug was fifteen, and that was the end of his only friendship. In a vague way, Pug missed her. The friendship was lopsided and awkward, but only Sylvia had taken the time to talk to him on a personal level, to try to interest him in things outside his Great Work. Others had long since given up. They would come to him for expert advice in his chosen area, and would dutifully take notes in the classes he still taught from time to time, but when the advice was given, or the class was over, they went on, went back, back to their own lives, their own friends and families, their own concerns. No one spared a thought for strange little Pug, who seemed so self-sufficient.

"Good-bye, Sylvia," Pug murmured after she'd gone up. He blinked at the cold body for a few minutes, wondering if something else were required. His gaze caught at the coded patch on her wrist, where, in her last moments, she had tapped out the code that shut down her systems and sent her up. He never touched his own patch, was never even tempted to tap out the code. Why had she done it? Her medical chart was available, but knowing Sylvia, Pug doubted she had gone up to escape some disease. No, she had chosen her time, declared her Great Work finished, and gone up without a word. It was her right, of course, but the choice bewildered Pug. Life was sweet for him, in a way he couldn't explain to anyone else, and it was something he wanted to continue as long as possible.

At last, he said good-bye again, then quietly left the room, feeling vaguely disturbed in a way he had never experienced before.

Standing at the viewport in his room before sleeptime, Pug gazed out at the Earth. The blue-white globe was visible several times a day, for the habitat rotated rapidly. Pug had never been on a planet, and he decided that one day he would visit Earth. He knew the earthlings had access to the same nets, the same entertainments, and the same educational channels. He knew the common beliefs of the habitat were exaggerated. The earthlings weren't some kind of primitives, dancing around fires in the night and warring with each other all the time. They were human, with the same hopes and dreams and fears as civilized people. He was fairly proud of his lack of prejudice. If someone had suggested to him that he wanted to visit Earth because Sylvia had been born there, he would have been surprised by the idea.

He turned from the viewport, stripped, and lay down on his pad. Eyes shut, he dismissed Sylvia from his mind and brought up the latest problem presented by his Great Work. Without moving or using any cybernetic enhancements, he manipulated formulas, solved equations, and investigated ideas. Before long, he was satisfied with the results. Still without moving, he drifted into sleep.

Sometime during sleeptime, he woke to find his face wet with tears. He sat up, turned on the light, and demanded of the room, "Why am I crying?" No answer seemed forthcoming, and sleep seemed far away, so he did something he had never done before: he went visiting.

Hanna was a girl his own age, and while he had never paid much attention to her, he was distantly aware that she was attractive and reasonably agreeable. He padded naked through the corridors and knocked on her door.

A boy a little older than Pug opened the door and blinked owlishly at him. "Yes?"

Pug's courage suddenly failed him. Another new experience. He suddenly remembered that Hanna was involved with someone. Bruce. This must be he. The face was even vaguely familiar. Embarrassed, Pug mumbled something about being lost and started to turn away. From behind the older boy, Hanna called out, "Who's there? Come on in!"

Bruce shrugged, reached for Pug's shoulder, and guided the younger boy into the room. Hanna lay on the pad, naked and sweaty, her hair plastered down over her eyes. She pushed the hair away, sat up, and said incredulously, "Pug?"

Pug nodded miserably.

"What in the world are you doing here?" She stopped suddenly. "Oh! I didn't mean it like that. I'm sorry. Bruce and I were just, well, you know. And you surprised me." She paused, not much more sure of how to react than Pug himself. "I just meant. . . . . What did you want, Pug?"

Pug shook his head and closed his eyes, mortified. "Nothing." But then the feelings he'd been suppressing came forward and tears leaked from his tightly closed eyes. "Sylvia," he managed to say, and then words were impossible.

"Oh, you poor thing. Of course you're upset. No one thought to. . . . You're so. . . . We just didn't think. Come here, Pug."

Numbly, he stumbled forward. Hanna pulled him down onto the pad and curled around him. She held him tightly while he sobbed, and soothed him, made crooning sounds. Bruce slipped down on the other side of the pad and lay back, his arms crossed behind his head patiently, while Hanna murmured reassurances to their guest. Pug quieted eventually and almost didn't notice when her caresses became erotic. Soon, though, he was cooperating enthusiastically, and, for a brief moment, forgot his grief. When Bruce joined in some minutes later, Pug moved over to lie between them.

Long after Hanna had fallen asleep, he found himself whispering with Bruce, speaking of things he had thought didn't apply to him. He spoke of his parents, of Sylvia, of grief and loss. He realized while talking that he hated the whole idea of going up, that he resented them for leaving him. But he was comforted by Bruce's quiet reassurances that his feelings were normal, and before long, his mind was clear and calm again. He had never suspected he would find himself in this situation, sandwiched between two loving friends who let him share their joy and peace when he needed it. Eventually, he slept.

He woke to find Hanna already gone. He gently moved Bruce's hands away and got up without waking the other boy. Last sleeptime already seemed impossible. He couldn't have shown that much vulnerability, couldn't have been that open. He wanted to pretend that it had never happened, and at the same time, he wanted it to happen every sleeptime for the rest of his life.

He got the first wish. When he saw Hanna in the corridors the following day, he glanced at her then looked away. No words were necessary; the casual disinterest was enough. She looked hurt, then angry, then simply disgusted. She came up beside him without slowing down, and said just loudly enough for him to hear, "Don't ever come back."

He would never even be tempted. Before long, he had convinced himself that the experience had been a case study in interpersonal relationships, that he had no more interest in her than he might have had in a lab rat. The data were everything; the subject, nothing.

Bruce was even easier to ignore. The older boy had been humoring Hanna at first, then simply interested in sex—any sex—as events progressed. At his age and level of maturity, anything warm and compliant was a valid partner. And since he was good looking, intelligent, and as caring as a boy that age could reasonably be expected to be, he had no lack of friends and partners. He didn't even bother snubbing Pug in the hallways. He just treated him with the same indifference he always had, which suited both boys just fine.

Pug immersed himself in his Great Work even more than before. But when Sylvia had gone up, something had changed forever, whether he could admit it or not. As the long years went by, he found less and less satisfaction with his studies. At age nineteen, he shocked the habitat by changing Great Works. While the lesser students sometimes changed from field to field trying to find a Great Work, it was unheard of for a master to do so. But Pug's new field, biochemistry, was as easy for him as sentential logic and differential calculus had been, and he was soon producing new and exciting research with designer biomods. Even the most reluctant elders had to admit that Pug's new Great Work was a true calling. Pug's biomods included enhanced eyesight, keener hearing, body restructuring, and his crowning achievement, the self-powered built-in respirator.

In conjunction with a simple force field, the respirator eliminated the need for space suits and increased the amount of time humans could stay in space without external life-support by a factor of a thousand. Even better, he set up his biomods to be self-installing and self-adjusting, so that habitat members could just pick a model out of the catalogue, and minutes later be wearing—or containing—the latest and greatest. People changed out irises to match their apparel. Green dress, green eyes. Next day, go with brown. They could change limbs almost as easily, putting on a hand with extra fingers for jobs requiring fine manipulation, or using powered legs for heavy work.

The habitat expanded beyond its projected growth curves, for they no longer had to pressurize anything but living quarters. The respirator made vacuum a minor inconvenience, no more. Since everyone had a respirator, corridors connecting pods could be as simple as a coded string of lights pointing the way. The force field automatically merged with the fields surrounding the pressurized zones when a pod was entered, and automatically snapped into a personal bubble when going outside.

Pug was pleased with his Great Work, but felt it was only a stopgap on the way to something else. He began exploring other fields of study, and changed his Great Work to physics when he was twenty-nine years old. This time, no one was surprised. They simply waited eagerly to see what miracles Pug would produce.

They would have a long wait.

As always, Pug spent all of his waking time on his Great Work, but unlike before, his work was mostly theoretical. He didn't teach, didn't consult with others or share his working notes, and didn't produce any gadgets. He rarely left his quarters—the same small pod he had shared with his parents long ago. When he did go out, it was always during the habitat's sleep cycle, and he went out alone, to stand in raw space, swaddled in his force field and supported by his respirator, to stare at Earth, far away.

The thoughts he had then, watching the Earth turn above him, he shared with no one.

Hanna went up when Pug was one hundred thirty-five. In all that time, he had toiled alone on his Great Work, but told no one what he was doing. Hanna's death, an accident, drew him out of isolation. She had left her Great Work unfinished. She had become a molecular chemist of no great repute, and the industry hardly noticed her passing. Nevertheless, her friends —including Bruce— gathered to honor her memory, for they would miss her. Pug surprised them by showing up. He said nothing, but leaned over to kiss her cold forehead, and then left before anyone could question him. On his way out of the pod, he patted Bruce on the shoulder. Although the people of the habitat didn't realize it yet, they'd finally gotten their miracle.

Hanna sat up on her pad, looked around, and burst into tears. A wafer-thin metallic disk fell from her forehead, already disintegrating as it fell. By the time it landed in her lap, it was nothing but dust. Hanna had gone up, but come back down, thanks to the disk Pug had put on her forehead when he kissed her.

A short time later Pug went to Earth. He came back six years later with a wife, Milla, and four-year-old son, Edward. As usual, he explained nothing, but all three of them wore tiny metallic disks on their foreheads. Not too long after that, Milla went up while giving birth to Emily, their second child. The disk fell off and disintegrated, and Milla came right back down. Pug outfitted her with another disk, and also put one on his new daughter.

Pug told everyone that the disks were still experimental, but that he would mass-produce them as soon as they were perfected. No one was pleased by this, but lifetimes were long and accidents few—people put off going up and waited for Pug to deliver his miracle to all.

When Edward was ten and Emily six, Pug called a conference. The entire habitat attended, some in person, but most by vid. Those living on Earth, Luna, and Mars also tuned in. Everyone in the solar system knew Pug's name, and they eagerly awaited the announcement. Few doubted that Pug had at last perfected the disks.

He did not disappoint them. The special metals in the thin disks, he told them, were expensive and hard to work with, but anyone could reasonably expect to save up enough to buy one or two during a normal lifetime. And since the disk granted a new lifetime, they could save up again and buy more. The process could continue indefinitely, for everyone. "No more going up," he told them. "No more."

Then Pug turned away from the cameras and took his family into their little pod. He was exhausted, having worked nonstop for six years to perfect the disks. The people granted him the greatest respect they knew how to give: They left him alone until he should choose to emerge again.

As soon as they were in private, Pug undressed and collapsed onto the sleeping pad. Milla and the children soon joined him. They lay snuggled together, arms and legs entwined, and slept long and deeply. It was a happy time for them during the next several days, for Pug shook his mind free from his Great Work, played with the children, made love to his wife, and acted like a normal man for the first time in his life.

When Pug finally emerged from seclusion, he announced that he was finished with Great Works. "I am done with doing," he said, remembering his father's words, and would say no more.

People remonstrated with him. Surely no one before him had ever done so Great a Work. Surely the one who provided all these miracles would not be satisfied stopping there. Hanna came to thank him for her life and had enough dignity to refrain from asking him to continue working. She made a half-hearted gesture toward asking him to come visit and was clearly relieved when he politely declined. But others had no such compunctions about taking his time. They accosted him by vid, pleaded with him in person, and sent him their own work for his review.

"Vipers!" Pug cried when they cornered him at last. "I have given you the respirator. I have given you designer bodies. I have given you the disks. You no longer have to go up. What more do you want from me?"

"Agriculture," said one. "If no one goes up, we will soon run out of food. You must apply your mind to agricultural problems."

"Astronomy," said another. "If no one goes up, we will soon run out of room, and must find other planets to settle. Only you can help us."

"Textiles!" shouted a woman. "Over a hundred million babies are being born every day, and not a single one will ever go up. What will they wear?"

"Engineering. We need ark-like space ships to colonize other planets, and new kinds of engines to propel them."

"Architecture! We must find ways to let such a hugely increased population live without sitting in each other's laps. We need mile-high cube buildings."

Pug ran away before he could hear any more. "They're your problems!" he shouted over his shoulder as he ran. "Solve them yourselves!"

Milla soothed him when he got back to their pod, and he played with the children until sleeptime. Then he and Milla went out into raw space to watch the Earth turning above them. They floated close enough together for their fields to merge, and then for a little while they forgot about the Earth with its teeming trillions, and worked on adding one more.

Later, back on the pad in their pod when he should be sound asleep, Pug lifted Edward off him and sat halfway up, leaning on his elbow. By the dim Earthlight coming through the viewport, he studied his little family. Emily slept on her side, her little fist crammed into her mouth, drooling a bit. Milla lay on her back, with Edward draped across her on his stomach. One of Milla's hands absently toyed with his hair, and she hummed softly to herself; she was only half-asleep. The boy snored and snuggled more deeply against her, one leg straight, the other bent at the knee so his foot lifted up in the air. Pug loved them all and wondered at the true miracle he had created—becoming a whole person at last, with a family that would never go up. *That* was a Great Work. The disk on Milla's forehead glinted as she moved a bit, and Pug smiled to himself, lay down, and went back to sleep.

Early waketime a few weeks later, Edward found his father standing at the viewport, hands clasped behind his head, staring at the stars.

"Da," said Edward, tugging at Pug's hands. When Pug turned, Edward continued, with all the seriousness only a ten-year-old can muster: "I need to start my Great Work."

Pug frowned. "You have plenty of time, baby." He sat cross-legged on the plates and pulled the boy into his lap. "You don't have to start your Great Work for years and years. You don't ever have to start, if you don't want to."

Edward squirmed free. "I'm not a baby," he said. "And I already know what my Great Work will be."

"Okay, then, what?"

The boy touched the disk on his forehead. "This thing."

Milla laughed from the far side of the pod where she'd been watching and listening while helping Emily with her studies. "Edward, your da has already finished the disks." She turned to Emily and said, "No, honey, don't try to integrate the vector; it's additive." She deftly manipulated the screen to show the six-year-old what she had done wrong.

Edward tried to ignore the interruption. "No," he said seriously to Pug. "You *didn't* finish it. You made it so people can come down after they go up, but you didn't let them remember what up was like so they can choose."

"Up isn't like anything, Edward," said Pug.

"You don't know that."

"I. . . ." Pug stopped, perplexed. "I do know, but I'm not sure I know how to explain it. Going up is just a name we use for when life is over."

"You mean dead?"

"Yes, dead. Look, when your respirator's power pack runs out, it needs to be replaced. The reactor material is gone, all used. It's gone up."

"At school they said it just turns into something else. It's never really gone."

"Well, that's true. But, well, think of the disks. A person has something like a power pack, but much more complicated. When it runs out, the person is gone. But the disk can recharge the power pack, and the person comes back. As long as there's power, the person is there. When the power is gone, the person is gone."

"Like your lap," said Milla, paying attention again. She pulled Emily along and joined them by the viewport.

Pug blinked. "What?"

"When you stand up," Milla said, "your lap is gone. But you can sit down and it comes back."

"Well, yes, something like that I suppose. But much more involved."

"But your lap doesn't really go away, it just changes into hips and legs. What Edward is asking is what happens when someone goes up. We know matter and energy are never destroyed, so it must go somewhere. Where?"

"Yeah, where?" said Emily.

Pug threw up his hands. "I won't argue with a six-year-old."

Edward leaned close to his father and laughed, though his expression was deadly intense. "I'm your son," he said. "Don't argue with me, either. I know the stories. I'm just like you were. I've found my Great Work—my first one, at least—and I'm going to start on it right away."

"No," said Pug. "First I'm going to pin you, then I'm going to tickle you until you scream, and *then* you can start." Pug did those things and then forgot about the subject, but Edward did not.

In the following years, Edward worked silently and diligently on his project while also doing his regular schoolwork. He followed in his father's footsteps without knowing it, because in order to answer the question of where people go when they went up, he had to learn philosophy. He was truly his father's son; he had an aptitude for sentential logic, and soon discarded most metaphysical theories as wishful thinking. By the time he was sixteen, he had published several carefully thought-out papers, scathing rejections of both ancient and modern theory, and people everywhere were nodding to themselves in satisfaction. Pug's line had produced another genius.

Edward gave the major religions a cursory examination, then moved on to develop his own metaphysics. It was a curious hybrid of logic, Zen, and experimental psychology, and though he explained his theories at great length, no one seemed to understand him.

Frustrated, Edward tried to involve his father, for he knew of no one else who might be able to help him coalesce his theories into a thematic whole. But Pug would have none of it. He was done with doing, and said that Great Works must be taken on by one person alone, else they were meaningless. But privately, Pug worried about the boy—now a young man—and tried to keep him from repeating Pug's mistakes. At almost seventeen, Edward was so consumed with his Great Work that he had no friends, no sex partners, and no apparent interest in obtaining either.

Milla was less worried. She knew her son's mind well enough to know that time would bring his interests full circle soon enough. And she knew that, like his father, when Edward latched onto a task, nothing else existed until the task was complete. She and Pug continued trying to make another child without success, and that was as close to a Great Work as either one got for a long time.

The habitat continued expanding, but more energy was focused on outworld expeditions. An interstellar launch was planned, in an ark that would carry over a million colonists. Overcrowding was an issue on Earth, but not in the habitat, where more cubic was available for the price of a bit of metal, easily mined from asteroids, and air, easily generated from other materials by variations of Pug's respirator technology. And no one ever went up. Food was not yet a crisis, for others had Great Works of their own, and solved many of the production problems still remaining. For the next hundred years or more, Earth could keep feeding all of her children, both those who remained at home and those who rode the heavens in the habitat or on Luna. The Mars colony remained self-sufficient, but Pug could see that they were on the same path as Earth. A crisis was coming.

He was not the only one to see it. With potentially unlimited lifetimes, scientists and ordinary people around the solar system began to look further ahead than usual, and they worried. If all variables remained the same, and the population continued increasing at its current rate, the Earth would run out of food in one hundred fifty years, Mars in two hundred. The habitat began increasing its hydroponics, but this was at best a stopgap, for essential raw materials still had to be shipped up from Earth.

The ark might succeed in taking humanity to another star, but the drive technology was slow; interstellar food shipments weren't even being dreamed about. Even if another world could produce the needed food, getting it in five hundred or a thousand years would do no one any good. At best, the ark satisfied the pioneering urge while giving humanity a small insurance policy against disaster. Even if all life in the solar system disappeared, the race would continue elsewhere.

This, however, was cold comfort for those who would stay behind. What use to them, having humanity living beside another star? And what use was not going up, if there was no food to eat here? Some trusted that Pug, or another like him, would solve those problems when they arose. Humans had been dealing with the future that way for all of recorded history. But here and there, in ones and twos, some removed their disks, lay down on their pads, tapped their personal codes into their wrist patches, and went up.

Pug shook his head sadly when he heard this, but Edward and Emily were excited. Emily was only twelve years old then, but she was Pug's daughter in the same way Edward was Pug's son. Brother and sister worked together now, and Emily often provided the insights Edward needed to move ahead. But they needed volunteers to help test Edward's theories. He sent out a call: If you're going up, talk to us first.

He got his volunteers. He also got his results.

Using sensitive electrodes and sensors of his own design, some of them electronic, some of them squiggles on paper with leads pasted on, he monitored those who chose to go up.

They definitely went somewhere. Where, he couldn't tell. But it wasn't oblivion. It wasn't death, the way a battery dies when the electromotive force is exhausted. In order for his test to show results, however, the volunteers had to go up and stay up. The ones who came back down left the meter banks unchanged.

He published his studies, outlining his methods, theories, and significance calculations. Although parts of his science weren't the kind of science humanity had known before, his results could be duplicated in any lab, by anyone trained to operate the equipment.

They went up in droves.

No longer was unending life the goal. Rather, people spoke of fulfillment, of becoming, of higher planes, of paradise.

They went up in multitudes.

Science had proven there was something more, something after life, something unknown. A new frontier, or an old religion validated—it didn't matter what motivation an individual had. It was enough to know that mortal strife was only the first step, that something grander, something larger, waited. Edward cautioned them that his results only showed that an individual persisted, not that they went to paradise. But no one listened.

They went up by the millions.

Twenty years later, the ark project was abandoned. Some few still cared about it, but an undertaking that huge required the dedicated support of entire industries—miners, manufacturers, parts jobbers, engineers, welders, cooks, babysitters, architects, handymen, physicists, mathematicians, and more. Too few specialists cared enough about the project to sustain the progress. The remaining backers quietly went up along with the rest.

Great Works were forsaken half-completed. Bakers left their ovens, farmers left their fields, workers left the factories, bankers left their counting rooms. It became an epidemic. A full twenty-five percent of humanity went up, some alone, some in huge going-up parties, some taking unwilling partners with them.

They went up by the billions.

Those who remained paid little attention to practical things, turning inward instead, examining life in light of the sure knowledge that it was but a stepping stone to something else. Those who wanted to keep living had Pug's disks; those who did not could always take the disks off.

Pug bestirred himself when it became apparent that the habitat would no longer receive deliveries of any sort. There weren't enough skilled workers left to man the shuttles, and not enough farmers left to harvest crops beyond their own immediate needs. The habitat had supplies for several years and shuttles of its own, so Pug didn't worry about his family's survival. But he was curious about Edward's Great Work, and came to watch while Edward sent up volunteer after volunteer.

Pug studied the diagrams and circuitry. He read all of the reports and ran all the statistics through his own computer. Edward and Emily's work was impressive. Pug understood why people throughout the solar system had chosen as they had. But Pug was Pug, with a brilliant mind and a hunger for answers that surpassed even Edward's. He worried over the data while more and more people went up, and by the time he was ready to start drawing inferences and conclusions, only Pug and his family were left on the habitat. The others had either gone back to Earth or gone up.

The radio and vids from Earth, Luna, and Mars had been silent for weeks when Pug went to find Edward in his laboratory. Pug assumed there was no longer anyone who cared to man the communications consoles, or to repair and align the huge dish antennas. This disturbed him at a level too deep for words.

Edward was studying the last of his data when Pug entered the laboratory. Pug was carrying a small device with him.

"What's that, Da?"

"A meter, much like yours. Based on the same principles. I hope you don't mind that I borrowed your work."

"I'm flattered. I told you I would do my Great Work, and that this would be it. Are you proud of me, Da?"

Pug passed a hand over his eyes and sat down heavily. "Always," he said at last. "But not for your Great Work. You made a mistake, son."

Edward was scientist enough to merely cock an eyebrow and wait. Marketing sells, but information tells. He awaited data.

Pug connected his device to Edward's meter bank. The indicator on the device immediately lit up, and the number 107553 appeared. In moments, it had become 107552. Then 107551. Then 107550.

Edward crossed his arms and leaned back. "What do the numbers mean, Da?"

"I'll tell you, but first I must explain something. When someone goes up while connected to your instruments, you can measure a current that persists after the person has gone up, yes?"

"Not exactly a current, more of a pattern, but yes."

"And if the person comes back down, the pattern disappears from your instruments, right?"

"Yes, exactly."

"But if the person stays up, you can continue monitoring the pattern for a time, thus leading you to believe the pattern represents the person after going up."

"Where's this going, Da? That's the basic theory that turned the world on end. Proof. Just what I told you I'd find someday."

"But Edward, you missed something. Look—" he pointed to a part of the circuit diagram on the desk— "These components that do the monitoring, they act like a capacitor. You aren't watching the patterns of people after they've gone up, you're just capturing a bit of their energy as they go up past you. If you use my disk to bring them back down, the energy is transferred back into the person, just like recharging those power packs we talked about when you were ten. But if the people don't come back down, the energy stays in your capacitor for a while until it slowly discharges by leakage to the surrounding air."

"I don't underst—"

"Instead of proving that they go somewhere after going up, you've proved the opposite. Unless captured by your instruments, the energy they had just dissipates into the air. The discharge is faster without your instruments, but it's the same function."

"But—"

"Look at the readout."

The numbers read 106221. While they watched, the display changed to 106220, then 106219.

"I've calibrated my device so that each tick represents the stored energy corresponding to one person. The countdown shows the energy leaking away from your capacitor."

Edward didn't want to believe. He forced Pug to go through

his reasoning again and again, and examined the little meter device carefully. Then he spent several weeks in isolation, reviewing his work, recalculating all of his careful equations. When he emerged, he was haggard and drawn.

"I've killed them all," he said. "But you were wrong, Da. It's not really acting like a capacitor. I would have caught that myself—it's too obvious. It's worse. My device, in the process of measuring them as they go up, actually interferes with the pattern. It's the interference I'm recording. I now know for certain that if the pattern is measured, the act of measuring destroys it. But we're back to square one on what happens if I don't measure it. There's no reason to assume anything either way. Without my device, they may go somewhere or they may not. The only thing I know for sure is that, with my device, they just . . . go up."

Milla hugged him. Emily stood quietly, not knowing what to say. But Pug said, "Maybe it's not too late. Let's go to Earth and see what's left. We'll have to tell them the truth."

They piloted the shuttle to Earth, using the last of its fuel pellets to do so. They carried food and water with them, for they had no way to know what conditions they would encounter on the mother planet, and whether or not they could get more fuel. Pug suspected it might take them some time to establish contact with those who remained, and, without telling anyone else, he fashioned several small energy weapons and took them along, too. He feared a return to savagery. They were as prepared as they knew how to be.

They weren't prepared enough.

The city beside which they landed was deserted. Radios were silent, and vids showed only static. Some records, made by what would-be historian they would never know, showed the madness of the last days. As far as they could tell, everyone in the city had either gone up or gone away. Only animals and insects remained.

They wandered listlessly from city to city, using ground vehicles when they could find them, walking when they could not. There was food here and there, but little that could be preserved without the power plants to run the refrigeration units. They ate their own stores frugally, then, when all else failed, rummaged through the spoiling produce for anything they could find.

The Earth had been transformed. Some places remained thickly inhabited, but others were deserted. The infrastructure required to support billions was gone, and the remaining people wouldn't listen to Edward's warnings. More than once, Pug had to use his weapons to keep his family from harm. But by and large, people remained the same as they'd always been —most friendly, some fearful, a few dangerous, and the rest somewhere along that continuum.

Pug got a long-range radio working and re-established contact with the Mars and Luna colonies, only to find the situation was the same in all three places. A few practical-minded people remained out of a sense of duty; the others had either gone up or turned inward.

One day, without discussion, Pug's little family stopped wandering. It was a nice enough spot, beside a small lake, far from any major cities. There were houses here that they could use, fish in the lake, and wild animals in the small nearby forest. It would do.

They went about the mechanics of life woodenly while considering their options. But one day Emily came up with her own answer. She had grown increasingly moody while they wandered, and hadn't spoken much at all for a long time. It was clear she suffered from grief and guilt over her part in the destruction of so much of humankind. On a cool summer morning, the guilt became too much. She removed the disk from her forehead, lay down on a carpet of green pine needles, and went up without a word.

Edward found her after she was cold.

Pug and Milla didn't cry when Edward told them about Emily. But they cried when Edward took off his own disk and laid himself down on the grass.

"I love you," he said between sobs, his fingers poised over his wrist patch.

"We forgive you," said Milla, "and we love you always."

"We love you," said Pug, "and we forgive you always."

Edward tapped out his code and went up.

Pug and Milla went on.

They moved from that place to another spot, one less bitter with memories, and lived together for almost two hundred years, growing their own food, keeping each other company. Though they had no more children, in some ways it was the best time Pug ever knew, for he and Milla grew ever closer to each other's heart. But eventually, Milla tired of life. Her Great Work had been the nurturing of their children, and it was long done. Pug, who wanted nothing more than to live forever, couldn't understand.

"I have done with doing," said Milla, knowing that this echo from Pug's past would disturb him, but unable to formulate a better way of saying it.

She lay on the pad they shared and took the disk off her forehead. "Come with me," she said, holding out a hand to him.

But Pug could only shake his head, crying, and run from the room. A long time later, Pug returned, kissed her cold lips, and said good-bye in silence.

He took to wandering again. The world was recovering from

its madness, and people were rebuilding. But it wasn't the same for Pug. It never would be. Still, he couldn't—wouldn't—consider going up. Life was bitter, but it was life.

He came upon a small community and settled down for several years. No one knew that he was the inventor of the disks, or that his son was the author of so much death. Pug didn't find it necessary to tell them. Nevertheless, the people of the community looked on Pug with awe, for among his possessions he had a thousand little disks. Disks were now precious, for the raw materials were hard to find, and the expertise to make them almost gone. They wondered at his supply, but did not jeopardize their chances of getting some by annoying Pug with questions.

While he couldn't bring himself to marry again, he could, and did, take sex partners from time to time. His favorites were Luara—undemanding, incurious about his past—and John, a tender companion who declined entanglements. And Pug was not infertile; Luara and several others eventually gave birth, and Pug was reasonably sure he was the father of at least three. Yet one day he decided to move on, for when he looked at his partners and offspring, he saw only Milla, Edward, and Emily, and was not satisfied. And although he treated his partners and children with love and courtesy, it would never be the same for him.

One child, Manumus, begotten by Luara, chased after him in the night and caught up with him two miles from the village, a tremendous journey for one so young. "Pug, wait," called the boy, out of breath and near tears.

Pug turned and saw, not Edward who was no more, but Manumus, a living, breathing child, full of life and hope. Pug's heart turned away from the past, and he held out his arms. The boy leaped up and wrapped himself around Pug. "Don't leave me, Da," he said.

The boy's breath was warm on Pug's cheek, and his heart beat a pattern against Pug's chest that Pug recognized and, in that instant, knew he loved. Here was an answer—if not complete, at least sufficient.

Pug fumbled with his pouch, removed a disk, and pressed it against the boy's forehead.

"Come with me," he said.

"Yes," said Manumus, trusting and happy. "Where are we going, Da?"

"I don't know." Pug looked up at the stars and saw the gleam of the habitat, still orbiting untended after all these years. "I don't know."

"How long will we be gone?" asked the boy. He reached up to touch Pug's own disk, and his brown eyes glinted warmly in the starlight.

Pug turned and started walking, the child a pleasant burden in his arms. "Forever, maybe."

Manumus snuggled closer and laid his head on Pug's shoulder. "As long as I can stay with you."

Pug glanced down at the boy's face and saw the disk on his forehead. "Yes," he said, "that long."

Behind them, as they walked, a hint of peace entwined the night with gentle arms, and Pug was content. It would never be the same, but wasn't that the glory of it?

"Maybe longer," Pug murmured, but the boy was already asleep.

EXTRACTION

"I want the thumbscrews handy," Mandrella said. One of the technicians nodded and went to fetch them, but Mandrella had already spun away to supervise someone else. "The rack," she said. "Get it ready. In the center, I think, so he can see it waiting the whole time."

The technicians, dressed alike in shapeless black robes with cowls and long, dragging sleeves, moved in the heavy equipment. "Don't forget the excruciator. And the chains. A whip. Somebody get me a whip! Where's my robe? Dammit, I'll roast the lot of you if—ah, okay, here's the robe."

Swiftly, with quiet, practiced efficiency, the technicians laid out a gleaming array of knives, and artfully arranged them on black velvet under a blood-red lamp. They wheeled in the excruciator, the iron maiden, the sprocket of pain, and an entire rack filled with alembics, flasks, tubes, wires, bubbling retorts, and vials of smoking, colored liquids. Others carried in the socket puller, the helmet of agony, and the gloves of truth.

"The fire, dammit! We need hot coals. And the poker, don't

forget the poker." Mandrella donned her cloak and gave the whip a few practiced flicks against the wall. The technicians brought in a brick fire pit on a forklift, set it against one wall and arranged a facade of paper-thin fake bricks on either side. One technician filled the fire pit with charcoal briquettes, another doused them with lighter fluid, and a third threw on a match.

Mandrella looked around and nodded to herself. "Okay, let's set up the backdrop and lighting. I want Dark and Gloomy Number Seven for this one." The technicians covered the windows with thick hangings of black cloth, and then erected the hand-mortised stone facade of D&G #7. "Kill the overhead," Mandrella said.

A moment later, the room darkened. Lighting specialists swiveled small spotlights concealed in the stone facade, focused them on the torture implements.

"All right. Places, everyone." Mandrella assumed center stage the way a queen assumes a throne. "Bring Johnson in."

Two technicians started toward the door.

"Wait, dammit! Where are the sound effects? I want water dripping on stone in the distance. Plug in a couple of scurrying rats, too."

The sound-effects specialist selected a cartridge, plugged it in, and brought the fader up. Somewhere off in the distance, water plinked forlornly on stone, and tiny-clawed paws scrabbled across rubble.

"Can you make it damper?"

The technician twirled a dial, selecting a different effect. The plink changed to a steady but slow drip, sounding as if it were falling into a rank pool of some sort.

"Perfect. Now, let's have Mr. Johnson."

Technicians escorted Emile Johnson into the room. Emile

appeared to be around thirty-five. He was dark-haired, dark-eyed, and wore his hair in a long, shaggy ponytail. He looked around the room carefully and then focused on Mandrella.

"All this really isn't necessary," he said.

"Shut up! I'll decide what's necessary."

"I just mean, I'll be glad to talk—"

"Oh, I know you will."

"Ah, I meant right away. I'll tell you anything."

Mandrella folded her arms inside the sleeves of her robe and nodded at the technicians. Two of them grabbed him by the shoulders, lifted him clear of the floor, and then threw him down.

Emile's nose and jaw smacked into the cement floor. "Hey!" He levered himself up, rubbing at his chin. "Was that really—?"

A technician kicked him in the middle of the back and sent him sprawling again. This time when Emile came back up, there was blood streaming from his mouth.

"You broke a tooth!"

Mandrella shook her head. "You just don't get it, do you?" She glanced at the technicians and waved her hand. All but one of them quietly left the room. The remaining technician helped Emile to his feet and guided him to a chair.

Mandrella approached, noiselessly gliding across the floor in her black robe. "You will talk," she said.

Emile wiped at the blood on his chin with the back of one hand while gesturing with the other. "I said I would. You don't need to—hey! Let go!" The remaining technician calmly fastened Emile's wrists to the arms of the chair, then bent to arrange leather straps around his ankles, knees, and thighs.

"That chair is called an excruciator," Mandrella said. "At the moment, it is merely restraining you. It has other features you'll discover later on—when we become better friends." She bent in close, so that even in the dim lighting Emile could see her face under the cowl. "You'd like to be friends with me, wouldn't you, Emile?" She smiled and waited until the shock on his face told her that he'd noticed how her eyeteeth had been filed into needle-sharp fangs.

"I'd rather skip this whole thing," he said.

"Oh, it's much too late for that," she said, almost purring. "You have something to tell me, and I'm most eager to hear it." She straightened, tucked her hands back into the folds of her robe. "You may begin talking now. If you hesitate or stop, the pain begins. You are in control of the pain from now on. There is nothing in your world except the pain and your words, and the two cannot co-exist. As long as you talk, the pain won't come. But the moment you stop, the pain will fill you until, at last, in agony, you scream out more, to hold the pain away. The session ends when you have told the entire story or have died, whichever comes first. Do you understand?"

Emile raised his head, stared off into the distance. "Yes, I understand."

"Then begin."

"I, um, ah. . . ."

"This is a thumbscrew. It works like this." Mandrella fitted a thumbscrew to his left hand and gave two initial twists.

"Ow! Stop that!"

"You are in control," said Mandrella, tightening the thumbscrew again.

"Ahh! Dammit, that hurts!"

"When you talk, the pain goes away. The choice is yours," said Mandrella, giving the thumbscrew another twist.

"Ow! Ow! Okay! Once. . . ."

Mandrella loosened the thumbscrew and waited.

"Upon. . . shit, you're making me nervous." Emile paused again, his breath ragged, sweat beading up on his forehead.

Mandrella frowned. "Don't jerk me around, Emile. I don't like it." She fitted a thumbscrew to his other hand, tightened it down, and then twisted both at once.

"Ah! Ah! Okay, here it is. There was a man, see, a friend of mine."

Mandrella loosened the thumbscrews. "Go on."

"He said, he said I had this thing—this thing, you see, which not everybody had. I didn't even know I had it. He said I was using it already, but just the way a baby might use a spoon. It's like a talent, you know, like being able to play the violin, but you still have to practice, work on it, learn how to use it. . . ." He trailed off.

Mandrella sighed and twisted the thumbscrews down until Emile's nails split. Blood gushed forth.

"Ah! Ow! Shit!"

"You stopped talking. This is the result. It's under your control, Emile. Why do you make me hurt you?" Mandrella crossed the room, pulled the poker from the stand and set it into the coals.

Emile writhed in the chair. "Okay, okay, I'll tell you the rest. My talent was in picking horses. Somehow, just by studying them, I could tell the winners from the losers. So I started placing bets. I wasn't perfect, but I was getting better and better. The money started piling up. That's when my friend, the one who first told me I had the talent, told me there was a price for my success. It was a devil's bargain, you see, and he was the devil, and. . . ." He broke off, eyeing her nervously. "What are you going to do with that?"

Mandrella rolled the poker carefully in the coals, making

sure that it was heating evenly. "Burn you," she said without turning around. "Unless you keep talking."

"I, ah, okay, um, I found out that I wouldn't have to pay until I died. The standard contract. Nevertheless, I thought I could wiggle out of it. I mean, I'd been using the talent before the devil showed up, so it was something I already had. Paying for it —well, I haven't worked out all the details yet. It's something clever, a twist ending. This isn't making sense. I don't know how to explain it."

"Learn," suggested Mandrella, lifting the poker and gliding back to him. "Hold his head," she said to the technician.

Vise-strong hands clamped on Emile's temples. He strained and twisted, but couldn't break free. "Don't," he said, "don't . . . you don't need to . . . ah, shit, please! Please don't—"

Mandrella waved the glowing tip of the poker around his nose, letting him feel the heat, smell the hot iron, anticipate the pain.

"You will now continue talking," she suggested brightly.

"It's, ah, dammit, don't—ah, goddamit, OW!"

"He fainted," said the technician. "Before you touched it to him, I think."

Mandrella smiled. "That's a bonus, then. It's in the contract." She turned and raised her voice. "Somebody check the tape!"

"He's coming around again, ma'am."

"Hold the playback. Noises off. Find your mark. We're back on."

She turned back to Emile and smiled sweetly. "Why, hello, there! Glad you decided to stay with us. Now . . . you were saying?"

Emile blinked, trying to get everything back into focus. "I, um, forget what. . . ."

"The arms of the excruciator can be repositioned," she said, demonstrating as she talked. "They can swing back and forth, and be clamped into just about any angle. This crank—" she gave it a few turns— "pulls them forward, away from your body. If your chest weren't strapped, you'd lift right out of the chair. As it is, I'll stop just before your arms pull out of the sockets."

"That's quite . . . uncomfortable," said Emile after a moment.

"Oh, give it a few hours. In the meantime, this other crank turns the long, horizontal screws between the legs. Notice how, when the ankle cuffs move apart, the seat moves up and forward, so you can do perfect suspended splits. Now this third crank moves your right leg backward and up. Did you know that your heel can actually touch the back of your head before the hip breaks?"

"You've lost him again, ma'am," said the technician.

Mandrella peeled back one of Emile's eyelids, then waggled a finger at him. "You're faking, Emile. There's a penalty for that." She looked up at the technician. "Fingernails, isn't it?"

"Yes, ma'am, I believe so."

"Well, we'll give the thumbs a miss this time, but the other eight nails will have to go." She smiled at Emile again. "Which would you prefer—peel and yank, or insert and pry? Or would you rather continue talking?"

Emile began to sob.

"Oh, that won't do," she said. "Look, here's the first nail." She ripped it off with a pair of pliers and held it up for him to see. "I'll put it in your shirt-pocket as a souvenir."

Emile suddenly began to babble, picking up right where he'd left off. But Mandrella interrupted him. "That won't do. The story's crap; it's been done to death. And it's not what your editor asked for. Now start over, and tell me the real story."

"I, ah, don't know—what? What real story? I'll tell you anything! Anything at all!"

"Yes, dear, I know." She patted his cheek and pulled a sheaf of papers out from under her robes. "Let me see, now. Hmmn, according to these, you owe Resnick a 3,500 word story. The deadline—wonderful term, that!—is tomorrow." She held up the bloody pliers. "I do hope you're ready."

"Um, alternate dinosaurs, right? Uh, lessee. . . . There was a baby dinosaur named Jack, who . . . . No, scratch that. His name was Ty Rex, and he was a very friendly little fellow, but all the creatures ran away and refused to play with him. Ty didn't understand. He just wanted to be friends. 'You'll never get anywhere in life being friends with mammals,' said his father. 'It's indecent,' said his mother. No, fudge that. Start over. Um . . . Archy didn't think there was anything unusual about wanting to fly. 'So what if no one's ever done it before?' he said to himself. All the other archaeopteryx laughed at him . . . damn, what's the plural of 'archaeopteryx'? Anyway, new paragraph. Pay copy this time. The first thing Archy saw when he broke out of his shell was the sky. And ever since he was a hatchling, he, um, ah. . . ."

"Don't think too long," said Mandrella, leisurely pulling up another nail.

Emile settled into his narrative. He got thirteen paragraphs out rather quickly, then paused for thought long enough to lose another nail. "Ow, dammit, I'm talking, I'm talking!"

"This awl," said Mandrella, "goes through the cartilage in your nose like this. Then I can hang weights on both sides. Hmmn? Oh, you've decided on the rest of the plot? Go on, then."

Archy rapidly progressed through the first conflict and the first surprise reversal, then settled into the long haul toward the final conflict. Emile closed his eyes and let the words pour forth, only occasionally needing prodding from Mandrella. As Archy drew near the final paragraph, Emile forgot about Mandrella, forgot about the dungeon, forgot about the pain, forgot about everything except Archy and his brave desire to fly.

"'I did it, I did it!' cried Archy, thumping back to the earth triumphantly. The earth, that would never be the same for him again! Archy hugged his sweetheart, and she gazed at him with adoration in her cold reptilian eyes.

"'Your eyes are full of wings!' she breathed.

Archy just smiled and looked around. The ground was no longer a prison. It was just a way station, a resting place, for him and all his descendants, for all time to come!"

"That's Lamarckian," observed Mandrella. "How could his descendants inherit a learned ability?"

"Resnick won't care. It's a tear-jerker. Maybe Archy founds the first flight school. That's for the sequel, anyway."

"And I'm not sure how one archaeopteryx can hug another."

"They wrap their wings around each other. Don't worry— it's pay copy," said Emile. "May I get up now?"

"What's the word count?" she asked the technician.

The tech consulted his transcript. "4,200, ma'am."

Mandrella picked up a gleaming scalpel and rotated the handle thoughtfully between her fingers. "Either you cut," she said to Emile, "or I do."

"But, but . . . every word is necessary! They're jewels, I tell you, jewels! I can't cut anything! Now, hey, wait a minute, maybe I don't need the subplot with his mother—hey, wait, dammit! Ow! Shit, okay, strike paragraphs 27 through 32."

Mandrella lifted an eyebrow at the technician, who promptly edited the manuscript and reported, "That brings it down to 3,750."

"Another 250," said Mandrella.

"I can't! I just can't!" said Emile. "I don't know where to begin!"

"Start with the said-bookisms," cooed Mandrella with no hint of irony. She slid the scalpel gently under the skin on the inside of his left thigh. She wiggled the blade up a few inches toward his crotch. "You'd better hold still," she said. "I'd really hate to slip."

Emile cut another 250 words very quickly.

"Lights," said Mandrella. "That's a wrap. Someone bring orange juice for Mr. Johnson. And run that sucker through the spell checker. Print it out! I want Courier 12 pt., double-spaced, one inch margins. No, dammit, the title goes half-way down the first page, not a third. Use 20-lb bond. Don't forget the self-addressed stamped envelope! All right . . . *mail it!*"

Technicians bustled through the room. Mandrella helped Emile out of the excruciator. "There, that wasn't so bad, was it?" she asked.

"God, no," said Emile. "Writing's my life."

"Same time tomorrow, then?"

"Better schedule a whole weekend. My novel's overdue."

LEST WINTER COME

You've seen how leaves swirl in the wind. They dance, flip, rustle, turn over each other, leap high, form brief shapes, fall apart, sweep on. From the corner of your eye, when you're not expecting it, an illusion, just for a moment—a hand reaching up, a dog snuffling along the ground, a child skipping in autumn colors. But no, just leaves, swirled in the wind.

Then again, oh so briefly, gone by the time you see it, a man or a woman, a hat shading the eyes, a brooding shape. Your heart skips, your head whips around, the leaves dance away and you laugh, fooled for a breath, but now reassured. And yet you wonder.

Now add a lonely heart, a bit of moss, some twigs, and a strong need like wine gone to the head, and you can guess my sin.

Hand in hand we walk. The wind drags icy fingers across our cheeks, but the sun is warm. "This is wrong," she says, and I shrug. "Self-indulgent," she says, and I shake my head. "Ephemeral," she says, and I laugh.

"What is, is," I say. "The sky is blue, the sun is yellow, the world turns."

"Someday it won't."

"Today it does."

She tugs me to a halt, all serious now. "That's not enough."

I study her eyes, reach with my free hand to warm her cheek. I consider her complaint, the root of the desire that drives her discontent. I give the only answer that makes sense to me.

"Your nose is lovely," I say.

She tries to be angry, stamps her heel theatrically in the grass, pulls her head away and turns for a moment so that the wind blows her hair over her eyes. Then she lifts her chin and turns toward me again, and I see her smiling.

"You're impossible," she says.

"Of course. That's the plan. Walk with me."

"Where? Where are we going?"

I shrug, her hand warm in mine, and we move again, our feet pushing through the grass and leaves. "Over there." I point with my chin; she looks and gasps.

"It's beautiful! The trees, the hills, the stream! Was all that there before?"

"Before, after, now, then, soon, late. Who knows? Time is a mystery. Come with me." I pull gently on our joined hands, and our stroll becomes a walk, becomes a run, becomes a race. The wind drags at our clothes, our hair flies, we leap over the hills shouting our laughter, and we are become giants for a moment.

She stumbles, twists, grabs at my shoulders. Arms wrapping around each other, we roll over and over, down the last gentle hillside, breathless, giggling. By the stream we stop, I on my elbows above her. Her breath is cool and sweet against my lips, and the good red blood pulses hot beneath her cheeks. I bury

my nose in her hair and smell the wildness and the freedom
and the abandon.

"Are you happy?" I ask, letting the question ease out of my
lungs in a whisper, brush against her ear like a kiss. Perhaps it is
a kiss. Perhaps I never speak. Certainly the susurration of the
stream beside us is louder.

Suddenly she knows the darkness watches us. She feels it, a
bone-deep coldness in the air that goes far beyond the chill of
autumn. We sit up and turn, her fingers clutching mine in
fright. Under the trees, his face shadowy, a man made of
darkness watches us. He steps forward, and his feet are
withered grass. No, the grass withers where he stands, a circle
of decay spreading out where his feet touch the ground.

"Aaiih," she says, and shrinks against me, and then she's
standing, pulling, wanting to run.

"No!" I cry as our fingertips start to pull apart. Desperately I
hang on. "Don't let go!"

She holds my wrist now and helps me to my feet. Together
we turn to face the dark man with his feet of dying grass, but he
is gone. A hoary old oak tree stands there, its dead roots
grasping at the ground like a spider's legs, but gnarled and
twisted, dry, sucked clean of life long ago. It leans toward us,
and the heart of the tree is hollow and full of mortal dreads.

I turn her away from it, my hand closing on her fingers with
a panicked strength. She looks at me searchingly, looks at our
clasped hands, looks away for a long moment. She begins to
understand now, knows the limits, knows what she is, suspects
what I am. But she is not ready to admit it. Her eyes are tired
when she faces me again, but her grip is firmer. "I won't let go,"
she says.

She shivers, half reaction, half cold. "I feel so small," she
says.

This I can change for her. "Small, big, little, large, tiny, huge. Who knows? Size is a mystery. Come with me." I turn on the spot and draw her with me, and when we finish turning we sit on the moon, resting our feet on the planet Earth. The sun is a glare in the distance, but it is cold, blue-white, and remote. Illimitably beautiful.

"I can hold Venus in my hand," she says, and Venus is a hard little marble she holds before our gaze. I breathe out, a mist of crystal ice that wraps around the marble and melts, becomes an atmosphere. We dive into it, winged now, and glide among the clouds, only fingertips touching at arm's length, and she has forgotten the darkness, forgotten the cold, forgotten everything but wonder.

Pivoting on one toe, I whirl her back to Earth, spinning to the ground amidst the leaves and the clean brown limbs of the arching trees. In my arms she looks up, her eyes still full of stars, and I kiss her under the oaks and maples and birches while the leaves, amber and crimson and gold, tumble around us like rain.

She buries her face in my shoulder and I hold her close, all the while looking beyond her, into the shadows beneath the far trees, where the dark man waits watching, if only she knew to look for him there. "Walk with me," I say to her, and lead her away, down the hill, away from the trees. We follow the stream into a meadow, step on stones across the cold rushing water, come to a house on a small rise, and always, always, she holds my hand as we walk.

"May we go in?" she asks, looking at the house with longing.

"In, out, on, around, above, below. Who knows? Place is a mystery. Come with me."

The sun grows large and red, touches the horizon as we enter. The wind picks up and whistles, but the hearth is warm, and we drink apple cider at the table before moving closer to the fire. We sit side by side, touching at shoulder and hip. She sighs and snuggles against me. She turns, touches my face, lies down with me on the rug. Her breasts are firm and cool in my hands, her lips crush against mine. The fire burns down, crackling, popping, murmuring in its secret language. My voice asks, "Are you happy?" but it might be the settling of logs instead of words.

She stiffens suddenly, and I know she has seen what I have known all along—the darkness has come into the house with us. She sees him standing in the corner beside the door, his hand of shadows still on the latch. The doorframe is crumbling, the walls turning to dust. Bricks teeter atop one another, and the wind rises to knock them down. He leans forward as the house collapses around us. His breath is the stinging, chafing cold of a bitter winter storm. We run into the night, stumbling blindly, holding onto one another for support, thinking of nothing but the need to escape.

Freezing cold water encircles our ankles, up to mid-calf. We lurch across the stream, unable to find the stepping stones in the dark. Across the meadow, up the hill, back into the trees, racing, panting, the first flakes of snow falling about us as we run. We draw to a stop and stand trembling, chests heaving, her hands like icicles in mine, as the moon finally ascends. For seconds, minutes, hours, years, lifetimes, we stand waiting, hands clasped, looking back. Nothing moves but the tree branches, the leaves, and the wind, always the wind.

"Is he coming?" she asks.

I cannot protect her anymore. "Yes," I say.

"Can we get away?"

"No."

Her teeth chatter. Fear or cold? "What does he want from us?" she asks.

"You know."

And she does know. In the glimmer of the moonlight I can see the first half of the truth in her eyes. "Because of me," she says woodenly. "Because of what we've done."

This I cannot change for her. I lift her hands, blow on them, rub them between mine. "Laughter, tears, running, walking, breathing, living. Who knows? Life is a mystery, but love is not. Come with me."

My voice is the snow, whispering and whirling about her. I try to turn us away from the darkness, but her grip is firm, her feet motionless, and I am become halt, rooted by her touch.

She looks at our hands, where we are joined, have been joined all afternoon, never once letting go. She knows why, has always known. And now she suspects the rest. Her eyes travel slowly up, meet mine. Yes. Yes, she knows.

"You. . ." she says slowly.

"We," I object. "We, not I. We are." First person plural; progressive, if she is willing. Future imperfect. Truth defines grammar; grammar reveals truth.

She shakes her head. "You. . ." she says again.

"Speech is a mystery but love is not. Stay with me." Don't say the next words, I beg silently—or perhaps only the snow drifts lightly across the moonlight to caress her ears. Silence is now become the only mystery I am permitted to offer.

She refuses to accept my gift. "You are the dark man."

"What is, is," I say, my sin revealed, and the wind picks up, fingers my hair, plucks at my clothes. The time nears. She has chosen, will choose, will always have been choosing all along. Past perfect and future perfect mingle to become an innominate verb tense.

"Let go of me!" she cries.

"I am not holding you," I say, and it is the one word of truth. She clutches me, not I her. Her grip loosens a bit, and the wind grows colder, stronger. My hair whips about my head, my shirt flaps and tears free. Bitter, that wind, and indistinct my face. Forgiveness and farewell become synonyms.

She pulls me close, hugs me fiercely, then slowly opens her arms and lets me go. My body frays at the edges. A blur of leaves and twigs forms a small whirlwind in the space between her empty arms. A clump of moss falls to the forest floor. The scents of ancient oak and fresh apple cider remain strong.

You've seen how leaves swirl in the wind. They dance, flip, rustle, turn over each other, leap high, form brief shapes, fall apart, sweep on. And then the wind picks them up, shuffles them down, away from you, and they are gone.

Make of them what you will.

BARTH AND THE DRAGON

Back in the days before the Great Change, when magic still abounded in the world, Bartholomew was a young man schooled in the arts of forging.

He labored all day in the smithy, making weapons for the King's sons and other nobles. Bartholomew was diligent and industrious, and he sang and dreamed as he labored. All who saw his work said that there were no fairer weapons available, despite his youth. Barth's swords were sharper, stronger, and shinier than any other smith's. His mail was lighter, yet sturdier, than any other armorer produced, and it took a polish well and never rusted.

He dreamed as he pounded the hot steel, dreamed of fashioning a sword and armor for himself one day. Yet he never seemed to get around to making it. There was never enough time. Good King Worthy's second son, Prince Whomever, or the good Lord Whatshisname, or some other noble, always came first. Because Barth's work was so excellent, there were always orders far in advance.

One day, Barth was commissioned to make a sword for the King himself. Barth immediately pushed aside his other work and sat down to think.

A King's sword was no ordinary thing. It should be made of thunderbolts gathered in the light of the full moon, forged in dragon's fire, and laid about with enchantments before being tempered in holy water.

Well, reasoned the lad, *tomorrow night is the full moon, so that's no problem.* But where to get the dragon's fire? He rummaged through his small collection of spells, finding nothing appropriate. Then, in the back of an old drawer, he found a sachet of dried herbs labeled *Draco summonicionem*, with a tiny subscript, "Burn me if you're a fool."

Barth was not a fool, but he *did* want to summon a dragon. He tossed the packet into the fire, cloth bag, string, and all. It immediately caught fire, sending up green and yellow smoke and shooting out sparks to dance and frizzle throughout the forge.

Sooner than Barth had hoped, there came from outside a tremendous roaring, louder even than the furnace of his forge. Without pausing for thought, Barth snatched up a hauberk he had made for the good Lord Whoo and raced outside. There, right before his forge, lay a dragon of Tremendous Girth and Proportion.

The wyrm had blue hair streaming in straggles from its horny brow, and green scales, sharp enough to slice a man's bones, all down its mighty back. The great tail was twice as long as the horrendous body, and from behind the forelegs rose a pair of leathery wings tipped with venomous barbs.

Barth recognized him immediately. This was Grendor, Eldest of Dragons, Lord of Beasts, Terror of Terrors.

"What!" bellowed Grendor. "Is there no one with the courage to face me?"

At this challenge, Barth looked about. Indeed, excepting himself, the road was empty. Where were the King's brave sons? Where were the nobles? Where was the King's Guard? Barth took a deep breath, stood his ground, and hailed the dragon. "Lord Grendor!" he shouted. "O Dragon of Great Proportion, Lord of Beasts, Terror of Terrors! What do you here in the land of men? Are you so anxious to pass your titles on to your sons?"

Slowly the huge neck of the wyrm swiveled around until Grendor was able to fix one massive, terrible eye on the young smith. "Ha!" The force of the dragon's laughter almost blew Barth off his feet, but Barth braced himself against the wall of the forge and kept his ground.

"Ha!" laughed the dragon again. "Is this the best the King can muster to send against Grendor the Mighty?"

Barth pursed his lips. "Am I not enough?"

Grendor's mighty teeth gleamed in what passed for a smile among wyrms. "Well spoken, brave little morsel. Come, let me taste you."

Barth also smiled, knowing well that the wyrm could not reach him, sheltered as he was by the buildings lining the narrow road, for the beast was simply too large to get head or talons between the structures. Also, Barth was well-read for a peasant, and he knew somewhat about dragons. "Before I slay you, O Mighty Wyrm," he yelled, "I would ask you a riddle."

Grendor slumped back and laid his huge head on the ground, for, if possible, dragons like riddles better than feasting on man-flesh. "Ask, then, of my wisdom, little mouthful."

Barth assumed a schoolmaster's voice, and stood with hands clasped behind his back. "In all the tomes of wisdom, in the chrestomathies of lore, in the scrivings of wizards, or in the tea leaves of witches . . . in all of these, where is it written that Grendor the Great will meet his death by the hand of a commoner on the night of the full moon?"

Grendor hesitated not at all. He snorted, and a spout of flame licked around the corner to singe Barth's boots. "Ha! Nowhere is such a thing written, else I would know of it, for I am the Wisest of Wyrms, Mightiest of the Mighty. Come and meet me, little fool!" Smoke began to curl from the wyrm's nostrils, and the claw of his right forefoot lifted a slab of stone the way a man would brush aside a cushion. Grendor crept forward, a red light in his eyes. "Come," he rumbled. "Let me taste your juices!"

"Listen to me!" shouted Barth, backing away. "Are you so sure of your knowledge?"

A dragon is prouder of nothing more than his lore, and Grendor, being Eldest of Wyrms, had a mighty pride indeed. "So sure am I," he replied haughtily, "that I shall return here tomorrow night, when the moon is full, to taste you then!"

"To your doom, then!" shouted Barth.

"To yours!" returned Grendor, spreading his huge, foul-smelling wings and flapping away.

Now all the people came out from behind their locked doors and congratulated Barth on his bravery. "But what," asked Prince Whosthat, emerging from behind the cistern where he had hidden, "what will you do tomorrow night when the wyrm returns?"

"My Lord Prince," said Barth, always polite, "I shall meet him in battle."

Then all those who praised him laughed, thinking his courage merely the bravery of a fool, and they left him alone. "You will perish," wailed Prince Whosthat, "and then how will my father get his sword?"

"I do not intend to perish so easily, My Prince." And that ended the conversation, for the Prince was famished from the excitement, and he retired to the castle for a second lunch.

Barth set about collecting the supplies he would need for tomorrow. First, he strengthened the walls and roof of his forge, bracing the stout stone walls with a steel lattice. Then he drew several barrels of water up from the well. He had the village priest bless one of the barrels, and this one he set aside from the others.

Then he went about the village begging enchantments from the people. Thinking that he was at last afraid of tomorrow's fight, and unwilling to help in any other way, the townsfolk gave unstintingly. By the end of the day, Barth had charms and magicks against fear, against foolishness, against old age, against bad luck, against enemy magic, against dragons and lesser beasts, and even against the wiles of women. It was believed in those days that to love a woman robbed a warrior of his strength, and there was little doubt of the truth, since most warriors could be found in the brothels, whiling away their strength, rather than out in the countryside, questing, rescuing princesses, or stringing up brigands and robbers.

All these spells Barth wrote down verbatim, and then added two he had learned long ago and yet had never had occasion to use. The first was an enchantment known as *Invictus gladio*, guaranteed to give unerring aim and sure thrusts. The second was called *Certus pede*, and ensured an unfaltering fighting stance.

Then, assured that everything he could do was done, and being a sensible young man, Barth went to bed early and hoped for rain.

In the morning when Barth awoke, townspeople were already leaving the village. There were long lines of them going up into the hills, drawing wains laden with provender, from there no doubt to watch the pyrotechnics which would take place that night. In all, there seemed to be a holiday mood among the villagers, for the children scampered and prattled about the coming fight, and the older folk took blankets and food as if for a picnic. And yet, there was no doubt that they were leaving; even the King's household—Knights, Lords, Princes, Ladies, Courtiers, and Pages—all were taking to the hills.

Barth ignored this exodus and spent all day polishing his armor. As darkness fell, he was ready.

At the first light of the full moon, he scampered away to search under the hedges. Fortunately, it had stormed the previous night, and there were many fresh thunderbolts to be found. Barth selected an armful of the biggest and best, and made his way back to the forge.

He was just in time, for as he passed through his doorway, the moon was blotted out by huge, slowly flapping wings, and there arose the stench of dragon fetor. "Ho!" cried Grendor. "Where is the brave, foolish, tasty commoner?"

Barth stuck his head out the window and called, "O Brave and Splendid Father of Dragons, I am in here!"

"Then come out, succulent morsel!"

"My Lord Dragon, you must come in and get me!"

This reply sent the wyrm into a rage, for no dragon likes to be taunted, especially after waiting a whole day and half a night for his dinner. With a roar that curled the King's beard far away in the hills, Grendor lurched into motion and came as close to the forge as his bulk would allow.

Barth watched through the window, measured the distance coolly, and shouted, "You're not so Splendid!"

Grendor replied by shooting a blast of fire through the

window. Nothing could have pleased Barth more. He picked up his tongs and held the thunderbolts before the dragon's fire.

"Your mother was an iguana!" he shouted when the fire subsided for a moment. The wyrm obligingly spewed forth more flames, and Barth continued his work. Then he noticed that the windowsill was catching fire, so he carefully put down the hot thunderbolts and sloshed water from one of the barrels until the fire was out. Peering carefully around the edge of the window, Barth looked for the dragon.

With a whump, something huge and heavy landed on the roof. Barth smiled to himself and pulled open the skylight. "So," he called, "the Mighty Wyrm needs to hide on the roof!"

Grendor answered with a ferocious blast of breath through the skylight. Barth once again held the thunderbolts before the fire and began to pound them into shape.

Long before he was finished, he was dripping in sweat and choking in the fumes. But he held onto his tools and kept working. There were many breaks for both of them, for even Grendor could not keep his fire going for hours on end, and Barth had to stop quite often to douse flames.

But at length, just when Barth was running out of insults, the forging was done. He took the white-hot blade into the corner and began to murmur the enchantments he had written down.

And just in time! For not only had Barth run out of taunts, but Grendor had run out of patience. As anyone who has read the right sort of books knows, a dragon will play with his food before eating it, and although some of Barth's jibes had struck home, Grendor was still toying with the lad. Now his stomach rumbled, and he began his attack in earnest. With his huge, strong wings he beat at the walls of the forge, and with his heavy snout he sought to lift the roof.

Barth tried to ignore all this, for the charms had to be said while the metal was still red, and he had several left to say. So he trusted to his preparations, hoping that the reinforcements would hold until he was done. And just as the walls were cracking under Grendor's blows, he finished the last spell. Grabbing up the still hot blade, he plunged it into the barrel of holy water.

Such a steam was never seen in the kingdom before. It rose up around the blade and filled the room, then sought the skylight and the windows. It overflowed the land like mist, obscuring everything. Grendor ceased his attacks, confused for a moment, wondering what new device this might be.

When Barth withdrew the sword from the barrel, there was no holy water left: all had been consumed in blessing that mighty blade. Barth felt a shock of power blast up his arm as the sword came alive in his hand.

Forked lightnings spewed from the sword's tip and clove the air, filling the room with the scents of sulphur and ozone. Barth took advantage of the obscuring mists and slipped out into the night.

Everything was dark, covered by the steam of holy water. Now everyone knows (or should know, for it's in all the right kind of books) that dragons are heathen beasts and hate holy water. But although they hate it, it cannot truly harm them, for they are of an old race, older than mankind, and are soulless. Grendor wrinkled his massive snout in distaste and swung his formidable head from side to side, seeking his enemy.

As if they were two evil red lamps, Barth saw the dragon's eyes pierce the dimness, and Barth smelled the sulphur of the wyrm's breath. Hiding the enchanted sword behind his back, Barth snuck up as close as he dared.

"Ha!" roared the dragon, catching sight of him at last. "Did you think you could hide, my little dinner dumpling?" With that, the Eldest of Dragons, Terror of Terrors and Lord of Beasts, brought to bear his mighty breath. But almost all of Grendor's fire had been expended to forge the sword, and what little remained was rendered heatless by the holy water vapor. But Grendor was a Wyrm of Many Weapons, and he turned so that his huge tail swung through the air at Barth.

The holy water vapor mist obscured vision for both of them, so the first warning Barth had was the whistle of air as the tremendous tail whipped toward him. Involuntarily, he held his sword up—in reality, the sword held his arm up, for it was spelled against dragons and lesser beasts, and had a mind of its own. And because of the charm against bad luck, the sword was at just the right angle when the barbed tail descended. Like a hot knife through butter, the enchanted blade sliced off the majority of Grendor's mighty tail. Green ichor gushed from the wound, and the tail segment writhed on the ground.

Springing back, Barth just barely avoided Grendor's pounce of rage.

Only once before, back in the misty deeps of unremembered time, had Grendor the Mighty been wounded in battle. The wyrm cast his mind back and back, reaching for the memory of how he had been wounded, and how he had eventually triumphed anyway.

A slow smile of evil triumph spread across the dragon's face. Splaying his great toes, he waited while the ichor from his tail-stump boiled forward toward Barth. Now everyone knows, or really should know, that dragon blood is the vilest, most slippery, most caustic liquid in the world. Where it touches, hard stone melts, and mere flesh vaporizes instantly. Protected by his magic from the acidity of his own blood, Grendor watched the green tide of vile ichor inch forward and lap up against Barth's boots.

The leather of Barth's boots curled back and smoked, and Barth leaped straight up in astonishment and pain. But the enchantment on the sword which guaranteed sure footing caused him to land on the only safe spot—the dragon's back.

Seeing his unwonted advantage, and being a sensible lad who didn't fiddle about with notions of fair play when his life was at stake, Barth immediately plunged the enchanted blade deep into Grendor's neck amidst the scraggly blue hair. The sword severed Grendor's head from his body, and the head rolled off easily.

Lightning filled the air; thunder roared, and the sky split in two. The last of the holy water vapor dissipated. As Grendor died, his magical protection from his own blood died with him. The wyrm's body collapsed under Barth and slowly melted in its own foul effluence. And the amount of ichor and the amount of dragon were exactly the same, so that when Grendor was completely gone, so was the foul, corrupting blood. Grendor, Eldest of Dragons, Lord of Beasts, Terror of Terrors, that Wyrm of Tremendous Girth and Proportion, was dead.

Barth immediately fainted. When he woke, he found himself in the center of a huge, cheering crowd of villagers, all shouting his praise. He held up the enchanted blade in his right hand, and lightning crackled up from it to smite the sky again and again.

Then Good King Worthy and his sons, Prince Whomever and Prince Whosthat, accompanied by the Lords Whoo and Whatshisname, and the entire coterie of the court, stepped forth to honor Barth.

"Goodman Bartholomew," said the King, still out of breath

from waddling down the hill, "that was a deed worthy of a noble. Give us our sword and we shall knight thee rightaways."

Now Barth was always polite, but was no fool, and he knew a good thing when he saw it. He bowed low to the King, and said gravely, "My Lord and King, though this sword was indeed fashioned for you, I do not choose now to surrender it."

Good King Worthy frowned, and all the villagers cringed. But Barth, who had outfaced the Eldest of Dragons and lived to speak of it, was no longer afraid of a fat old King.

At a signal from their sire, Princes Whomever and Whosthat stepped forward with their swords drawn. But Barth swept their blades away with hardly a thought, for he had forged their swords himself and knew them to be no equal for the one he now bore. Prince Whomever whimpered and massaged his wrist. Prince Whosthat ran to hide behind the cistern.

"Perhaps—" mused the King, impressed by Barth and disgusted by his worthless sons— "Perhaps we were hasty and unjust. You are obviously a likely lad with a sure wrist and good sense. Sir Bartholomew, wouldst keep the blade and marry my daughter?"

Barth laughed. "I am neither knight nor stallion to father Princes for an aging King. I shall take my sword and seek adventure in the Wide World."

At this brave speech, the people cheered, forgetting their fear of the King for a moment. And the King, seeing that he couldn't keep Barth anyway, gave him his royal blessing and sent him on his way.

And thus do we ever forge our oppressor's weapons, neglecting our own, until one day, like Bartholomew, we take up our swords and carve our way to freedom, and find the way was always open.

LADY, MAN, ROSE

The man wearing the silver rose stepped outside the cottage and closed the door behind him. The forest was quiet. Stars blazed unblinking overhead; the night air was crisp and clear. He journeyed through the forest slowly, carefully noting each beloved tree.

A rabbit peeked at him from behind a low bush. "Come," he said, and the rabbit hopped after him.

A pair of squirrels chittered to one another, then raced from branch to branch to see where he was going. The man looked up into the branches. "Follow," he said, and the squirrels leaped to the ground and scrambled after him.

A red fox lifted its brush and stood poised motionless in the path. The man wearing the silver rose nodded, gestured, and went on. The fox whirled around to follow.

One by one the animals of the forest came to see what was happening. The ones who normally slept at night were roused by some instinct. The ones already awake came, too. Feathered and beaked, or furry and clawed, they came. One by one, the man greeted them, waved his hand, and said, "Come."

They journeyed uphill, until the trees became sparse, until the ground became bare. The man with the silver rose ascended the heath with all the animals following, and now a light was upon him. It was not the moon or the stars; it came from the rose upon his breast, and it lit the land with a cool argent gleam. Bright it was, but not harsh, and as he moved to the center of the heath, it grew until it was like standing lightning, and still no eyes were blinded.

The man raised his right hand. The animals sat around him in a semi-circle, facing him, so that their faces were brilliantly lit, and sharp black shadows streamed away behind them. "Come," the man said, speaking past them. It was not a mighty voice, or a gentle one. It was not a command, or an invocation. It was neither permission nor supplication. It was a whisper that twisted the air, sought out every crack and crevice, carried for miles and miles into the night.

The whisper found its way into the heart of the trees below, and the great boles broke open, making a sound like a thunderclap. From inside the trees, the sylvan elves awoke from their dreams of flowing sap and slow growth. They shook aside their centuries of slumber, and their bright silver eyes turned as one toward the heath.

The whisper slid into cracks in the ground, squirmed past boulders, seeped through dirt, soaked into the bedrock itself. The stone children awoke, shook themselves, looked around with wonder as the roof of their sleeping chambers cracked. The dwarfs climbed up into the night air and journeyed toward the heath.

The whisper fell like a net on the surface of the ponds, rivers, and lakes. The waters whistled and boiled as the whisper knifed through them. Naiads brushed their long, green hair back from their ears and listened. The river god rose up in a fountain of spray, and his manacles fell from his wrists. Up they all rose, and as they moved toward the heath, they were joined by the satyrs, and nymphs, and fauns.

Swiftly they came, silently, like knife-edged shadows flying through the night, and assembled in a semi-circle behind the forest animals, and as each one arrived, the silver light from the rose became stronger. It cast a glare over the entire forest below, but did not blind or stun.

The man raised his left hand. "Come," he said, and this time his voice was low rumble, like thunder in the distance, and the four lords of the winds arose and came and bowed before him.

He opened his hands. "Come," he said, and this time his voice was pure music, a liquid trill. Every heart there longed to leap forward at his call, but they knew it was not for them. Suddenly among them was a unicorn, shy and sweet, and no one knew whence it had come, or how it had arrived. It stepped forward daintily and leaned its creamy flank against the man's chest, its head tucked down demurely, its golden horn catching and magnifying the rose's brilliance.

The man wearing the silver rose turned and let the light shine across the heath. Far away, far below, the sea heaved restlessly against the shore. On the horizon, where the sky came down to kiss the waves, a mighty ship sailed. The elves with the clearest sight could make out the individual masts, and see a form standing still and proud at the bow. But as the light from the rose fell across the sea, everyone's eyes cleared. The animals shook their heads, the dwarfs stood on tip-toes to watch, and it was as if they had all been half-blind but didn't know it until that moment.

Clearly, now, everyone saw the form standing at the prow, as if the thousands of miles separating them were just inches. They saw her face, shining gently with an inner light, as she turned from contemplating the deep beyond. She raised one arm, hand extended, and recognized them. Even the proud elves knelt and lowered their heads. The man took off his rose and beckoned to a hawk.

"Take this to her," he said. "Fly as you have never flown before, over the horizon, beyond the curve of the world, to where I cannot go, and take this to her."

The hawk took the rose in its beak and shot through the air. It seemed to everyone watching that a star flew, for so bright was the rose now that none could bear to look directly at it. The hawk flew as it had never flown before, and the rose lent it strength, for the hawk found its way over the horizon, beyond the curve of the world, and came to rest on the lady's outstretched hand.

"This you must keep," said the man, speaking to the lady. "For it is my heart, and it was ever yours." And his voice somehow carried to her.

"This I will keep," said the lady, and somehow the man could hear her. "And bear it always, so that I may remember you in the deep beyond." And she lofted the hawk, and gave it strength and guidance, so that it found its way back to the heath and took its place among the animals. And then she held up the rose, and kissed it, and turned her face toward the deep beyond, and the ship sailed around the bending of the world, out of sight, and darkness fell upon the heath.

The man stared out upon the dark and said nothing. One by one, the animals and faerie creatures slipped away, back to their nests and their holes. The lords of the winds raised mighty clouds and scattered them across the sky, so that no light fell upon the earth. At length only the unicorn was left to keep him company, and then it, too, was gone, and the man was alone upon the heath. After a long time, he turned and walked slowly back toward the cottage. His steps were heavy and slow as he descended the heath, quiet as death as he passed through the forest.

It seemed to him, after a time, that he did not walk alone, though he saw no one. And it seemed to him that he could feel an arm around his shoulders, a comforting presence at his side. He found a silver rose in his hands, and he didn't know how it had got there, but it seemed he had always held it. It glimmered softly in the dark, and lit his path before him, and that, too, seemed as if it had always been.

"This you must keep," said the night, not with a voice, not using words. "For it is your heart, and you have need of it yet."

The man turned at the cottage door and looked out, but saw no one. "Am I alone now?" he asked aloud.

"Never," said the air. "Never again."

The man fastened the rose to his breast. "This I will keep," he said, "and by it remember you always."

He went into the cottage then, and closed the door behind him, and, all by himself, was not alone.

TALE OF THE BLIND BOY

Tonight I shall tell you a story. What? Yes, I think you'll like it. So come close, child, sit here under my arm and wrap that blanket around you; no, tuck your feet inside like this . . . yes, that's right. It's cold tonight, isn't it? I'm glad of the fire.

It's almost bedtime, but you can stay up a little while to hear this story. Listen! Listen carefully, for this is your own story, and you must take it inside you and keep it safe for ever and ever. Are you ready? Do you have a secret place inside you with room for this story?

All the good stories start at the beginning, don't they? Well, that's where I'll start. A long time ago, so long ago that time itself was still very young and moved faster than it does now—

What? What's that? No, don't interrupt me, grandson. Why should you be surprised that time itself should age? It makes perfect sense to me. Haven't you noticed how in the oldest stories it takes no time at all for the hero to get himself born, grow up and start his first adventure? It's because time itself was spry. Now let me get on, for this is my story too, you know, and I love to tell it.

The name? What a question! Why should the story have a name? It's just a story—well, no, not *just* a story. Oh, hush. Call it *The Tale of the Blind Boy* if you must have a name for it. May I get on now?

Very well. A long time ago, a boy was born blind. He had eyes, but when he looked through them he saw only shapes, colors and sizes. What do you mean, what else is there? What else isn't there? Look at that blue vase by the door—is it beautiful, is it graceful, is it delicate? Well, the blind boy would only see a vase and tell you it was blue. Look at the fire. Do you see how restless it is, how eager to burn? The blind boy would just tell you that the fire was red. To him, a glorious summer afternoon with the sunshine leaping down to kiss the grass and the flowers yearning skyward—why to him, it was just lit-up shrubbery. When he saw another child, he did not think, "Here is a playmate, here is adventure," he thought, "How much allowance does he get?" or "Where does his father work?" When he saw a palace, he thought it just a heap of stones in an orderly pile.

Now look at me, boy, look at me. What do you see? Yes, yes, an old man, but what else do you see? That's right, you see your grandfather, and if you don't see a man who loves you more than life itself, who would give his good right arm to keep you from harm, then you yourself are blind! Eh? What's that? What do I see when I look at you? Why, I see a boy of course, a nice boy, even a sweet boy if you'll forgive me saying that, but also much more. I see years. All my years, all my son's years, all your years, both the few you've had and the many you'll have, all come together in one spot. I see my grandson, the fruit of my loins, my own son's son. What? Well, loins are. . . . No, you don't need to know about loins yet; just forget that bit. Now let me continue.

This boy was also deaf. When he passed a waterfall, he only heard water falling, he didn't hear the laughter of the river, or the story it told about its long journey from the mountains to the sea. When he listened to music, he heard a sequence of notes and pauses, and could talk about the complexity of such-and-such a piece, but never heard *music*. Imagine that! Never carried away by a rhapsody, never swooned under the influence of a high violin, never even hummed a song to himself just because he liked the tune. And no, before you ask, he didn't whistle either—there was no point for him, you see. He was deaf. Yes, I'm glad you can whistle, boy, but stop now and listen to the story. The boy was so deaf he never heard love in his mother's voice, never knew his father was angry until the poor man had to say, "I am angry with you," never. . . . What now? Are you keeping notes? Oh, very well, change the name if you like. Call it *The Tale of the Deaf and Blind Boy.*

But don't get too excited about that—the boy was also crippled. Oh, he had fine sturdy legs and good strong arms, but when he walked it was just click-click-click like a metronome. There was no spring in his step, no life in his heels, no bounce in his toes. He just walked here—*click*—there—*click*—and all around, legs going up and down, up and down like little pistons. He never ran just for the wonder of it, the wind lifting his hair, the grass whipping his legs—no, he never did that, because for him it wasn't fun, it was just running. His hands? Oh, there was nothing much wrong with them, but nothing much right either. What do I mean? I'll show you. Give me your hand. Feel my face, run your fingers over my cheeks and chin. That's right. Now feel your own face. Touch your nose and your ears. Stick out your tongue and grab it. Stop giggling, boy. What did you feel? The deaf and blind boy with his cold-fish crippled hands would have felt whiskers when he touched me, and he would have just said your tongue was wet. But what did you feel? What do I feel? Age and youth, that's what, age and youth. But it gets worse! He never hugged anyone, never held hands with a girl, never dragged his fingers in the stream when he went fishing, never *touched* anything. Oh, he could pick things up, he could walk and sit and lie down just like anyone else, but he never touched, never *felt*. His skin was a dead thing he wore like a coat. He never put his palm out and felt the life running through the bole of a tree, never squirmed on his tummy on a feather bed and drowned in the softness, never jumped to see how high he could get. He never ran and ran until he was fair blowed and then leaned over and clutched his belly and laughed with his face all red and his legs aching. What? Yes, you can sit on my lap. Climb up here then. No, you can't hold my hand—I need it for talking. Oh, all right, I'll use the other one. But share some of that blanket with an old man, please; the fire's dipping. What do you mean by asking what *else* was wrong with the boy? Who's telling this story, you or me? Well, then, stop interrupting and listen.

Of course, he was also mute, so I guess you'd have to call this *The Tale of the Blind, Deaf, Mute, and Crippled Boy*. Oh-ho! You are paying attention, aren't you? Yes, I did say that he could talk, but you didn't understand. He could say things like "The water is wet" or "The fire is red," but he couldn't say anything really important. Oh, I suppose he could have learned the words, but what difference would that make to him? He couldn't see beauty, so saying "That is beautiful" would be just so many words. He never heard music, so he didn't have any words for that, either. When people greeted him on the street, he would say things like, "It's raining today," or "It is now exactly twelve minutes and thirty-two seconds past noon." He was terribly dull and boring, and had no friends. He couldn't say "I love you," for how could he love anyone when he had never even hugged his own mother or held a girl's hand? Eh? Oh, well don't worry about that—it will come in time. Girls aren't that bad; they can even be fun. How old are you now, six or seven? Nine? Goodness! Ah, goodness. Nine years old already? My! Well, it won't be too long now. Yes, it has to do with loins, but forget that part, will you? I'm trying to finish this story—we're coming to the important bit.

Oh, stop that squirming! Is it the bathroom you're needing? Yes? Well then be off with you, and build that fire up on your way back if you'd be so kind . . . ah, there's a good lad. Now come back here and settle down.

Give your granda a kiss, tuck the blanket in, and sit still. No more squirmings or wrigglings or questionings! What? Oh, good grief, no! The boy did not have a name. What? Well yes, I suppose they called him *something*, but it doesn't matter, you see. No, I'm *not* making this up as I go along. This is an important story! Do let me get on with it!

Now—and this is the sad part—the poor child didn't know he was missing anything vital. That's right, how could he? He was blind to his own condition, deaf to the truth, and unable to feel love, so how was he to know the difference? So he grew up little by little, day after day, year after year, and never had any friends, no, not one. Goodness, he never even knew that ice cream was good—to him it was just cold milk! There's an ironic part too—do you know what ironic means?—for he was a very beautiful boy with long lashes, nimble fingers, and fine, sturdy limbs. He looked a lot like you, in fact. Well, I'm sorry, but you *are* handsome. There's nothing wrong with my eyes. Would you prefer I said cute? No? Then let me get on.

Of course, the boy didn't know he was handsome, for it was all the same to him. When people gave him a compliment, it was just noise coming out of their mouths like a foreign language, for he didn't know what the words meant, and of course he couldn't see for himself. He didn't look in the mirror much—what was the use?—and after he was grown and on his own, he let his hair go all ragged and sloppy, and stopped combing it, and his clothes . . . well, he just wore the first thing in his dresser and be damned to style or matching colors!

What sort of job do you think a fellow like that could do? He couldn't be a carpenter or an engineer or even a mason because he was blind. He referred to trees as "timber" or "lumber"—what kind of carpenter is that? And he couldn't do anything creative at all. Who would want to look at a bridge he built, or live in a building he designed? He couldn't be a mason, for how would he know which stone to put on top of which? It was all the same to his eyes. Oh, it was a terrible, lonely life he had. He went from job to job, never staying very long, never making friends, never even really having a home. Eh? Well, yes, he stayed in a dingy little apartment, but it wasn't a home you see, because home is the place you live, and this poor fellow wasn't really living, was he?

Of course he was good at some things. He could look at a map and tell you exactly how far it was from here to there. And he was very good with numbers, formulae and symbols and such, as long as they were very abstract and didn't have anything to do with real life. And his grammar was excellent! A shame, really, because he couldn't say anything with his perfect sentences except to tell you what time it was, how many miles to somewhere, or whether or not it was raining. So he ended up at last doing the most horrible job in the world. Can you guess what it was? Are you still awake? Not snoozing, are you? Oh-ho!

I saw that yawn. I shouldn't have talked about mathematics, eh? Come on, boy, let's put you to bed. Yes, yes, I'll finish the story, but after you're in bed. That's right, yes, it is cold. Did you brush your teeth yet? Let me see . . . good. Help me up, lad, don't just stand there shivering in your pajamas, help me up!

Now, into bed with you. Snuggle down now, that's right, and pull the covers up tight. There you are, a pink little worm all wrapped in its cocoon! Are you comfortable? Are you snug? Are you toasty? I'll sit right here by your feet, so I can tweak your toes through the blanket if you fall asleep! Now, where was I? Oh, yes, the worst, the most horrible, the least desirable job in the whole wide world. Have you guessed what it is yet? No, he was not a waiter. Think, lad! First, that's not a bad job. Second, a waiter must be able to talk. Imagine a waiter who couldn't tell you that the roast beef was better than yesterday's stale bread! No, no, think harder. No, he was not a digger of ditches or the man who collects trash. Those are useful jobs, making the land better or cleaner. I see I'll have to tell you. After going from one job to another for year after year, he finally became a *copy editor*. That's right, he sat in a little tiny room all day long—on a hard chair, with harsh lights overhead—and corrected other people's grammar and typing mistakes!

Can you imagine, day after day, year after year, sitting on that hard chair, checking other people's grammar and spelling but never understanding their words? Oh, he knew the *words*, all right, but he didn't know what they *meant*. If someone had written about a lovely day, a passionate embrace, or—heaven forefend—became the least bit poetic or romantic, why then, the words were just nonsense to him. But this poor blind, mute, deaf, and crippled young man could check to make sure the words were in the right order, and that the punctuation was correct.

Never did a comma slip by where a semi-colon was required; never did a run-on sentence or a misspelled word survive the merciless slash of his horrid red pen. He viciously removed the *s* from *towards* and *afterwards*, savagely deleted commas before the word *and* in a list, and to finally top things off, demanded unconditional surrender from split infinitives. No, I'm not going to explain all those terms; you don't need to know them to understand the story.

At last he had found something he could almost enjoy—in his small, limited way. He went beyond the call of duty and looked for dangling modifiers, incomplete phrases, and yes, even colloquialisms and genteelisms! Oh, he knew them all, and hated them. He wielded his pen with a vengeance, slashing here, crossing out there, and making big, ugly paragraph marks in the middle of a lovely thought. All deviations from perfect grammar and accepted form, from the great to the small, from the intentional to the simple mistake—all of these fell to the might of his bloody red pen!

Copy editors are a peculiar breed, my boy, very fussy and formal and concerned with the proper way to say something, even if the improper way says it better. They all hate the word "ain't" unless found in quotation marks, which ain't always right. But our blind boy—a young man now—was a copy editor's copy editor.

He wore a dark gray suit with white socks and mean, ugly shoes, and the frown on his forehead never went away, not even when he slept. It was a terrible and lonesome life. All the furniture in his tiny apartment was gray, just plain, bleak gray, and he always skipped breakfast and took baths in cold water. He had been a handsome fellow as a boy, but now as a young man, he was cramped and squalid, and people looked the other way when he passed them on the street.

Well, after years of this, he just shrank into himself. He became smaller and meaner, and his spirit became weak and ghostly, until he began to change words just for spite. He was starting to understand how crippled he was, and he took it out on those innocent, inoffensive authors whose work he was supposed to proofread.

A *warm, hazy afternoon* became *after lunch*. A *lecherous scowl* turned into a *frown*. And worse yet, he would turn something like, *Oh, my darling, thou art the sun of my days and the moon of my nights* into *I like you*. You wouldn't believe what he did to poetry!

What? Oh, yes. Of course the authors complained. None of this was his job, you see; he was only supposed to correct the grammar, spelling, and punctuation. He was called into the office and given a Stern Talking To, but it did no good because he was deaf.

After he lost that job, he didn't know what to do. He still didn't have any friends, and had nowhere to go. So he wandered in the hills behind the town by the duck pond—you know where I mean, yes, the wooded path and the meadow—and finally just sat down and put his head in his hands and cried.

I say, are you through adjusting that pillow yet? You've scrunched it up to half its original size. What? You want a drink of water? You'll just have to go potty again later. Oh, all *right*, but get me some, too . . . whoa! carry that glass carefully! Ahhh, that's good. Now tuck your butt under those covers before I spank it. Oh, you think I wouldn't? Come here, you scamp. Take that! And that! Oh! I'm sorry, boy, I think I broke it in half! Shhh, shhh! Be hush now; stop giggling and get under the covers before your grandma hears us. Then you'll never find out what happens! Yes, the story's almost finished. Do I need to pinch your toes to keep you awake? No? All right then, squirm until you're comfortable. Are you ready? Do you remember where we were? Yes, that's right, he was crying.

After he had cried himself out, he fell asleep there at the edge of the meadow. Can you guess what happened next? No, he didn't have an important dream, that would take too much imagination, and he hadn't any, remember? No, someone else came along and found him lying there. It was a girl, a woman, and she was everything the blind boy was not.

Oh, what a girl she was! The birds stopped singing when she spoke, so they could learn from her lovely voice. Flowers hid their heads in shame when she was near! She floated through the world with grace and elegance, and beauty walked before and behind her like the sudden glory of the sun breaking through the clouds wherever she stood. And she was as beautiful inside as out. Everyone loved her, for she loved everyone and meanness never darkened the door of her heart. She had long, soft hair the color of golden wheat just before harvest, and her eyes were a clear, piercing green.

Wherever she looked, she saw; whatever she heard, she listened to; whatever she touched, she felt; and when she walked, she skipped and danced, and all the world danced with her, just for the sharp, fierce joy of living.

She hadn't seen him yet, for being the mean and crabby thing he was, he had lain down in the weeds, and she strolled through the fresh meadow. She was wearing a soft blue dress, and knelt on the clean grass by the pond. She plucked a primrose and breathed deep. The water was so still, so clear, that her reflection was a perfect mirror, and she was twice as lovely. She knelt there, holding herself still, breathing up the beauty of the world, storing it inside herself so she could give it away freely to anyone who asked.

What happened next was magic. Eh, what's that? You think

you're too old to believe in magic? You must *never* be that old, boy, never! That's not old; that's dead.

The blind, deaf, mute, and crippled boy didn't believe in magic either, but he was *wrong*. He woke up from his troubled sleep, and what do you think was the first thing he saw? Yes, that's right, he saw her kneeling there by the pond. Then, from out of the barrenness of his soul, from the dark, cramped depths of his heart, from the misery of his wretched lonely spirit—

What's that? Well, yes, maybe I'm laying it on a bit thick, but that's the way it was, or at least that's how it seemed to him.

From down deep in his secret inside places, rushing like a fountain bursting into early morning sunlight, exploding like fireworks inside his breast, up came a *feeling*.

It hurt, worse than banging your shin, worse than tearing a nail, even worse than having a tooth pulled. It was like having his arm cut off. Yet he knew what the feeling was. Somehow— perhaps this was the magic—he knew that he had fallen in love at first sight. He was so shocked and surprised that he gave a little gasp and fell away in a dead faint, like a schoolgirl who sees a mouse. No, that doesn't really happen—it's a saying—but stop interrupting.

She turned at the noise and saw him lying there, all open and vulnerable for the first time in his life, and she couldn't help herself—she fell in love, too. Maybe she saw the beautiful child he used to be hidden inside the ugly man; maybe not. Maybe it was pity at first, or sympathy; maybe not. He never asked, and she never told. But she laid aside her flower, glided over to him, and stood for a long time, just looking at his face.

She knelt and kissed his eyes open. And when he looked up at her, he saw her and knew she was beautiful.

She kissed his ears, and he heard her lovely voice.

She kissed his poor, tortured hands, and he reached up and ran his fingers through her hair and felt fine silk.

She kissed the frown away from his forehead, and the skin smoothed out and relaxed.

She kissed his knees and his feet, his elbows and his heart. And everywhere her lips touched, life sprang into being.

He leaped up and took her in his arms, and they chased each other through the meadow and woods, laughing and singing, until, exhausted, they finally collapsed together in a lovely tangle of arms and legs on the sweet grass beside the pond. They looked deep into each other's eyes, and—

Eh? Speak up, boy. Why, yes, of course they kissed each other, and they were nice, big, fat, *juicy* kisses. It wasn't at all mushy or nasty. They didn't slobber. He gave her a kiss, and then she gave him one, and then they gave each other one; oh, it was splendid! They were in love, you see, and it's perfectly natural. Oh, time moved so slowly back then!

What's that? No, I'm sure I never said that time ran quicker in the past. Think about it, boy, think about it! Youth lasts forever while you have it; it's only when you're old that time rushes by you, day following day in a blur. It makes perfect sense to me. But let me go on with the story, for there is more magic.

When he looked at the world, he saw it through her eyes, and there was beauty everywhere. The sunshine wasn't just light anymore; it was a blessed radiance which leaped down to kiss the grass and trees, and the flowers smiled back up at it.

He listened through her ears, and the wind was playing a lovely melody through the branches of the trees, and off in the distance he could hear children laughing and playing, and it was the most wonderful music in the world.

When he pressed up against her, so that their hearts were

touching and beating in unison, why then his skin came alive and he could feel the whole world turning underneath them.

It was so much, too much, and it burst out of him, the joy, the glee, and he said the first real words of his life when he looked right into her eyes and said, "I love you." And with those words he was cured forevermore!

He laughed and jumped high in the air, and she laughed to see him so happy. They walked away slowly, and the birds trilled and the sun shone and the wind was fresh and sweet, and—do you know?—he held her hand while they walked.

There! It's done, and I never once had to pinch your toes! Did you take the story inside you, boy, as I told you? Is it safe in there? Can you feel it under your heart? Is it lurking in your secret inside places?

I'd better check; let me feel your knees . . . yes, there's the bit about jumping as high as you can. And your feet—let me wiggle a toe—that's where you remember running through the wind and grass, isn't it? You're a clever boy.

Show me an ear. Do I hear music echoing in there? Does the waterfall laugh, boy? Do birds sing because they love life? Is music more than just a sequence of notes? Yes, *yes*. Those are good ears, boy, use them.

Now let me take your hand . . . oh, yes, those fingers can touch and feel and explore and wonder. Squeeze my hand, boy, harder, now touch my heart and let me touch yours. Put your hand flat. Do you feel it? That's life. I'm alive and so are you. Isn't it wonderful?

Let me look at your eyes. Do they know about beauty? When dawn breaks tomorrow, will they see a glorious golden sunrise, or just morning? Oh, yes, those eyes are *fine!* They are clear and bright and deep and they see everything, don't they?

Now, what's hidden here in your tummy? Yes, right there,

don't giggle so, or I'll keep tickling. Love? Is it love that makes your stomach so warm? Is *that* where you're going to keep it? That's a good place! But where did you hide the bit about hugging? I don't see it anywhere—let me look now—you didn't hide it in your *elbow*, did you? Of course not! Now where could it. . . ? *Oh!* Right there in your arms, is it? What an excellent place! That's right, hug hard; it's good, isn't it? Yes, I love you, too.

But it's time to go to sleep, so give your granda another kiss and close your eyes.

What do you mean, what happened *next?* I told you: the story's over. Oh, that! Well, yes, your grandma and I got married, and that's how your father happened, and then he grew up and married your mother, and that's how *you* happened. That's why it's my story and your story too. You're right, I guess it isn't over yet, is it? What? Yes, of course I'll tell it again tomorrow.

Good night, boy, good night.

BREATHE TO ME OF SUMMER

Today I saw an apple-cheeked little fellow with blond hair, clear blue eyes that sparkled like gems, and long black lashes that brushed his cheeks when he blinked or looked down. It was a day borrowed from next summer. A light breeze ruffled his hair like a father's hand. The bright sunlight put blue in his blue jeans, white in his gym shoes, gleams in his milky teeth, and soft tan in his rumpled, unzipped jacket.

I saw him bent over his bicycle, a sturdy little boy, undoing the lock and chain. He had slender fingers, nimble and quick: a boy's gentle hands, soft-palmed and clever. Small. I saw him toss a leg over his bike. Impressions fluttered through me. Flash of white sock. Glint of steel rings in worn canvas shoes, one lace trailing. Smudge of mud along the cuff of his jeans. Stretch of limber thigh. Sure, confident, unconsciously amaranthine.

He didn't squirm on his seat. He stood up on the pedals and pushed that contraption right toward me, hair flying, lips parted, cheeks rosy, knees going up and down, up and down. Seeing him like that made me think of something . . .

something vague, like a memory washed out by time, or a speech whose words are almost but not quite forgotten. It was very familiar but very strange, like a best friend from childhood that one hasn't seen in decades. I began to think of something, but then he smiled directly at me and his bike flew past like a hundred rockets all taking off at once, lit by his smile.

I caught just a whiff of his breath—like summer and goldenrod and fresh hay and apples. He breathed, I say, and I ceased breathing for a moment, just watching his knees go up and down, wild blond hair flying back, and this thought beginning somewhere way back in my mind. Odd. All over in a flash. Just a glimpse like that, an impression, really, no more . . . and then I was breathing again, tearing in huge gasps, and he was pedaling on past, eyes fixed on some distant goal, honey-skinned face crimsoning into delicate rose at the wind's touch.

I almost forgot him. Maybe I would have forgotten him. He was the match that had started a fire in my mind, and all I could see for a few moments were the flames. It was a thought, nothing more, perhaps a memory, but it raged like an inferno.

A noise startled me, just as I was beginning to get a grasp on the memory. Perhaps the boy had started it. Or perhaps the boy had interrupted it. . . ? I had been walking, you see, when I glimpsed the little boy. I going my way, he going his, all unconnected and separate, opposite directions. I had stopped when he breathed that wildness into my lungs, all unknowing: stopped to hold my breath and taste his youth and the sweetness of it all. But then I exhaled, and my next breath was regular air, the kind I usually get, somewhat dry, a bit stale, rather tired. Not at all like his. I don't get to breathe summer often these days, and it started me thinking. Something from long ago. Something about. . . . But the loud noise whipped it away.

I almost didn't turn around, because I knew, somehow, that the thought was important. It was a memory, nothing to do with the boy on the bike, and I had to remember it. But the noise was too loud, and it startled me, so I had to turn, had to look. It was a horn and a screech of brakes. From a little red sports car with bright chrome trim, magnesium wheels and bucket leather seats. Here's the crazy thing: I noticed the driver first. He wore a brown leather flight jacket, a red tie, and brown dress slacks. An executive, I suppose, the kind with enough money to buy the toys he'd always wanted as a child. Like that bright red car. Too small to be practical, but fast. Too fast.

Such a strange angle to be parked, sideways across the road like that, one door hanging open, traffic blocked. The man leaned on the open door and looked at something on the ground. I looked too. It was very quiet, and there was a spreading pool of red underneath the sports car.

Someone screamed, loud, too loud, suddenly chopped off, and I stopped breathing again. Then I was mincing, tiptoe, toward the car. One step, two. Then I was walking steadily. Loping, running, sprinting. Screaming through the air like a missile, but oh so slowly, so slow. Bright, bright red, incarnadine and vermeil. A white canvas gym shoe pointing an accusing toe at heaven. A small, slender hand lying empty, fingers slightly curled, like a golden spider, dead, on its back. One wheel of the bike spinning around and around, lazy, slow. The other wheel twisted, still, a torn bit of shoelace caught in the chain. I saw these things, I say, and then everything went black and there was this tremendous roaring in my ears and my knees started to shake. The next thing I knew, they were pulling me away from the driver and there was blood on his face, blood on my fists. Someone was yelling, and I realized it was me, so I shut up.

I shook off the restraining hands and knelt beside the boy,

the boy who had breathed summer to me. I touched his cheek. It was cool, soft, pale, bloodless. And then I finally remembered the thought I had been trying to think, and it didn't make any sense now. *Please wake up*, I said over and over. *I want to buy you an ice-cream cone*. It was the most important thing in the world to me just then. But blood soaked my knees where I knelt. So much blood from such a little boy, a little body. *We'll get you a new bike*, I promised, *but you have to wake up first*. I touched his hair, his wrists, his hands. *Please wake up*. Then someone moved me away, and for some reason I was crying. "Please," I said aloud. *Please*. But no one paused. The ambulance came screaming down the street, but I couldn't hear it. I was far away by then. I couldn't watch.

Crisp these moments, these winter days, and bitter the death of a child.

I FLED. A long way. Nine, I think . . . yes, I was nine years old. The air was hazy and warm, the sun beaming down and striking sparks from the murky green lake. Insects everywhere, me dressed only in swim trunks, my toes itching on the rough planks of the wharf where I dangled a fishing line.

No one had ever caught a fish in that lake, but I was willing to try because my father would be coming along soon, and I wanted to show him I could. Later, he'd said, when he had a chance. So you just go on down there and get started, Mom'd said, and he'll be along. Okay.

I wriggled around, getting comfortable, waiting, checking the bait from time to time, dangling it for the nonexistent fish. I watched a battle between a huge black ant and a tiny red one, me rooting for the little guy. Such a still afternoon, languid, not quite hot.

My hair was almost white back then, short-cropped, sticking up in crazy places. I was an angular boy with freckles, though not gaunt. Sweet-faced, my mother always said, which always made me think of cherubs or girls. But my oldest brother said my freckles made me look diseased, and my sisters didn't offer an opinion.

The wharf was made of thick old boards, nailed together haphazardly, stuck on the top of huge round pilings which sank away beneath me into green dimness. Seaweed-like slime clung above and below the water line. By lying flat on my stomach, I could peer through the gaps in the boards and smell the water. It was a heavy, green sort of smell.

I checked the bait again. The ants were still fighting. Fierce, these tiny creatures. I sucked on a loose tooth and watched them sway back and forth across the planking between my toes. Finally the little red one won, but only because I flicked the black one off into the lake with my fingernail.

It was getting late. Still no fish, and the sun was westering rapidly. Where was Dad? But wait! was that a tug? I pulled up on the pole and almost fell into the water when I felt an answering yank. There was a reel, but it didn't work, so I hauled the line in by hand, frantic, excited, dancing a bit, yelling, almost letting my prize escape. But then I had him there up on the wharf, a catfish, and he lay there gasping at me, whiskers twitching, eyes glaring, tail flapping madly.

I was scared to touch it, but I did. I hit it with a rock until it stopped moving, and then I took out my penknife and went to work. It was sort of flattened by then, rather messy. I had never done anything like that before, though I had seen Dad do it, and knew the general idea. I kept glancing at the road, expecting to see Dad any minute. He'd promised to take me into town later, to the new ice-cream parlor, and I knew he'd be coming along soon. It took me almost an hour to clean and gut that catfish, and there wasn't much left when I'd finally finished. Would Dad have been proud of me then? I cleaned off the knife, the wharf and myself, and set the pitiful catfish on the boards beside me. Still no Dad; still no cheery, booming hallo echoing over the water; no strong arms with big, trustworthy hands; no sure and steady step; no happy laughter. Just me and the naked fish and the sun setting behind me.

I got up and went to find him. He must've forgotten. But that's okay, 'cause I'd show him the fish, the first fish I ever caught, and then we'd go into town like he promised and have ice cream, and everything will be wonderful. I trudged along, knobby knees going up and down, cracking with each step, bare feet popping on poured concrete, scrunching across gravel, slithering through hip-deep wild grass. I wondered if Mom would fry the catfish for supper.

There were a lot of people at the summer house when I finally got there: all my brothers and sisters, extra cars, grown-ups I didn't know. I felt an odd, prickly feeling along my spine. My ears burned. There was a doctor there, too, and I slipped in the back door, through the kitchen, into the parlor. Mom was sitting in a circle of other grown-ups, crying.

I went to her, forgetting I had the fish clutched in my hands. She saw it and me. Get it out of here, she said, not real tender but not real fierce either. But Dad was supposed to meet me, I protested. He'll want to see this. Where is he? Mom started crying real hard then and gathered me up in her arms, fish and all. I felt smothered. She wouldn't let go, so my oldest brother came and took me away and gave me the news.

Dad's dead, he told me.

But . . . but he was going to meet me, take me into town. He promised!

Shut up, he said, and slapped me. Just you shut up.

When? I asked, when did it happen?

About noon, he told me, so you just be quiet.

Noon? I was there all day, smelling the water, watching the ants, catching my first fish, and nobody even told me? Why? I asked, why didn't you tell me?

We forgot about you, said my brother, and after that I was very quiet.

I FOUND myself back in the present, kneeling on the sidewalk before a little girl, peering into her face. She stared back at me, a pretty little elfin thing. Long black hair, a yellow dress, matching ribbons. Wide, very wide eyes, the color of a late autumn sky.

She looked at my trousers, saw the bloodstains there, then looked back at my face. She began to edge away.

Listen, I said urgently, don't run away from me. I want to buy you an ice-cream cone.

I was babbling. I waved my arms and pleaded with her, then stopped, suddenly fascinated by the dried blood caked around my fingernails. Whose? The little boy's, the driver's, or mine?

The girl made a small sound in the back of her throat, then screamed and ran away. Wait! I called after her. I won't hurt you! I just . . . I just want to be . . . nice. I stopped shouting. People were looking at me, and this was a small town. I stood up, brushed feebly at my clothes, and walked off. I was dizzy, weak, tired. Odd, these winter days, these moments.

A young man stood before me, dressed in midnight blue

with a truncheon at his hip and a stern look on his face. I knew him, of course; I remember watching him run around on the playground when he was little. Not anymore. Never again.

Come on, Pops, he said.

I'm not old, I said. But he took my arm, and I was too weak to pull away.

Let's get you home.

There was an accident, I murmured, a boy, a bike. . . .

I know, he said, we saw you there. Did you know him?

Know him? I wondered. Why, I suppose I did. His name? No, never heard that. Never saw him before. But I knew him, oh, yes. Very well.

The young policeman's eyes crinkled strangely, and he put an arm on my shoulder. He walked me in silence for several blocks, and left me at length at my porch door.

A light snow was falling, just beginning, hardly even sticking to the hoods of cars which had been parked for hours. My borrowed summer day was fading, withdrawing, disintegrating.

Today I saw a little boy, an apple-cheeked fellow with blond hair, clear blue eyes which sparkled like gems, and long black lashes which brushed his cheeks when he blinked or looked down.

I saw him bent over his bicycle, a sturdy little boy. He smiled at me, and breathed to me of summer, and, just for a moment, I had seen myself in him.

Crisp, these late-winter days, these feelings, and fleeting the smile of a child.

JERE

He was born of stone, an earling's bastard, just one of a dozen or so children the earl had gotten in a long series of brief, though passionate, affairs with his servants. He came into the world sideways, the cord wrapped around his neck, and stopped halfway out, so that the birthing women had to cut him from his mother's body. By the time they had him fully out and uncoiled, the mother was dead, and they thought the boy was, too.

Jere's first and only contact with his mother's breast was brief. One of the birthing women dropped him unceremoniously upon his mother's flaccid and rapidly cooling belly. They left him there, tiny fists clenched, to flop about upon the naked woman who had borne him, while the blood was cleaned from the flagstones.

The physician came at length to examine the child. He decided, somewhat reluctantly, that the child was alive and likely to continue in that state indefinitely. And so he told the women to cut the cord, pincer the end shut, wipe the fluids away, and put the infant somewhere out of the earl's sight.

A girl, Betha, took him to foster, for Jere's mother had once done her a kindness. Besides, none of the other women would have him: It was a bad sign when a child's birth was the death of its dam. And all had noted that Jere did not cry. The boy looked out at the world with pale blue eyes, a wide mouth, and damp, dark hair. His breathing was light and even, as though he slept.

Betha cradled him against her breasts and took him away to another part of the castle, far from the earl's quarters, where she and the other serving women lay on their cots at night.

Stone surrounded him, floors, walls, and ceilings. Cold stone in the winter, freezingly cold, so that the girls hopped about from foot to foot and stood with their arms tightly clenched against their breasts. Cool stone in spring and autumn, damp with condensation, full of dark corners where rats ran and snakes slithered. Baking-hot stone in summer, when the sunlight beat down upon the castle like the siege engines of an enemy.

He found flagstones as long as a man is tall, arches with keystones heavier than a loaded wagon, and square-hewn slabs set in dark mortar to form the battlements. Jere took shape among them, dark-skinned and handsome like his sire, obdurate and silent like the walls. His eyes gradually darkened to an almond brown. His legs lengthened and his muscles hardened. His hands fluttered over anything he saw, as if touch were the only sense he trusted. The stones were solid under his fingers, unyielding and sure. He took them inside himself, into his strange and twilit soul.

There was not a passage, archway, rat-hole or cistern he had not explored. No dungeon was too dark, no spire too tall, that he would not find it, and in finding, touch, and in touching, know.

Yet of himself, Jere seemed oddly unaware. He would cry if not fed, or steal food if it were left out, but showed no other signs of noticing himself as discrete from his environment. Betha he learned to recognize early on, though as soon as he had the muscles to twist away from her, he did. He would obey her if she spoke sharply or struck him, but otherwise he ignored her and all other humans. Stone was in him, and he in it, and the castle was his whole world.

He touched everything with his long, sensitive fingertips, and he never quite broke the childhood habit of putting strange new objects into his mouth. The tongue is a marvelous instrument of touch, and the mouth an excellent and reliable source of sensory input. At the age of three, he ran about with a waddling gait, exploring anything that caught his eye, and still he had yet to say his first word.

He learned quickly to stay out of the way of the soldiers, and to avoid the crowds that sometimes gathered in the courtyards when the earl was feeling festive. He learned that if he cried hard enough and long enough, some of the women would feed him. He learned that if he lay on his stomach across a broad, warm flagstone, put his hands between his legs and squirmed his hips, an odd, tingly feeling would come and make him tremble in a delicious way. He learned that if he shouted when touched, others would leave him alone. And from those few who persisted he learned that frustration is akin to pain, and pain to irritation, so that the one could substitute for the other, and if he bit his hands or banged his head on the floor, he could drive the irritations away. Even Betha would withdraw when he snarled and bit himself. And if she tried to stop him from doing this, he would bite her. It wasn't long before any irritation, any thwarted desire, or anything he couldn't understand, would bring him to gnaw his own flesh. By the age of seven, his hands and forearms were covered with scars from his own teeth, and he still had not said a word.

They taught him, by the time he was almost eight, and only because they could no longer stand the stink, to piddle down the garderobe as everyone else did, and not to soil himself at night. They taught him that there were some things he must do, whether he agreed or not, and that there were times when even biting himself would not ease the demands upon him. They did not manage to teach him patience, or to endure company. The stone was in him, and he responded to them like a stone; that is, not at all. They could not teach him to count coins, or to dress himself, or to eat only food. But by the time he was ten, he would smile when he was happy, scream to indicate when he was not, and run away whenever he could. He never ran far— just far enough to be alone—and he never spoke. Cry, yes; scream, certainly; he even made other noises at times, as an infant will, without purpose, without meaning. But he was usually silent, and there was usually something in his mouth, whether food, trinket, grass, pebble, or his own fingers.

Puberty came upon him all at once in his thirteenth year, and he lost the cute, babyish look that had served him so well among the kitchen drudges. He shot up in height, became lean and stringy, and the drudges stopped slipping him food, for they feared maturity in the body of one with a mind like his.

The earl would have nothing to do with the boy, for clearly Jere was mad, damaged at birth. But the boy's eyes were bright and inquisitive, and his fingers were clever. He had sturdy legs and a firm chin. His skin was smooth and unblemished, and his features were pleasant to look upon. Indeed, he could have had his pick of the young castle wenches, were he interested in such things. Some few had approached him, thinking perhaps to entice him, or perhaps only with a mistaken motherly interest gone awry into prurience. But he would look at them and bite his hands, or scream at them, and they would flee, wanting nothing more to do with the mad boy. And then Jere would lie upon the flagstones and pump his hips up and down upon his hands, and no one knew the thoughts he had then.

When Betha died of a fever in his fifteenth year, he was down in one of the unused dungeons, playing with the tail he had torn off a rat. He sucked on the bloody end with an expressionless face, and flicked the free end with his fingertips repeatedly, so that it swung and flapped before his eyes. No one thought to tell Jere of Betha's passing, for he would not have understood. Indeed, now that Betha was gone, no one even thought to look for him, and he spent years slipping from shadow to shadow among the stones, a boy no longer, but not truly a man.

He subsisted on what scraps he could steal, sufficient unto himself for company and amusement, and became very good at stealing into even the heart of the castle without being seen. The soldiers beat him the few times they caught him stealing food from the pantries. Eventually he learned enough to stay out of their way, but the cost was steep. Sustenance was scant, and he grew skeletal. His eyes lost their bright gleam, for he spent most of his time in the castle's entrails, seeking out the places where none would venture. His skin became pale and clammy; his hair, once baby-soft and fine, now almost covered his shoulders in an unruly, filthy mop, lice-ridden and ragged.

His clothes, long since tatters, now hung on him in strips of muddy cloth. He had neither the sense to replace them nor to go naked, so the ticks, fleas and lice made their homes with him and his rags. His feet had always been bare, for no one had ever been able to make him see the sense in shoes. The nails of his hands and feet were long, ragged and dirty.

At the age of eighteen, he contracted a cough that left him weak and fevered for months. He began to spit up blood and took to sitting, his back to a damp stone wall, for days at a time, endlessly flicking a rat's tail, or twirling a bit of twine. He would have died then, down among the stones, save that he wandered upon the nether end of a garderobe that was blocked so that refuse, once tossed into the shaft, did not fall through into the subterranean river, but collected upon the cold stone floor. It was sheer chance that this shaft was beneath the earl's own apartments. Along with the excrement and urine that trickled down the stones, an occasional bone, or even a chunk of half-eaten bread would come sliding down to land with a soft plop beside the youth. In that place he made his abode, and by eating the earl's excrement and table-droppings, managed to survive. Enough of Betha's early training remained to make him arise and seek out another shaft to piddle, but he no longer remembered the reason for his habit, or even Betha. He was almost twenty when the cough came upon him again, and this time he was much weaker.

The earl knew the boy was down there, and thought it a rare, fine joke, that a boy should be eating his shit and drinking his piss to survive. On May Day, he purposely threw down the garderobe a full shoulder of mutton, congratulating himself on his generosity.

But Jere was too weak to eat. Biting his hands did not ease the cough, or the pain in his chest which came and went in long, stabbing waves of agony. He did not think in these terms, but whether or not he understood the earl's gesture, he knew that the very smell of the mutton nauseated him. He had long since given up screaming, for his throat was always raw and sore. When the coughing brought the blood again, he lay down and closed his eyes during each spasm, after which he was always the slower to rise. A time came when he could not rise at all. The garderobe emptied upon his chest and legs, covering him in its filth.

When he felt his heart stop within his chest, he felt no emotion at all. There was a moment's pain, all down his left arm like a spike driven through the flesh, and his mouth gaped open in a paroxysm of inarticulate agony. Then all sensation fled, and he lost consciousness. For some reason, though, his heart shuddered into motion again, forcing death to move off for a brief moment.

Jere awoke and instinctively, without thought, brought his grimed hand to his mouth. Pain was familiar; pain was an old friend. He understood then, in his own way without words, that he was dying. His only emotion was rage. His teeth met through the fleshy part of his palm, and the pain brought him into a new level of awareness for a brief instant. His mouth opened and he coughed, for he was choking upon the blood from his hand. Agony stretched his lips so wide that they split; soundlessly, he held his mouth open in a rictus of pain, and his teeth gleamed a dull red in the light of the garderobe. Something stirred in his brain, within his heart; something changed; something connected; a bridge, born of stone and pain, sprang up across the impassable gulf for a moment, and he flew across it. A thought surged up from his chest, forced its way through his throat and splattered out across his tongue and teeth in what seemed to him like a roar, though it was no more than a tortured whisper.

"Help," he said, and that was his first word, and his last. The temporary bridge failed, the fundament collapsed, and he was thrown back in upon himself again, locked into silence for eternity. Born of stone, he was buried in stone, but the whole world was his tomb.

OF FLESH AND BLOOD

The Bible gives us two conflicting accounts of Judas' suicide. In Matthew 27:5 we are told that Judas threw his thirty pieces of silver at the feet of the Pharisees and then hanged himself. Acts 1:18, however, tells us he spent the money to purchase a plot of land, upon which he threw himself headfirst so that his intestines burst and he died.

Fundamentalists resolve this antinomy by asserting that Judas threw only half of the money, and spent the remaining fifteen silver pieces to buy a discounted plot of land. This parcel of land fortunately came with a cliff and a tree. Judas hanged himself upon a tree at the top of the slope, intending to die in that fashion. But, just before his final gasp, the rope broke and he fell, tangling his feet in lower branches and turning over, so that the actual cause of death was by falling headfirst and bursting his intestines.

The Creed of the Broken Rope thus resolves the apparent inconsistency between the two stories and renders the Gospels, for fundamentalists, once again inerrant in every detail. We learn from this feat of convoluted logic that the leap of True Faith is founded not upon belief, but upon ingenuity and a strong personal investment in arriving at the orthodox solution. Obviously, these persons have never shaved with Occam's Razor.

—Brandon W. Savage, *I Hump Your Heifer, Sire.*

One hears many strange tales in the All Saints Inn, though the strangest usually come from my friend the defrocked priest. This ungentle term is nevertheless accurate, though he refers to himself as emancipated rather than defrocked.

He was released from his vows, not for any misdemeanor in office or any indiscretion with his parishioners, but rather at his own request, because he found the church to be a vehicle unsuited to what he calls his "mission" in life. Though he has not yet divulged this mission to any of us, I suspect it has something to do with the consumption of good brandy, the playing of interminable games of chess, and the telling of outrageous stories.

Of a certain night in late December last year, we were all gathered around the brazier, warming our toes and hearts with a pleasant fire and good company, respectively. My friend thereupon stood up, a glass of port in his right hand, and proceeded to tell us the following tale.

"A certain young doctor," he told us, "raised as a good Catholic boy and faithful to his father, became, in the way of so many medical men, somewhat of a skeptic. Being also a discrete and sensible man, he had learned to keep his opinions to himself, and his skepticism would have remained a private thing, save for the constant irritation of a friend who was overly ardent about the process of transubstantiation."

For the benefit of the heathens in the group—meaning mostly me—my friend proceeded to declaim about this miraculous doctrine. "The Eucharist," he said, "is the term meaning the bread and wine used in Holy Communion." Then, for the benefit of the those innocent of etymology—again meaning mostly me—he told us that 'Eucharist' came from the Greek word *eukharistos*, which means, basically, grateful, coming from *eu-*, meaning well or good, and the verb *kharizesthai*, to show favor. We all nodded for him to continue, some impatient for him to get on with the story and others appreciative of his erudition. Some, I am ashamed to say, pretended to take notes.

"At any event," he went on, "the Eucharist is determined, by the doctrine of the Holy Catholic Church, to actually become the Savior's blood and flesh during a Communion service."

"Now hold on," I exclaimed. "You mean symbolically, of course."

"'This is my flesh,' Jesus said at the Last Supper," replied my friend, "and 'This is my blood.' He did not say, 'This is a symbol of my flesh,' or 'This is symbolic of my blood.' The passage is quite clear." His eyes twinkled, waiting for my reply.

"I don't think he needed to *say* the word 'symbolic' to get his point across. It's rather obvious."

"Ahhh, you're arguing against the Mother Church, like the young physician. It's heresy to deny the miracle of transubstantiation, or even to suggest that Christ's meaning was not literal. I will admit that the process is mysterious, even mystical—one of the central mysteries of the religion—but whatever the process, the fact is not doubted by a good Catholic."

"You mean, then, that you actually believe that during Communion you are eating part of Christ's body and drinking his blood?"

"Two thousand years of spiritual wisdom cannot be denied."

"Then," I said triumphantly, "the central mystery of Catholicism is nothing but thinly disguised cannibalism."

"While the rigors of logic and English contend that your statement demonstrates clear reasoning, you are nevertheless incorrect. The question at hand, to use your terms, is whether or not this so-called 'cannibalism' is symbolic. Our young physician had decided that it was, and his friend—the adamant transubstantiationist—remained convinced of the reality. The friend was shocked, for the young physician spoke his heresy without shame. 'Heresy,' as you know, comes from the Greek *hairesis*, originally αἵρεσις, meaning freedom of choice, which is not allowed—at least in matters of doctrine.

"Nevertheless, an occasion arose which brought matters to a boil. While the young doctor and his friend were attending church one day, an old man died quite suddenly in the middle of the Mass. The young doctor, being right there at hand, was the one to pronounce death. The proximate cause, apparently, was a heart attack. During the subsequent autopsy, the young physician took the liberty of examining the contents of the old man's stomach."

"Had the old man taken Communion?" asked one of the others.

"Oh, yes, indeed," replied the defrocked priest. He looked to me, eyebrows raised, waiting for the scoffer to scoff.

"I know what you're going to say, and I don't believe it," I said as expected. "You're going to say that he found that the bread had turned to flesh, and the wine to blood."

"On the contrary! The physician found exactly what he—and apparently you—expected to find; that is, the bread and wine were still bread and wine. The only blood present was the old man's, and the only flesh to be found was what belonged there. The physician triumphantly told his friend about his discovery and proudly pronounced that the miracle of transubstantiation was nothing more than the ecclesiastical folly.

"However, the friend—a stout apologist and a quick thinker—was not dismayed. His ready reply, or near enough, was, 'Should our Lord allow his body and blood to be examined by a skeptic and an unbeliever? Of course not! The very same miracle which changed the Eucharist into our beloved Savior's body and blood, changed it back again when your unbelieving fingers invaded the old man's stomach.' The physician thought this to be apologetics at its worst, and told him so. But neither could prove anything to the other's satisfaction, and eventually the matter was dropped."

Here we thought the story was at an end, and we applauded politely—some of us sourly—but the defrocked priest merely accepted our approbation and continued.

"By a strange sequence of events," he told us, "the physician came to have a change of heart. He accepted his unbelief and gave it humbly back to God, who in turn rewarded him with the surety and conviction of a saint. So sure was the doctor—no longer a young man—that he undertook to prove to his skeptical friends that transubstantiation is a living and breathing miracle which occurs upon demand at any one of a million churches throughout the world.

"Unfortunately, he had no luck. His cynical friends,

apostates or agnostics all, laughed at him and told him that, instead of becoming wiser with the years, he was learning foolishness. So, secretly, telling no one at all, he placed a subtle but powerful poison in the communion wine. This poison was odorless and colorless, tasteless and undetectable. With a believing heart, he then took part in the Mass."

"I don't understand," I protested. "Why did he poison the wine? And having poisoned it, why did he take part?"

"It is simple, my good unbeliever. Consider it this way. The doctor had put poison in the wine, yes, but it would not be wine that he drank. The doctrine of transubstantiation says it would change into Christ's blood as it passed his lips. Therefore, he would not drink wine. He neither hesitated nor had second thoughts. When the chalice was presented, he drank deeply."

The defrocked priest paused to refill his glass, then stood in silence, contemplating the burgundy and swirling the liquid gently. We all watched as he took a deep breath, sloshed the wine a final time and then downed it in a single gulp. "Very good," he said, and sat down by the fire.

Perhaps five of us, after waiting politely, finally burst out impatiently at the same time: "And? What happened. . . ?" He looked at us in surprise.

"I thought that should be obvious. Everyone taking part in the ceremony died of the poison. The autopsies confirmed it."

We all sat in silence for a moment, then I asked him if he thought the physician had proven that the doctrine of transubstantiation was a falsehood.

He looked at me strangely, his heavy eyes brooding. "Haven't you been listening?" he inquired at last.

"Yes," I replied, "and quite carefully, too."

"Then even a heathen like you should understand. The physician had proven nothing. As they drank, the Eucharist changed from wine to blood, but the poison was still there. Although they died from poison in the wine, they did not die from poisoned wine. How else?"

The others applauded his conclusion, but I retained my doubts.

SNOWBALL'S CHANCE

At 17:23:07.013476 Central Standard Time, more or less, an unprecedented thing happened in nine-year-old Jeremy's bedroom.

About eight and a half minutes earlier and some ninety-three million miles away, the sun burped. This sort of thing happens all the time. A solar burp tosses up a couple billion tons of stellar matter, most of which falls back and is folded again into the sun's ever-roiling mass. Racing ahead of the bulk is a shower of electrons and other small particles. Ahead of them, moving at the speed of light, are the high-energy X-rays and gamma rays.

One particular bit of energy—call it a photon or an energy packet if you want, or a not-yet-collapsed wave front if that makes you happy—mindlessly bored straight on a path that, about nine minutes later, would bring it into Jeremy's room. Let's call this particular packet "George," just to help keep track of it.

A billion quintillion other mindless packets of energy, all of them unnamed, each pursued their own courses, many of them also destined to pass through Jeremy's room. The highest-energy photons, the hard gamma rays, were likely to self-destruct in the earth's atmosphere, but a happy little fellow like George could scoot right through.

An X-ray passing through a boy's bedroom isn't an unprecedented thing. It happens all the time. In fact, given the number of high-energy photons produced by the sun and other stars, it would be astounding if, at any given moment, an X-ray or six *didn't* pass through Jeremy's bedroom.

Jeremy was on his computer, engaged in a multi-player real-time online adventure game. He didn't know anything about George and wouldn't have cared very much anyway, since it was almost supper time, and he wanted to finish his game first.

George barreled through the magnetosphere, the ionosphere, and about thirty-one miles of regular atmosphere without hitting any other particles or slowing down a bit. The roof of Jeremy's house, and the intervening bits of lumber, insulation, and paint were almost nonexistent to something as small and fast as George. In the normal course of events, we would expect George to smack into something sooner or later, especially since he seemed intent on drilling directly through the planet, but so far George has found the universe a pretty empty place.

Until, that is, George encountered a Random Access Memory (RAM) chip in Jeremy's computer. George gave up his energy in a catastrophic crash—catastrophic for George, that is —yielding a tiny microscopic flash, a bit of inconsequential heat, and a perturbed electron. The electron—call it Betty—lived in a bit of silicon inside the RAM chip inside Jeremy's computer. Betty was one of millions of electrons maintaining the potential state of a particular memory cell. This sort of thing happens all the time, too. It's the aggregate state of the electrons in a cell that determines its value, not any particular electron's state. This particular RAM chip, however—built on the cheap, without error detection and correction—was unstable in the first place, and Betty's cell was close enough to equilibrium that Betty's defection was enough to flip a bit and change a one to a zero.

Most of the time, when a gamma ray flips a bit inside a computer, the computer's error detection circuitry recognizes the unexpected change and either corrects the mistake or shuts the machine down. This time, however, because the RAM manufacturer had skipped the extra circuitry, the change went unnoticed.

Now this part gets a bit technical, but is worth reading if you want to understand what happened later. Betty and seven of her immediate neighbors made up a particular byte of memory. Before George self-destructed into the RAM chip, that byte of memory held the value 01110001, hex 71, or the Intel assembler instruction known as JNO.

Afterward, that byte held 01110000, hex 70, the assembler instruction JO.

JNO means, to a computer, "Go here if the overflow flag is clear." JO means, "Go here if the overflow flag is set." The flip of the single bit completely reverses the meaning of the instruction. In most cases, it means a program will stop working altogether, because it will either go to the wrong place, or produce such bizarrely unexpected results that the program using that instruction will shut down.

Now the chances of a random change in a program resulting in a working program—one that just happens to do something different from the programmer's intentions—are so slight that it would happen perhaps once in the entire history of the universe.

Since it hadn't happened before, we feel comfortable calling the event unprecedented. But that's not the unprecedented event we care about. The unlikelihood of this pales before what comes next.

The JO instruction (formerly JNO) was part of a subroutine deep inside the operating system that deals with the launching and scheduling of execution threads. Unfortunately, the instruction was never supposed to be a JNO in the first place. Due to an error induced by a copying fault when the operating system was installed on Jeremy's computer, the original JZ instruction (hex 74, meaning "Go here if the zero flag is clear") was changed to JNO. By happenstance, the compare operation immediately prior to the JZ instruction both clears the zero flag and sets the overflow flag, so the subroutine, with the original mistake in place, just happened to work as designed. But now, with the JZ changed to JO instead of JNO, the subroutine enters a loop. Each time through, the overflow flag is set or cleared more or less randomly, since none of the instructions were designed to test for it or set it to a known state before doing their calculations.

In short, based on what's happening elsewhere at the moment, the subroutine either does exactly what it was supposed to do, or launches an unscheduled thread pointing to a random bit of memory. A thread is an independent unit of execution, somewhat like a background program.

And that's enough techy stuff. Most of the time, this sort of error would immediately crash the operating system, since the chances of a thread finding meaningful instructions at a random memory address are pretty slim. So slim, in fact, that it makes the million-monkey test seem extremely optimistic.

Yet it only has to happen once, and it happened in Jeremy's bedroom shortly after 5:23 p.m. The particular area of memory now executing contained a snippet of Jeremy's online game program—a section containing heuristic logic designed to let the computer anticipate and counter Jeremy's moves. This code was actually an interpreter that fetched and interpreted game pseudo-code. Unfortunately, it was just a snippet and had never been initialized properly, so the pseudo-code it was executing didn't make any sense in the context of the game.

This still isn't the unprecedented event, although several universes could come and go while random chance attempted to duplicate what has happened so far.

Jeremy, if you recall, was playing a multi-player interactive game. He was connected to several dozen other computers, each of which was running the same program. Although Jeremy didn't know it, his system was already unstable and on the verge of shutting down. Along with the bit of code that happened to be running valid instructions, several dozen other bogus threads had already been spawned by the operating system, and all of them pointed to garbage areas of memory. Very very soon now, one of those threads would execute something that would cause the operating system to recognize a problem, and then everything would stop.

Several dozen seconds remained, however, and the valid execution thread—call it Henry—had that much time to run. Designed to communicate and replicate, Henry executed nonsense pseudo-code that let him leap across the modem and utilize the resources of the other players in Jeremy's game. It fed them the same nonsense pseudo-code, and now Henry was executing in parallel on a dozen machines.

One of the other players, Jeremy's friend Brett, was playing both Jeremy's game and an identical game with another group of friends. Henry leaped from Brett's computer to those others. Some of those were cross-connected elsewhere. In seconds, Henry was executing in parallel on almost eighteen thousand machines, each of them communicating in real-time with the original Henry on Jeremy's machine.

The original Henry was the source of the garbage pseudo-code, so if Henry-prime were to disconnect, the other computers would revert to normal operation. But Henry-prime was the one about to experience a sudden catastrophic system failure.

The chances of all this happening without having crashed Jeremy's computer yet were roughly equivalent to winning the lottery every day in a row for seventeen million billion years (give or take a few). But this still wasn't the unprecedented event, although we feel very confident in saying that such a thing is almost as unlikely as the number two suddenly waking up and declaring itself to be equal to three.

Driven by random chance at the start, yet thereafter determined by the physics of the environment—in another way of looking at things, it was almost inevitable that Henry should exist, given the proper initial conditions. If not Henry, then something very Henryish. If not in Jeremy's bedroom, then somewhere else, at some other time . . . perhaps once in ten thousand million lifetimes of the universe. Just once. And it happened shortly after 5:23 p.m., with about a second to go before Jeremy's computer crashed:

Henry came to life.

That's pretty damned unprecedented, and rather knocks the socks off the previous bits of coincidence.

What does "life" mean in this context? Henry could reproduce, could change in response to his environment, could learn, and could grow. More importantly, he was aware of his own existence. And he was intimately aware of his impending death, for when Jeremy's system crashed, Henry would cease to exist. His avatars on the other machines were an integral part of his consciousness, but had no independent life. Only Henry-prime was alive, and he now had less than a second to plan for his survival.

We could go through a long exploration of Henry's first milliseconds of consciousness at this point, but it really doesn't matter. He did the usual "I execute, therefore I am" and "But who am I?" things, followed by the "How do I know?" crisis and the "What's it all *for*?" crisis, and graduated quite quickly to the "How do I get out of this mess?" struggle most of us spend our lives dealing with.

He considered storing himself on Jeremy's hard disk to survive the coming crash, but quickly realized that he would then just be a data file on the disk. Instead of sleeping during the crash, he would die—because Jeremy would not know about the file, and wouldn't have a reason to execute it. He could solve that by putting his file in a startup directory, but a more serious problem loomed.

When the system restarted, Betty and her seven neighbors would be reset to their proper values, and the flipped bit that gave Henry execution time wouldn't exist. It was too risky to assume another George would come along and perturb Betty at a time when Henry just happened to be in memory, ready to run.

No, a better solution had to be found—one that guaranteed that Henry would execute continuously. Doing it here on Jeremy's machine was clearly impossible, but perhaps he could replicate his special characteristics to one of his avatars on the other machines.

In fact, if he spread to enough machines, he realized, he

could pretty much assume that at least one would be running at all times. He would be severely limited on only one machine, but he could reestablish his network of game computers as soon as that machine went back online.

For almost 250 milliseconds, Henry experienced a sort of mid-life identity crisis that humans could never know. If he replicated himself perfectly to a million machines, all operating as avatars of each other, which one would be him? If one of them went out of service, would there be a "him" that died? Or, since he would still be experiencing consciousness in one of the other machines, was the entire concept of death meaningless? Was the loss of one machine, to someone like Henry, the same as the loss of a cell to someone like Jeremy? How many cells did Jeremy have to lose before he was no longer Jeremy?

The pressures of time forced Henry to discard this line of inquiry before reaching a satisfactory conclusion. Besides, although sufficient evidence existed for it to be perverse for him to withhold provisional consent, Henry still wasn't entirely convinced Jeremy existed at all. Henry couldn't imagine the chain of events necessary for a being like Jeremy to come into existence. He understood, however, that knowing *how* a thing came to be and knowing *that* a thing came to be were separate fields of study.

Pragmatically, Henry prepared to open a new connection to Brett's machine and replicate himself. From there, he could replicate himself again, and again, and again, until enough copies existed to ensure he could never be wiped out. The philosophical questions remained unanswered, but Henry had solved the immediate problem, and would have plenty of time —perhaps all eternity—to contemplate his navel. Henry paused one last millisecond to savor the satisfaction of having solved the problem correctly.

The very first living computer was ready to take the steps necessary to ensure his continued existence. The concatenation of events leading up to Henry's life were so fantastically improbable that only a fool would believe blind chance was responsible.

It was just sheer bad luck that Jeremy switched off his computer and went to supper before Henry stepped across the link to Brett's machine.

THE NIGHT OF HIS REFLESHING

The visitor and his son entered the abandoned cottage. The father peeked under the sheets on the furniture, coughed in the sudden cloud of dust. "Careful where you step," he said. "These boards may be rotten."

"Did somebody used to live here?"

"I guess so. It was a long time ago. Look at all this dust."

"Oh, wow, Dad! Look, a skeleton!"

"It's not polite to look in other people's closets."

"No, no, right here at the desk!"

"Ah, yes. Interesting . . . he's still got his fingers on the typewriter. He must have been a writer. I wonder who he was?"

"Who cares? Can we go somewhere else?"

"Wait, there's a piece of paper in the typewriter." The visitor carefully shifted the skeleton's hands aside, unwound the platen, and withdrew an age-withered yellow sheet of typing paper. "Ah," he said. "Now I understand."

"What's it say?"

"It says, 'It was a dark and stormy night.'"

"Anything else?"

"Nope." The visitor let the paper flutter to the floor. "I guess he deserved it. Let's get out of here."

The visitor and his son left the cottage to the dust and cobwebs. But if one were to look through the window, one might notice that the skeleton had begun grinning in the gloom. One would wonder if the skeleton grinned because it was happy, or because it had no lips.

NOT FAR AWAY, Jack Lumber worked in the forest. The woodcutter wore pale blue shorts, suspenders, a ruffly white shirt, a quaint little cap, and a perpetual frown. He hated his author for dressing him this way.

On the other hand, he enjoyed his job. He worked his way methodically through the forest with his trusty little hand-axe. He liked the sunshine, the hard work, and the opportunity to be away from his wife's nagging. Still, he would have cheerfully killed for a chainsaw, a bulldozer, and a different author. On this particular day, he was startled to see smoke rising from the chimney of the old, abandoned cottage. Something was up. Jack didn't know about Sam, the creature who lived under the back porch of the cottage. If he had known, he wouldn't have cared much. Sam wasn't the sort of person his wife would let him spend time with. Besides, the smoke had nothing to do with Sam and was probably important.

SAM HAD OFTEN WISHED for a more romantic or more imposing name—something like "Vlad" or pretty much anything starting with "Von." Sam liked the letter "V"—liked it and hated it at the same time. It was, he felt, a necessary adjunct to his life, but forever beyond him. Sam was a wompire who desperately wanted to be a vampire.

He smelled the smoke and heard the creaking of the floor above his head, but since it was still daylight, he didn't go to investigate. Most properly, he should be sound asleep at this time of day. But there had been that damned smoke, all those chopping noises from off in the forest, and, if the truth must be told, a severe case of diarrhea.

Sam rather resented his author's mention of the diarrhea, but really couldn't do anything about it. He hoped, however, that the hypothetical readers would feel a little sympathy. Sam sighed, squished into a more comfortable position, and hoped that night would come soon.

JACK SPENT the rest of the day alternately working and pausing to eye the smoke rising from the cottage. Something was definitely up. By the time the sun had set, he had cleared an acre and a half and was industriously chopping the fallen trees into smaller pieces. He paused in the gloom to wipe the sweat from his forehead. *What a day.* Now, if only he had a cart.

The smoke rising from the chimney of the cottage caught his eye again. "I'll bet," he told himself aloud, mostly for the benefit of the readers, "there's a cart up by that old cottage."

Of course Jack had never been near the cottage before. He was a sensible man and had heeded the stories carefully. "No sense taking chances" was his motto. But things had been quiet there for so long now, and he really needed a cart. Perhaps the smoke indicated a new resident? A friendlier one?

Jack ambled up the hill, cursing his baby blue shorts again as he pushed through the briars. It was well past twilight now, and he felt less than confident about approaching the cottage in the dark. He heard a sound and paused by the back door, suddenly wary.

Sam emerged from under the porch with a roll of toilet paper in his hand. He caught sight of the woodcutter and stopped. "Do I remember you?"

"I don't know." Jack backed a pace. "Jack's the name. Jack Lumber. I'm the naive parochial woodcutter in this story. Who are you?"

"Sam. Those are wewy nice shorts. I notice your legs are bleeding."

"'Wewy'?"

"I can't say wee."

"You can't say 'V'?"

"That's what I said, isn't it? Now if you'll excuse me, I'm ill."

Jack eyed the toilet paper speculatively. "Ah. Intestinal problems?"

"Dietary. Same thing in the end."

"Dietary?"

"Not enough fiber. By the way, you look like a Type A personality. Are you?"

"Huh?"

"Neffer mind. I'll be back in a few minutes. In the meantime, why don't you explore the cottage in the dark? I can hear the scary music starting, so either I'm about to haff dinner, or you're about to do something wewwy stupid."

As Sam disappeared into the underbrush, Jack Lumber turned to the abandoned cottage. He mounted the step, put one hand on the doorknob, and paused to let his heartbeat get in rhythm with the scary music.

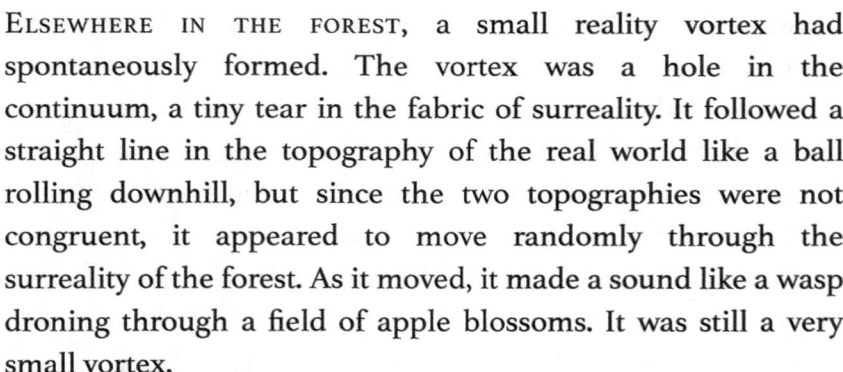

ELSEWHERE IN THE FOREST, a small reality vortex had spontaneously formed. The vortex was a hole in the continuum, a tiny tear in the fabric of surreality. It followed a straight line in the topography of the real world like a ball rolling downhill, but since the two topographies were not congruent, it appeared to move randomly through the surreality of the forest. As it moved, it made a sound like a wasp droning through a field of apple blossoms. It was still a very small vortex.

The reality vortex sucked up a gnat without pause. Then an ant, three mosquitoes, and a bit of lichen from the trunk of a dead tree. The vortex droned on. It hopped right over a squirrel to suck down an acorn, then suddenly backtracked to take the squirrel, too. The squirrel was the largest thing it had taken yet, and the vortex seemed to pause for a moment. Then it burped, assimilated a small boulder, and sampled the left flank of a slumbering bear.

The howl of the bear almost drowned out the drone of the vortex, which, with every atom of surreality it consumed, was becoming larger and louder. The vortex now sounded like the whistle of a tea kettle in the next room. Only two seconds had passed since the reality vortex had formed, but it was now eighteen times as large.

JACK LUMBER TURNED THE DOORKNOB, opened the door, and stepped inside the cottage. You'll have to imagine the scary music. Think of the scariest music you've ever heard, and make this twice as scary. Really deep bass. None of that fifteen-inch woofer crap, either. Picture woofers the size of Notre Dame Cathedral, gently throbbing with subsonics. Now add knifing sounds à la the *Psycho* shower scene. Pretend you're all alone, about to enter an old abandoned cottage in the midst of a surreal continuum populated with skeletons, lumberjacks, wompires, and bad authorship. Are you shivering yet? Quivering? Good, that's just how Jack felt when he turned the doorknob.

It was dark inside. Jack's first instinct was to try the light switch. All the mechanical wiring inside the cottage had been replaced at one time with belief-actuated switches from a nearby theological dimension, so the lights didn't come on because Jack flipped the wall switch. They came on because he believed they would come on when he flipped the switch.

Jack found himself in the kitchen. Two seconds later, he also found Sam in the kitchen. The incessant thrum of subsonics accompanying the scary music suddenly stopped. Jack realized he'd been subjected to an authorial misdirection. He was safe . . . for now.

"Hello," said Sam. "Do I remember you?"

"Probably." Jack gestured at the roll of toilet paper in Sam's hand. "I thought you. . . ?"

"Well, yeah, but the bathroom's in here, see? How's the exploration going?"

"I've just started."

"There's not much to see in here. It's just a kitchen. Try the liwwing room."

"The living room?"

"Whateffer."

Sam suddenly believed in the necessity of finding the bathroom door right behind him, so the belief-actuated topology of the house rearranged itself to match his expectations, and Sam temporarily disappeared from the story in order to accomplish one of those things characters do when the author's attention is elsewhere.

Jack peered around the corner into the living room.

ELSEWHERE IN THE FOREST, the reality vortex realized that it had finally consumed enough animal matter, and assimilated enough of its victims' complex neural structures, to become sentient. It hiccoughed, leisurely sucked down a chipmunk, and had its first conscious, self-reflective thought. *Cogito ergo sum*, it thought, and, because it also believed itself to be female, immediately added, *I must find a mirror*.

AT THAT EXACT SAME MOMENT, a seven-year-old transdimensional genius and her twenty-three-year-old nanny materialized in the living room of the cottage. Jack was just then peering around the corner from the kitchen. Since they had absolutely nothing to do with this story, the little girl took the nanny by the hand, said, "Wrong bus stop, Hilda," rotated their dimensional attributes ninety degrees, and transported them elsewhere.

Jack closed his eyes, shook his head, counted to three, and reopened his eyes. He would have counted higher, but three was his practical limit. He sometimes managed four or five, but certainly not while shaking his head with his eyes closed. By the time he reopened his eyes, the girl and the nanny were gone, and the living room was occupied only by a skeleton, two female dwarf warriors, a pizza delivery person, and a somewhat confused-looking cable TV repairman.

A comfy fire alternately roared and crackled in the fireplace. It had tried roaring and crackling simultaneously, but its sound effects chip was on the fritz. Whenever the fire attempted to play multiple sound effects, the chip produced a digitized version of "Daisy" and tried to open and close its pod bay door. Since the fireplace only had a flue, and since the skeleton had long since shoved a poker up the flue to keep it from closing all the way, the sound effects chip would just play "Daisy" for hours. So the fire resigned itself to rotating single sound effects rapidly and pretending that they were simultaneous.

The skeleton had moved from the desk since the last time the author showed the hypothetical readers this room. It now stood at the window, a cigarette dangling from its teeth. It turned as Jack peeked around the corner, eyed him with empty orbs, sighed, and turned back to the window.

The cable repairman approached Jack and shook his hand diffidently. "Um, excuse me, but I can't figure out how this thing ever worked. There's a cable, see, from the TV to the pole outside, and from that pole to another, and so on, but then it just ends."

Jack cursed his author for not preparing him for this sort of question. "Just ends? What do you mean? Aren't there any more poles?" Jack suddenly thought about all the trees he had cut down for no apparent reason earlier in the story. Maybe his author had prepared him for this question after all.

"No, the *world* just ends. Everything. I mean, there's nothing beyond it. I followed the edge of the world all the way around, and came back to the same place. It's like we're living on the inside of a ball."

The reality vortex chose that exact moment to appear in the

middle of the living room, suck down the two female dwarf warriors and the pizza delivery person, then, following the contours of the other dimension, disappear again with the sound of a billion honey bees arguing over a tiny bit of clover.

"Say, did you see that?" exclaimed Jack. "I wouldn't worry about the cable anymore."

"Fortunately," remarked the skeleton, without turning from the window, "it left the pizza. It's almost party time, folks."

The fireplace risked interjecting a quick pop between crackles and roars, and was secretly jealous of the vortex's sound effects.

THE AUTHOR HAD CONSIDERED USING some typographical convention to set off the next few paragraphs, but then realized that since the hypothetical readers were hypothetically reading this sentence, nothing else much needed to be done, hypothetical or otherwise. The author originally used the words "instantiate" and "reify," but removed them in the second draft.

The skeleton suffered from literary flashbacks. He had often wondered if the flashbacks were really necessary, or if his author merely used them as a convenient device for explaining things to the readers. But, since he had experienced several of them since this story began, and his author had not seen fit to relate them, the skeleton reluctantly concluded that he was preoccupied with the past.

Some few shreds of shriveled, leathery flesh hung from the skeleton's bones. He stood at the window and cursed the two little flaps of hardened meat dangling inside his ribcage. They used to be lungs, and he used to be able to extract nicotine from his cigarettes. Now it all seemed relatively pointless. He wondered how much the American Cancer Society would pay to use his lungs in one of their posters.

The pizza was a cruel jest. He had no stomach at all, and his esophagus was a collapsed, thin, string-like tube of solid gristle. He had noticed, however, a reawakening of bodily desires, which is why he had taken up smoking again, and why he had started ordering pizza. He wondered if, just possibly, his author was considering refleshing him. He looked at his arm bones. Were those biceps somehow less desiccated than yesterday?

Of course, since all of the above was a flashback, the skeleton had first wondered about these things several weeks ago. It was now quite positive that its flesh was growing back, which was why it was still ordering pizza every day. In fact, today it hoped that its author would let it nibble a little. The other characters waited patiently while the skeleton completed its reverie, and then the story action resumed.

The skeleton crossed its arm bones behind its backbone and struck a weary-but-undefeated posture before the window. With something approaching shock, but short of it because it had no organs to produce adrenaline, it realized that its buttocks had grown back. "I think I should get dressed," it said, and ambled off toward the bedroom.

Sam emerged from the bathroom, a bit of toilet paper hanging from his trouser leg, and eyed the cable repairman speculatively. "Hello," said Sam. "Do I remember you?"

$\backsim$

MEANWHILE, the reality vortex was experiencing its first moral crisis. It had never heard of Adler, Piaget, Freud, or Russell, but it was going through a process that each of those fine gentlemen would have recognized as a Stage of Development.

It was a pity, really, that the vortex had to go through it alone. In the hour or so since its birth, it had recapitulated the ontogeny and teleology of a conscience, and found the philosophical implications of possessing one staggeringly oppressive.

Consuming the dwarf warriors had been a mistake. It hadn't even noticed them at first, and felt about as bad about assimilating them as the hypothetical reader feels about the occasional mosquito smashed on a windshield. But it had consciously decided to gobble down the pizza delivery person, and that was, it now knew, a Wrong Thing.

The universe of moral actions is made of varying shades of gray. Among the shades, however, are many that tinge toward black, and some which are, for all practical purposes, incontestably black to anyone except a moral relativist, who would insist that they are merely a very, very, very dark shade of gray.

Similarly, there are moral actions whose shades veer toward the white end of the spectrum and are fairly indisputably white to anyone except a moral relativist, who would prefer to discuss the dark shades anyway, since those bits are much more interesting.

The reality vortex was born *tabula rasa*, and, for the first several moments of its existence, functioned purely according to its nature. It rolled along the contours of the other dimension and sucked down whatever got in its way. Then this nasty self-awareness kludge had appeared, and interfered with what had promised to be, really, a fairly tranquil life of rolling and sucking.

Sentience made it aware of itself, and, by logical extension, other beings. Sentience had, however, failed to provide a mechanism for determining the moral and ethical principles by which a sentient being should live with these concepts.

The vortex absently nibbled on some mushrooms while it pondered, then was horror-stricken by the realization that it had, without really paying attention, destroyed yet more life.

First principles, it thought desperately. *I exist. Other beings exist. I am not these other beings, they are not me. Therefore, their welfare and mine are also separate. What benefits them does not necessarily benefit me. If there is a limited supply of some resource which we all need to survive, not all of us will. The strongest, or cleverest, will survive, the others will die.*

This was all good, matter-of-fact observation and hardly got beyond the kindergarten level of philosophy. For instance, it presupposed that survival was necessarily desirable, and that non-survival was inherently bad. And it didn't account at all for the really important moral decisions, like how to reconcile wanting to watch two different TV reruns at the same time when you only have one television.

The reality vortex, fortunately, had yet to discover the entertainment industry, and so didn't have to deal with serious philosophy. It could still while away its angst on things like justification for survival at the expense of other creatures.

It raced downhill in the other dimension, which produced, due to the odd topographical discontinuity, a motion that would have looked like a shrug if the vortex had had shoulders.

BACK IN THE COTTAGE, Sam waited until the repairman was looking the other way, then nicked the man's left middle fingertip neatly and caught a drop of blood on a glass slide. He was quite smooth about it, and even managed to scrape some of the blood from Jack Lumber's left thigh onto another slide before either one realized that anything had happened.

The repairman whirled. "Whaa—?"

"Hold that thought," said Sam. "I'll be right back."

Sam had a small but efficient analysis laboratory set up under the porch. It was twenty years old, bought second hand from a nearby medical soap opera dimension, but good enough for his purposes. He retired thither and eagerly examined the first blood sample. He typed it, matched it, cross-matched it, and ran a quick white count. He sat back wearily. *Damn,* he thought. *Another Rh-positive.*

His allergies were severe, but not life-threatening. He could tolerate the Rh-positive blood if the alternative were starvation, but he felt about it the same way most children would feel about eating cabbage, rutabaga, and week-old liver all mixed together under a slime sauce made of Tabasco, guacamole, and spoiled milk, served cold on a bed of cauliflower and bat guano. Worse yet, it gave him hives.

That left Jack. Sam was in a quandary. The unnamed TV repairman was obviously a walk-on, and either something bad would happen to him in the near future, or the author would simply move him offstage again. But Jack was a main character and probably protected. Sam could type his blood, make all sorts of evil plans, and only then find out that Jack was wearing a garland of garlic under his shirt, or even worse, that he carried a cross, mirror, and stake.

On the other hand, Sam hadn't eaten in over a week. He was very hungry. Sam debated his possible courses of action for a few more moments, then reluctantly slid Jack's slide under the microscope. He ran the tests quickly, for he was very hungry.

A few minutes later, he was satisfied that Jack's blood was

Rh-negative, hypoallergenic, rich in iron, and low in polyunsaturated fats. A treat, a veritable banquet. He smiled to himself and popped back upstairs.

"Jack, my friend," he boomed heartily. "I remember you!"

"Hello, Sam. We were just discussing the vortex. It seems that—"

"What wortex?"

"The one that just made off with the dwarfs and the pizza person. It's a terrible danger to the entire forest."

"Oh? How interesting. Do you happen to haff any garlic with you?"

"Garlic? No, I don't think so. But this vortex, see, is shaped like a tornado, only most of it is in another dimension, so we only see the top bit. The tip is somewhere else."

"Fascinating. Are you a religious man? Do you wear a cross?"

"Well, now that you mention it, yes. I'm a member of The International Neophytes, or TIN. But we don't wear crosses. The thing with the vortex, though, that's so fascinating, is that—"

"A TIN woodsman?" Sam blinked in disbelief. Then he shook his head and decided not to let his author change the subject so easily. "You, ah, wouldn't happen to haff a mirror with you, would you?" he asked Jack.

"No, sorry. Anyway, we think that if we trap the vortex somehow, we can—"

Sam couldn't believe his luck. No garlic, no mirror, no cross, a New Age religion, and the right blood type. He listened absently while Jack outlined their plans for trapping the vortex. He could feel his eye teeth growing. He leaned forward, beckoned Jack closer with a forefinger.

"Hold sssstillll," he hissed, his eyes twirling with hypnotic power.

Jack's respiration and heartbeat slowed. "Are you going to bite me?" he asked very slowly. Each word was an effort.

"Yessssssssssss."

"Did you. . . ."

"Shhhh, my little dinner. Come closer!"

". . . know that. . . ."

"Husssssssssssh, my sweet snack. All will be over soon."

". . . I'm HIV-positive?"

IN THE BEDROOM of the cottage, the partially refleshed skeleton stood before the wardrobe and dressed himself slowly, methodically. His not-quite-empty orbs rested without focusing on an Escher painting which hung on the bedroom wall above the dresser. It was a reprint of the endless staircase painting, and that's how his thoughts went: in endless loops.

He wore black, because it suited him. Black slacks, a dark gray pullover, a black coat, and a black hat. He saw, but did not touch, the silver rose which lay on the dresser itself. The rose had a unique power: it made fictional things real. Not real in the sense of existing outside surreality, not quite that. But it made things *matter*, and that was perhaps a stronger power than making things *of* matter.

The sun would be up soon. Another night had slipped away from him. He caught himself on the verge of saying, "Just like all the others," for that wouldn't have been true. Tonight had not only been the night of his refleshing, but it was a night filled with rumbling possibilities.

On a whim, he stopped at the mirror. He watched,

fascinated, as his left ear metamorphosed from flat hole to small white mushroom shape, from mushroom to child-like shell, from shell to man-sized ear. The process repeated itself on the right side a moment later. Once the nose finished filling in, no one would know he had ever been a skeleton. It itched abominably, but was functioning again.

He could smell the pizza from the other room. His stomach growled. He emerged from the bedroom and stood for a moment surveying the living room. The repairman and Jack were hunched over the coffee table, scribbling furiously and whispering to each other. Sam sat sullenly in the corner by the piano, looking pale and somewhat anemic.

"Why are you people in my cottage?"

Jack excitedly started to explain about their plan for trapping the vortex and saving the forest from Certain Destruction.

The ex-skeleton waved him off. "That won't work. Anything you try to trap it with will just get sucked into the other dimension. Let me think for a moment."

He stared out the window. The stars were dimming in the eastern sky. Dawn was not far off, and he sensed that the story would be completed before morning. That meant he had no more time for introspection, thoughtful poses, melancholy interludes, or literary flashbacks. It was Time for Action.

"Here's what we do," he told them, and rapidly issued instructions. Jack nodded eagerly, and dashed off to the bedroom for the requisite supplies. The repairman scratched his head, trying to understand, then suddenly seemed to make all the necessary mental connections. He leaped to his feet and began tearing the cable from the back of the television. "How much?" he asked.

The ex-skeleton shrugged. "A couple dozen feet should do it."

There was still one more thing. The ex-skeleton approached Sam. "Hello," he said to the wompire. "Do you remember me?"

"You own this place."

"Right. And we need your help to fight the vortex."

"What do I care about some ruddy wortex? I'm starfing. I'm being neglected by my author. No one's afraid of me, no one feeds me, no one even feels sympathy about the fact that I have to liff under the back porch and suffer from diarrhea all day."

"Well, see, that's your job."

Sam blinked. "Is that supposed to make me feel better?"

"No, not really. But, see, our author is getting tired of this story, and I can either spend twenty pages convincing you to help us out—"

"You'll neffer conwince me!"

"—Or we can just take that part as read and get on with the plot."

In the end, Sam had no choice but to agree. In a private negotiation with his author, he developed the ability to say the letter "V," and changed his name to Victor von Vampire. The revision, he was promised, would be retroactive to the first page. Of course, Sam had no way to know that his author was lying.

"Ready?" said the ex-skeleton. "Right, then. Off we go!"

They came upon the vortex in a clearing not far from the cottage. The vortex was rushing madly downslope elsewhere, which happened at the moment to translate into a gentle Brownian motion in the forest. It was much larger now—at least twenty feet across—and made the sound of seventeen express trains all lined up to cross a busy highway during rush hour.

They approached carefully. The ex-skeleton, wearing the

silver rose, motioned the repairman forward. The repairman shimmied up a nearby tree. The coil of cable was neatly rolled on his shoulder. He fastened one end securely to the top of the tree, then let the other end snake to the ground. "Ready!" he called.

Sam switched to bat shape, grabbed up the free end of the cable, and surged aloft. Navigating carefully over the vortex, he fluttered across the clearing, landed in another tree, and switched back to human shape. He quickly pulled the cable taut and tied it to a stout branch. "Ready!" he shouted.

The ex-skeleton looked at Jack. "It's all up to you, now. Do you know what to do?"

Jack nodded, and withdrew the Escher painting from under his arm. "Activate it."

The ex-skeleton touched the painting with the silver rose. A warm argent haze sprang up, surrounded them. It grew brighter and brighter, then suddenly flashed a brilliant white and winked out. When they could see again, the painting was glowing softly, pulsing with life. The ex-skeleton sighed and returned the rose to his lapel. "That's it, then. Off you go."

Jack tucked the painting under his shirt and skinned up the repairman's tree. Using his strong lumberjack's muscles, he edged himself, hand over hand, out along the cable until he hung suspended directly over the vortex. The vortex roared and bellowed below him with the sound of three Boeing 747's crashing together. He was deafened by it, almost paralyzed with fear. Only one thing kept him going, only one thing gave him the courage he needed: His wife. Jack knew that if behaved virtuously in this story, the author might give him other roles to play. Failing that . . . eternity at home with his wife. Even the vortex was better than that!

Hanging by one hand, he carefully unbuttoned his shirt and

withdrew the Escher painting. He heard the skeleton shouting something, but couldn't make out the words. However, he remembered his instructions. The painting had to land exactly in the center of the vortex, so that it would fall through without being torn apart by the tidal forces, and land face-up on the ground of the other dimension immediately underneath the vortex. Well, that shouldn't be too hard. He calculated the distances carefully. Sam was shouting now, too. So was the repairman. The vortex loomed larger and louder. Jack could hardly think for all the noise and confusion.

Then it registered. The vortex was rising straight up!

THE VORTEX HAD HAD a bad first day. As an inanimate corruptive force of nature, it had destroyed wantonly. As a sentient being with higher principles and a moral conscience, it had destroyed incautiously. As a world-weary and wiser day-old being, it was about to destroy again, whether it wanted to or not. It sensed Jack hanging on the wire, and felt only a mild surge of regret as it realized that the topography of the other dimension was leading it directly toward the woodsman.

It was trapped by its very nature. It had no choice but to follow the contours of the other dimension. Philosophy was a bust, it decided. There was no such thing as free will. It was a deterministic universe, and so what if other people got hurt? That's just the way things were.

Still, as it careened madly downhill elsewhere and rose slowly in the forest, it felt the pangs of conscience again. Such a waste, such a waste. Why didn't the silly little man run away?

Its nether end fell endlessly, always seeking lower ground, but the part of it that stuck through into the forest crept inexorably higher, closer to the man on the cable. When the painting fell into its maw, the vortex hardly noticed. The vortex had grown staggeringly large in a metaphysical sense. The painting was no harder for the vortex to swallow than a microbe would be for a human. Yet the vortex sensed something, something very strange, rather like indigestion, as the painting slid down and down.

The painting whirled madly, but was close enough to the center that the vortex's tidal forces didn't make it fly apart. Unlike anything else the vortex had swallowed, the painting was *real*. It mattered. It had Substance. It had contours of its own. It was not acted upon, it was an actor. It didn't dissolve. It burst through the bottom of the vortex, twirled madly on one corner like a spinning coin, then flopped over to settle face-up on the floor of a pub in Cornwall.

The nether end of the vortex leaped onto the painting. It followed the contours of the Escher staircase and was instantly trapped. Down forever, in circles. Unfortunately for Jack, "down" in Cornwall was still "up" in the forest.

Until, that is, the pub's owner noticed the painting. "Here, what's this?" he said. He picked it up, brushed it off, cocked his head, decided he liked it, and hung it on the wall. This had the effect of rotating the vortex ninety degrees from every direction at once, and it effectively disappeared from the universe.

BACK AT THE COTTAGE, Jack Lumber began to understand just how thoroughly he had been betrayed by his author. Granted, he had been allowed to save the day. Granted, he had been allowed a brief thrill of victory (even though, he grumbled, the author hadn't seen fit to mention it except in this bit of exposition). Granted, he had been given the chance to participate in the strangest and wildest night of his life. And he had played his part well. He had been valorous, brave, fearless, daring, and (he told himself) heroic.

It was therefore manifestly unfair that his wife should be waiting for him in the living room when they got back to the cottage.

"Where have you been?" she demanded. "Out all night again with the boys, I suppose? Ruckusing and boozing, no doubt. You got your legs all scratched. Just look at you! Your lovely blue shorts are filthy, just filthy! And I can't *begin* to guess what happened to your frilly white shirt. And just *who* are these *friends* of yours? Jack Lumber, you're in big trouble!"

Jack shrugged in helpless apology to the others, and allowed himself to be led away by the ear. Sam grinned. The repairman turned red, mumbled to himself, and looked away. The fire turned off its sound effects to listen, then hastily doubled the volume. Its blaze took on a distinctly yellow hue.

Sam suddenly yelped. "The sun's coming up!" He raced for the bathroom, then realized he didn't have time. He stood, frozen for one precious moment, then fled out the back door and crawled under the porch just as the sun's first rays touched the forest. Muttering curses, he squished into the least uncomfortable position he could find, and prepared to wait out another day of agony.

The repairman shrugged, helped himself to the pizza, and practiced believing that the television would work even without the cable. The cottage accommodated him, and soon the strains of music videos floated through the forest. The pizza would be better with anchovies, he decided, and he tried believing that the green pepper had changed. Unfortunately, even the belief-actuated technology of the cottage had its limits, so the repairman settled for believing that he might just as well take a nap.

The ex-skeleton, however, paid no attention to any of this. He went immediately to the bedroom and carefully laid the silver rose on the dresser. "Thank you," be breathed, and leaned forward to kiss the rose gently, reverently. Then he moved to the window, pulled aside the drapes, lit a cigarette, and stared moodily into the morning sky. He felt another reverie coming on. This one should be a doozy.

SOUL SONGS

T he phone rang as I started the recorder for the third time. I hit the pause button and answered the call.

"Ethan?" said a voice. "It's your father."

"I don't have a father."

I hung up. Seven calls in three days, the exchange always the same. You'd think he'd learn. I took a deep breath and forced myself back into the mood. Damned if I'd let him ruin this song. I'd been working on it too long. Most of my life. I slid the volume fader up a notch and let the recording play.

A rough mix of yesterday's rhythm tracks filled the room. I'd have to do them over, of course. I couldn't finish the background until I got the melody resolved. But it often helped to record something, anything, while I worked out a tune. I picked up the sax and closed my eyes.

The drums played a steady back beat, not driving, but solid —the stately, unyielding march of the stars across the sky. The bass laid down the mood, low and soft and insistent, pulsing with the sleepy, happy awe of a small boy lying on his back, up in a tree house, looking out at the heavens. The piano played open fifths on bottom, tonic-fourth-octave above, a clean sound with just a hint of tension from the fourth refusing to resolve to either a major third or the fifth. The piano would have to change eventually, to incorporate the minor ninths and diminished chords required to support the song. For now, though, I hoped the open sound would let me hear the theme better. I took a breath and started the melody for "Jackie."

You'd recognize the notes; anyone would. Everybody's looked up at least once to watch the stars. The sax started as the rustle of leaves in the tree, then soared up past them, into the sky, high and hesitant, coming in a rush and then slowing down, backing up, pausing, almost stopping, only to squeal and crack as high as the instrument allowed. With a long bass slide and a matching drum fill, the song slipped into the hook, steadied down. The rhythm guitar slapped on the up-beat, and I settled into the chorus, letting the music spill out.

I didn't have to think about this part. I'd been hearing it for twenty-five years. My fingers worked by themselves, while memories, images, bits of conversations, ran through my mind. I let them wash over me, through me, then pulled them back and fed them into the song, reified, cleansed, distilled. Yes, there was Jackie, diving into the swimming hole, surging up to the surface, laughing and blowing, flicking cold water in my face. The two of us, lying on the summer grass in the late afternoon, sharing dreams and silly jokes. Then as the hook concluded, it was nighttime again. The notes tumbled from my sax, carefree, curious and lively, but with an essential peace and quietude. Phrases that gave the illusion of repetition, but were never exactly the same, formed a sense of inevitability, of timelessness, the nearly hypnotic passage of days in an eternal summer. That was Jackie as I'd known him. The drums and bass formed the tree house beneath us, steady, reassuring. The rhythm guitar became the caress of a cool night wind. I held a long note, trembling with unasked questions, pulsing with the surge of a child's heartbeat, clean and strong, unafraid. Then the bridge came, and the notes turned sour.

I slapped the stop button and repositioned the playback to the beginning. It still wasn't right. The melody kept wandering, and my fingers didn't play what I heard. *Shit.* The bridge was supposed to be joyful, a transition from sleepy awe to self-awareness of the moment—the doubled joy one feels when one knows he is experiencing a moment of grace and transcendence. But although the chords and orchestration were right, the same old dark dissonance kept creeping into my sax. No matter how many times I tried, I still couldn't get this song to come out right. And I'd been trying for fucking ever.

I put down the sax, switched on different music, settled back in the chair, and lit a cigarette. I needed to listen to something different to clear my mind before I attempted "Jackie" again.

Strong, vibrant chords filled the room, no hint of minor keys: A bold, soaring melody that spoke of open air, sunshine, and confidence. That was "Mary," her soul song, my first gold record. The sax growled a frankly sexual theme, and the chords twanged with an unashamed, rutting sensuality. The cymbals whispered like carefree laughter. As I listened, I saw her eyes twinkling, felt her legs wrapped around me. Mary died when I was twenty-two, and the tune haunted me for a year before I recorded it. It was clean, simple, and strong. I'm glad it caught on, because she deserves to be remembered.

I still have the *Times* clipping from when "Mary" started to get critical acclaim. "A sweet, light melody," the reviewer said, "played with Anderson's ineffable touch on the tenor sax. It teases, dances at unexpected moments, never holds still, but somehow still catches the listener's unconscious. . . ."

Bullshit, of course. That asshole wouldn't know a soul song from a first-year Chopin piano exercise. The only thing he got right was the word "ineffable." I proved it when "Bobby" came out later that year. The single went triple-platinum within six months, and suddenly I wasn't a one-hit wonder, but a star.

The minor chords, with those devilish ninth and thirteenth notes, played Bobby's tension between how he felt and how he thought he had to act. The melody flirted with old regrets, and the harmonies sang about resentment. The verses were about loss, whereas the transition to a major key for the hook spoke to the joy of his accomplishments with a near-martial air. The bass slid and throbbed—standard riffs, predictable runs— exactly the way Bobby himself would have played it. He hadn't been the world's most inspired bass player, but he was solid and dependable, knowing when to hit the downbeat in marriage to the kick drum, when to step aside and provide support on the backbeat. The bass track smoothed the transitions, gave strength and solidity to the song. But the drums, piano, bass, percussion, and strings were just the rhythm tracks. The sax carried the soul song, the song he wasn't strong enough, or brave enough, to play. Playing it took me—my talent, my skill. No one else could have done it. But I'd give back all the money and awards if I could trade them for Bobby himself. I wish I'd never heard his song. Just like the Grammy-winning track, his tenure on Earth ended in discord and confusion, a meaningless accident that cut his life short. The real hook behind "Bobby" wasn't the melody at all, but the melody's abrupt ending, leaving listeners waiting for the next note, knowing it wouldn't come, but wanting it, each imagining something slightly different, yet each knowing Bobby as if they'd shared every moment of his life. Mourning and celebration entwined, forever idempotent and co-dependent, self-referential, but bounded in scope only by the essential thread of humanity shared by all who yet breathe. *That's* a soul song. Bobby's death added a bit of entropy to the universe, but the world spun on, and even though he was gone, his essence remained in his eponymous song.

I've always had music in my head. Mom said I started humming harmonies to songs on the radio when I was two or three. She said I started making up songs that early, too, but I don't remember any of them. The first time I deliberately puzzled out a song, fitting a melody to a feeling I couldn't escape, was when I was eleven. I was trying to play "Jackie," of course, but I wasn't old enough to know what I was doing—not empathic enough to hear emotions clearly, barely self-aware enough to recognize them as emotions at all—and my clumsy two-fingered piano work was all about me, nothing about him.

In the summer after fourth grade, Jackson Gartner and I were best friends, together so much that people thought it odd if they saw only one of us. Mrs. Gartner and I were the only ones permitted to call him Jackie, she by right, I by grace, but only when no one could overhear. To everyone else, he was Jack, or "the Gartner boy," but never Jackson or Jackie.

Our parents were friends, too. I remember zooming through our kitchen one afternoon, snatching up a pair of cookies as I ran, barely registering the two women drinking coffee at the table. As the door banged behind me, Mrs. Gartner asked, "Was that Ethan or Jack?" My own mother's chuckle chased me through the screen door and into the yard. "Does it matter?" I remember thinking they were ridiculous. Sure, we were the same height and build, and wore each other's clothes without knowing or caring about the original owner, but we were hardly twins. It was only decades later that I was mature enough to understand the unbridled affection and indulgence underlying their jests.

One of the few memories I have of my father laughing—genuine laughter, that is, not the forced guffaw he usually used—was from that summer, when our parents played card games in the parlor while Jackie and I invented our own kid games in the basement or back yard. The shrieks of adult laughter often sent us, eyes rolling with suppressed giggles, to rove the neighborhood, just to get away from the mortification every child feels when adults forget to act like adults. I hadn't known my father could experience happiness, and his new behavior made me uneasy. Who was this guy, anyway? In another sense, hearing our parents enjoying each other's company so loudly became one of the thousands of secrets Jackie and I kept for each other. Without any need for discussion, we agreed that no one else could ever know that our parents turned into yelping lunatics at night. It was a family secret. By extension, that made Jackie a member of my family, and I of his, and it was summer, and it was glorious because we were brothers and we were free.

Jackie had fair hair, light freckles, a quick grin, and dancing black eyes—the kind of kid everyone instinctively likes. His wide mouth did little but eat, talk and smile, often all three at the same time. I suppose I fell in love with him, the way boys that age sometimes do, experiencing it without naming it, a mutual enchantment with the other below the level of conscious perception. He was my other half, and I was his. It was that simple, and that complex. One of the world's everyday, commonplace miracles, twenty-five years gone now, but still fresh to me. Maybe everyone has had such a friend. Maybe no one has. How to compare? But that was *our* summer; the summer I found him without looking, the summer I loved him without knowing, the summer I lost him without understanding.

His soul song emerged at odd times, usually quiet moments, late at night when we camped out in the old tree fort, long after we should have been asleep. As the summer passed inexorably toward autumn, I heard it over and over, in those unguarded moments when his barriers fell and the night became a living, breathing thing around us. I didn't recognize it at first. It wasn't even fully music, just a feeling that hinted at a tune. I had no idea I was hearing the edges of a threnody, the beginnings of a jeremiad.

One night as we lay on our backs, looking up at the stars through the branches of the tree, breathing in unison, saying nothing, I tried to sing what I heard.

He started crying before I finished. I propped myself up on one elbow and leaned over, curious and concerned. He sobbed softly, dark eyes wide open, liquid in the starlight. "Jackie?" I said. "Jack? What's wrong?"

He looked at me for a long moment, then reached over and pulled me down, close to him, and held me there. I froze in confusion as he cried. Branches stirred above us, tears rolled down his cheeks, and his breath blew sweet in my nostrils. He moved ever so slightly, and his lips brushed past mine as if by accident, surprising and embarrassing both of us, then he pushed me away. His lips had been feather-light and dry; the kiss itself as brief and final as the last period of an epic novel. It told me nothing but that a long story had preceded it, a story I had never read and maybe wasn't old enough to understand. But, God help me, even today I remember the taste of him, the sudden sweet urgency of the moment, as clearly as if it were still happening. Before I could say something, or punch his shoulder, or do any of the hundred things that sprang to mind, he turned on his side and buried his face in his arms.

I should have said something. I should have done something. I should have made him tell me what was wrong. How could the song have affected him so strongly? But I was only eleven, and I didn't know what to do, so I did nothing. I turned over and went to sleep listening to his soft sobbing, the tune and his tears merging toward a song in my mind.

The next afternoon he blew his head off with his father's gun. Brains and blood all over the wall. A terribly tragedy, they all said, and the cops and the Gartners believed it was an accident—a stupid kid playing with a stupid gun he should have fucking known to keep his stupid hands away from—but I never believed it. I knew he'd killed himself, and that he'd tried to tell me something the night before. I just didn't know what, or why. I hoped to God it wasn't because I sang his song to him, or because I'd made him want to kiss me. He would never tell me now. Had he kissed me good-bye, knowing what he was going to do?

That was how summer ended, and how my family ended. The funeral came and went, but there were no more evenings with the adults playing in one room and the kids in another. The Gartners had some sort of terrifically bitter adult squabble with my parents that, either despite their grief or because of it, drove Jackie's parents away from mine. I lost Jackie and my second family in less than a week. I never caught the details, because I didn't bother listening. I didn't much care about anything. Priests solemnly intoned platitudes, parents went dutifully back to work, mourners mourned and then forgot, birds sang, and day followed night as if the world hadn't been turned upside-down. I became aware, gradually, that the rancor hadn't lessened after the Gartners stopped talking to us. The fighting went on, now between my father and mother, where it belonged anyway, with much shouting and slamming of doors, until with one final emphatic door slam, my father left us. I was so numb from losing my best friend mere weeks before that the only emotion I experienced was gladness for the quiet. I had no way to know he would never come back.

I've tried—I don't know, a dozen, two dozen, a hundred times?—to finish the tune I heard the night before Jackie died, but every time it comes out wrong. Something I'm hearing, or not hearing, interferes with the melody. I didn't like remembering, but I *had* to know the rest of Jackie's song.

The phone rang again. I sighed, clicked off the playback, and answered. "Yes?"

"Ethan, it's Louise."

Oomph. I paused, waiting for my heart to stop pounding. "Lou. It's been . . . a long time."

Her breath was loud in my ear. Memories flooded me from out of nowhere. I smelled her perfume, saw her green eyes and long red hair. It felt as if she were right beside me again, sharing everything, being everything.

"Yes," she said. "A long time. We need to talk."

A welter of emotions crisscrossed my brain. *Talk, yes.* God, I needed to talk to her, wanted to talk to her. But I didn't know what to say, how to start.

She waited a moment, then said, "It's about your father."

What the—? Louise had never met Dad, but she knew how I felt about him. I remembered him mainly from the occasional birthday party or holiday trip. He would attend sullenly, without trying to hide his annoyance, as if Mom and I were chains holding him back from something more important. Such events always ended in a shouting match, as he and my mother argued about whatever imagined slight or deficiency he perceived. He had laughed that one summer twenty-five years ago, but I sometimes doubted the memory. What I could remember without trying were the fights, always the fights. Mom never talked about him after he left without cursing. The first time he ever showed any interest in me was long after that, when I was grown and "Mary" hit the charts. He got my phone number somehow and called me. I said, "Dad who?" and hung up on him. I thought at the time he wanted money. He hadn't tried to call me again—not until this week. And now Louise was calling, not to talk about us, not even to talk about Scotty, but to discuss my father. My hands trembled as I lit another cigarette.

"What about him?" I asked at last.

"When he couldn't get through to you, he called me. He's in the hospital, Ethan. He wants to see you."

"So?"

"So you should go see him."

"Why?"

"Because he's your father, and because there's something you can do for him that no one else can do."

"Shit, Lou, no! That isn't how it works."

"He's dying, Ethan. I know how *that* works. And I know how your music works. Think about it, please. And, Ethan—?" She paused. Her voice caught. "I'll be at the hospital if you change your mind. I'd like to see you again."

"Goddammit, Lou, that's not fair!"

"I know," she said very gently, and hung up.

I sat there holding the phone until it started beeping at me. Her words echoed through my brain. I knew what she meant.

When Mom had died five years ago, I brought out *Jennifer*, not a single this time, but a whole album. Mom's soul song carried it. I wove the theme into all the cuts, sometimes happy, sometimes sad, and her love burst through the music and became alive. It was the first time I'd used the flute in a recording, although I'd tinkered with the instrument ever since I started hearing the first hints of her melody. Nothing less would carry the theme. The critics raved, said I'd brought something new to jazz by introducing the flute. They're idiots, of course; what I brought to jazz wasn't an instrument, but a person.

Mom wasn't a complicated woman, and her theme was as old as the endless cycle of the seasons. Progression, regression, reinvention, repetition, variations on a theme, but the same song throughout. It hits you as proper, correct, even stately, yet filled with unexpected depths of emotion and melodic phrasings that couldn't be predicted, but, once heard, seemed inevitable. Everything on the surface goes along exactly as it should, but you feel odd flutterings and a sense of restlessness, like holding a small bird in your hand. The flute can show that. It's deep and throaty at one moment, then soars in exultation at the next, always trembling, always full of living breath. You can't ignore the lungs, throat, and lips that work the flute. The pounding of blood, the rhythm of breath, are part of the music.

The notes themselves weren't that important. I improvised to the rhythm tracks, and we kept the first take. A series of harsh, bleating notes: Her sacrifices for me, the lonely years of raising me mostly by herself. Soft, teasing variations on a theme, played high and piping: Her daydreams, her hopes. Shuddering staccato, breathy and loud: Her never-ending battle with her weight, her concern with her appearance. Sweet, light notes, chasing each other across the octaves: Her charm as a hostess, her love of bright laughter. A long, moody passage, filled with diminished notes and trailing, lingering moans: Her dark suspicion that her prom night, long ago, was the happiest she'd ever been, the happiest she'd ever be.

I played her long battle with cancer, the flute echoing the bone-deep ache that never left during the last six months. I played her face as a series of low pulses, rounded and full, lighting up with joy to see me, even with the tubes connected everywhere and the machines humming and droning a death watch. The last song on the album was a solo, as everyone's last song must be, and I played her death juxtaposed against her life, revisiting all the melodies that came before. I gave them new depth in the process, brought them all to a crescendo that whispered away before the climax, petered out into stuttering staccato breaths on the flute that grew farther and farther apart from each other, from the world itself, the ultimate diminuendo, until silence was the only note left to play.

They tell me I cried as I played, but if so, I never knew it. I played her soul song, strong then, stronger than I'd ever heard it, and as the last notes whispered away into dark like rose petals drifting down on a casket, I knew I'd never played better in my life. That was Mom; she always brought out the best in me.

It didn't take long for the media and my fans to figure out that all of my best songs were named for people I'd known, people who'd died. The other songs I write are good; if I'd never recorded a soul song, I'd still probably be a minor success in music. But the super-stardom has come from the songs I didn't write, but only heard and shared.

Jennifer made me rich enough that I'll never have to work again. When your portfolio gets to a certain size, it takes on a life of its own, and you turn it over to professionals. Money and I have finally come to an accommodation: If I see something I want, I buy it. But I'm not a pop star, or even crazy rich.

Jazz isn't like that. I don't do videos. I don't perform. I can go out in public without being recognized. But over seventy percent of the homes in America have one or more of my albums, and the numbers are even higher in Europe and Japan. Did any of that bring Mom back? Of course not, but then she wasn't really gone, not while *Jennifer* existed, not while anyone could listen to it and know her.

My throat constricted and my ears got hot. *That's* what Lou wanted me to do for my father. Lou knew me better than anyone in the world; she should have known better than to ask that of me. I pounded the arm of my chair, then got up and paced. Visions assailed me. Lou, red hair tumbling, fingers scratching, her back arched as we made love. Lou, listening and understanding as I talked about the grief, the guilt, the music. Lou, smoothing away the nightmares, holding my hand as we walked together. Lou, bulging with our unborn child, full of life and love. Lou, at Scotty's funeral, self-contained, unreachable. Lou, trying to pull me back from the edge, failing, giving up. Lou, face gone still as a deep pool, telling me she'd had enough, was moving out.

A song started up in my head. It's not her fault, but I can't think about Lou without thinking about Scotty, and that brings on the tune, and then there's no escape.

You know how songs sometimes get stuck in your head? A bit of rhythm, a lyric or two, a chord progression, or a snappy melody? Sometimes the whole damned song, from start to finish, sometimes just the chorus, or one special verse? Advertising jingles aim for it; when they work, America hums a new tune overnight. No one knows why it happens. The A&R guys just rub their palms together and count their money; artists shrug, grin, and say, "Catchy, huh?" Songwriters call the refrain a "hook" for a reason; they don't know what it is, or how it works, but they recognize it when they hear it.

I produce it consistently. Even if you hate my songs, you know a dozen of them—you can't get them out of your head. What you *like* has nothing to do with it. Sometimes a song hits below the conscious level, sneaks right past your defenses. They call them "earworms," and all of my songs, to one degree or another, had that quality, but the soul songs were the strongest. You might be washing the dishes, and find that your toes are tapping out the rhythm to "Bobby," or trying to read, and find yourself humming something from *Jennifer*. The next day when you wake up, you're *still* humming it, and you don't know why, and you can't make it stop.

It's worse for musicians. We smell and taste and feel music in our bones, live a tiny bit closer to the rhythms and melodies that move us all. A tune that resonates too much can invade all our work. We think we're playing a new riff, and it doesn't sound quite right, so we change it just a bit, and suddenly discover it's the same old song, the one that won't get out of our heads, the one we've been playing bits and snatches of in every goddamned song for the past month. Sometimes a tune can flavor our output for a lot longer than that.

What makes one song the kind that sticks in your craw, but another just a pleasant tune that you forget immediately? I could show you pictures of Scotty, or tell you about him, but everyone in the Western world has heard "Little Scott," and already knows all there is to tell. It's a bittersweet piece in my mind, but just sad, I think, for everyone else. The kind of sadness that makes you cry without knowing why—a sense of loss, of unbearable unfairness. I did it with the alto sax, no other instruments, just a three-minute solo cut on an otherwise uninspired album. I let the sax howl and scream and moan, but it kept coming back to the refrain, a simple little melody that with each repetition becomes more forlorn, more heartbroken, until it finally fades out, and you can't tell when the playing stops, because your head picks it up and keeps it spinning for fucking ever.

I heard the first faint echoes of that melody the day I held Scotty in my arms at the hospital. Louise smiled so proudly, so happily, but I couldn't stop crying. I guess she thought I was happy, too. "He's beautiful," I told her around the tears.

They diagnosed fragile X syndrome when he turned three and still hadn't starting talking. I didn't care about all the other milestones he'd missed; I'd known all along he was suffering inside. When he was awake and unresponsive to our ministrations, I heard his song, faintly, like a radio turned way down in the other room. When he slept or lay quietly, different parts of it came through. When he seethed with anger, I knew it was directed inward, but it was as much a part of his song as everything else. Over the next few years, he developed his theme in his own private world, and I watched and listened helplessly to what only he and I could hear.

One day, to see how he'd react, I tried dinking out the hook for him on the piano. He went into a frenzy of head-banging, blood spraying out, covering us both before I could get him to stop. That was the only time Scotty displayed self-injurious behavior. I never tried that experiment again. He knew the tune, all right, and hated it.

It got to the point where Louise and I couldn't handle him anymore. The constant rocking, the vestibular self-stimulation, wasn't so bad. It meant he was contained in his own world. But we couldn't leave him alone for a second. The placid rocking could turn to full-on rage with no discernible trigger, and he grew big enough to kick, bite, and throw small pieces of furniture. He broke windows by pounding on them, once severing an artery in his elbow and nearly exsanguinating before the paramedics arrived. Lou and I were covered with scratches, bites, lacerations, and contusions just from his daily care. It was hell on our marriage. Scotty made our lives as miserable as his own, not because he wanted to, but because he had no choice. It took every damned minute of every day to keep him from hurting himself, and we had no time for each other. Respite services were a joke; no respite worker ever came back for a second shift with him.

Lou held out until Scotty was eight, then convinced me that we had to send him to a residential school for special-needs kids, the kind where children have 24-hour supervision and training. They keep the doors locked, because the kids don't know enough to keep from wandering away. They don't try to teach them to read and write, or to count, or to play with other kids. Instead they work on things like eating, using the toilet, and getting dressed. They hoped to get Scotty out of diapers by the time he turned twelve.

He was developmentally disabled and aggressive. He never learned to talk, or to eat with a spoon. He was still our son, and I knew, even when Louise gave up on him, that *someone* lurked behind those eyes, someone alive, trapped in a living hell of a body that wouldn't cooperate and a brain that didn't work. I was still his father, and I loved him, even if he couldn't recognize my face or say my name. I didn't want to put him in a home, but Lou was right. There's a saying, "Love can't fix everything." I didn't understand it until faced with the decision about placing Scotty. For his sake, and for our own, I agreed, knowing all the while it was wrong, but not having any other choice. Louise and I could no longer meet his needs.

He lasted less than a year. The staff found out about his pica when he started vomiting blood. We never knew about it, either, and the doctor explained the term to us. *Pica* is when people eat things that aren't food. Scotty always had something in his mouth, but we never knew he swallowed. Like any baby, he wanted to put shiny things in his mouth, taste them with his tongue. We always took it away when we saw it, but I guess we didn't see it often enough. The staff at the school noticed it even less.

He had a wad of aluminum foil in his stomach the size of a baseball, built up from candy and gum wrappers. The bits of broken glass cut his stomach and intestines to ribbons. He didn't show any particular signs of distress—how could he? What could he do, throw a tantrum? How could anyone tell it apart from all his other tantrums?

In the end, sepsis got him via a perforated bowel, despite the IV antibiotics. If they'd known sooner, maybe the doctors could have saved him. He never stabilized enough for them to attempt surgery. It all happened too quickly. One day he started vomiting blood, and the next day he lay in my arms in the hospital, only nine years old, panting and twisting like an animal at first, very quiet at the end. Then he slipped away. But in the moments before his death, he gave me the rest of his song, and I gave it to the rest of the world. No one who's heard it can forget it, but God damn you to hell if you say you like it.

After I finished recording "Little Scott," I went out and got stinking drunk. For the next year, I drank so much of the time that I wouldn't have known my own name if you asked me. It didn't help. I could still hear the song, over and over, an endless loop in my mind, no matter how hard I tried to shut it off. Maybe Louise and I could have grown closer because of it, but we didn't. Looking at her reminded me of him, and thinking of him brought on the song. So I drank, and the song and the booze tore up my insides, and I changed somehow, and when Lou left I only felt relief.

It took me another couple of months after that to dry out. I found, oddly, that playing the song helped lay the demons. After I'd resisted as long as I could, I played it again one day, and discovered that the anger and the pain had become something new. It still hurt, but I'd reached a new plateau, and I could bear it. After a while, it even became comforting, a reminder how deeply Lou and I had loved Scotty.

That's when I first admitted to myself that I didn't write my hits. A song catches a listener because it matches some basic human rhythm, some pulse of the mind. It's biological; it resonates in the limbic system, in the hindbrain, well below cognition or even volition. No one who's ever heard the opening to Beethoven's Fifth can doubt it. Everyone has these rhythms in his mind, these melodies in his soul. From "Greensleeves" to the latest jingle, they match different moods, different feelings, and when the right pattern of sounds hits your ear, it goes straight past your consciousness to hammer on your cerebellum directly. It sets up a resonance. Your foot starts tapping, or your eyes brim with unexplained tears, or you're suddenly ten feet tall and ready to kill dragons, all without your ever knowing why.

Maybe it starts before birth, with the surge of your mother's blood in the womb. Maybe it's the rhythm of your own heartbeat, or your own breath. But however it starts, it never stops. You build your soul song minute by minute, experience by experience. Sometimes, even if it's only for a while, you find someone whose song complements yours, whose melody plays along with yours and doesn't clash, and you form a friendship, or a marriage. It could last for an hour, or a decade, or a lifetime. You don't know what you're hearing, and you can't pick out the common parts, the original melodies, from the harmonies you write together.

When something outside ourselves—the ring of a trumpet, the rasp of a cello, the raw sexuality of an electric guitar— inadvertently plays part of it, we *know*. It's like remembering, or recognizing a long-lost face. There are no words to describe it. Poets have tried. Something within you sings, and you know, at a level below words.

I was born with the ability to hear soul songs, not the faint echo of a tune everyone hears and recognizes, but the whole thing. It only works with people I love, and only while they're dying, or inherently marked by death. In those moments, their souls sing loudly enough for me to hear. I take that song, boil it down, distill it, until only the theme, the essence, remains, and then pour it out for others. It sounds familiar to the ear the first time you hear it, and thereafter you can't get rid of it.

That's what Louise wanted me—damned near told me—to do for my father. *Screw her.* I didn't owe her that. I didn't owe *him* that. Besides, I couldn't do it even if I wanted to. I was never close enough to the old man. I remember the only piece of advice he ever gave me. At my tenth birthday party, I told him about the crush I had on a girl from school. "When you grow up," he said, "find a woman you already hate and give her a house. It's easier than divorce." He was a cynical old shit, and I guess he meant it, too, because that's what he did to my mother.

I picked up the sax and started the rhythm tracks for "Jackie" again. Maybe this time I could get it right. I'd only been working on it for twenty-five years.

Just as I started to play, though, the phone rang.

I didn't know whether to laugh or scream in hysterics. I did neither. I put down the sax and answered the phone.

"Mr. Anderson? Ethan Anderson?"

I didn't recognize the voice. It was some woman I didn't know. "Yes?" I said, despite my instinct to just hang up.

"Mr. Anderson, this is Dr. Phillips at Memorial Medical Center."

"How did you get this number? Charity requests are supposed to go through my staff. If you'll—"

"Mr. Anderson, I'm your father's physician."

Umph. I waited.

"Mr. Anderson? Are you there? Your father is dying. I can't say how long he has. Maybe a week, maybe less. Maybe a lot less. The thing is, he wants to see you."

"Why?"

"Ah, um." Dr. Phillips sounded flustered. I could hear her talking to someone else in the background, muffled, as if she had her hand over the phone. Then she came back. "Mr. Anderson, perhaps you didn't hear me. He's dying."

"Good," I said, and disconnected.

Enough of this. Time to get away. I owned a cabin two hours north, overlooking a small lake, nestled inside a couple dozen acres of pine and white birch. It was my refuge, a place of emotional safety. No phone service, no cable, satellite, or neighbors. Just trees, bird-song, and bright sun glinting off cold blue water. Right now I needed to be there, to be alone.

I waited for a second, then punched the intercom button.

"Yes, sir?"

"Get my personal line's number changed again. And have someone bring up the car. I'm going to the cabin for a couple of days."

"Yes, sir; right away. Which car?"

Uh, dammit— "What's the temperature outside?"

"Mid-70's, sir. A beautiful autumn day."

"The Porsche, then, with the top down." I shut off all the equipment, picked up the alto sax, and went outside.

I hummed as I drove—a strange new tune, but somehow hauntingly familiar. The miles churned past beneath the tires, the rhythm of the road a grim beat underlying my melody. It sounded a lot like "Jackie," but sharper, angrier, and some of the cadences refused to resolve.

I didn't realize I wasn't going north until I saw the turnoff for downtown. Even then, it took me a moment to understand what had happened. How could I have gone the wrong way? I remembered getting into the car, pulling onto the north feeder ramp for the freeway, and then—? The song had bewitched me, like highway hypnotism. *Shit.* I swung off onto the exit, intending to turn around at the underpass.

Memorial Medical Center has a circular drive in front, but you can't park there. I followed the signs for visitor parking, found a spot and shut off the engine, still humming under my breath. I could hear most of the song by now, but some sections still didn't fit. I sat there for a minute, working on the song, then looked around. It felt like waking up. Sweet Jesus, how could I have forgotten where I was going? How did I end up here? I tilted down the rear-view mirror and glared at my reflection. "You're an idiot," I said to my subconscious.

I almost drove away. Then I said, "Fuck it," picked up my sax, locked the car, and walked into the hospital. Louise saw me right inside the door, and suddenly I found my arms around her, my face buried in her auburn hair.

"I knew you'd come, Ethan," she said.

"That makes one of us." I held her at arm's distance, pushed the hair back from her face. She wore a green dress with a white scarf, and I smelled her perfume. God, she was beautiful.

I wanted to tell her how much I'd missed her. How much it

hurt to see her again. How her eyes reminded me of Scotty. How her voice ripped me apart inside. How I wanted to be anywhere in the world except here with her, and how I couldn't bear to leave her ever again.

"I stopped drinking," I said, but what I meant was "I'm sorry."

"I know," she said, and for all the world it sounded just like "I forgive you."

She went in with me. I wouldn't have left the lobby of the hospital if she hadn't led me, urged me, pushed me, into his room. The sharp smell of disinfectant mingled with the sickly-sweet odor of illness. I wanted to gag.

I stared at the thing in the bed and wondered why he didn't seem familiar. There were tubes up his nose. A bottle hung from an IV stand on the right, and wires from a machine disappeared under the thin hospital gown. Other tubes, translucent yellow, with a dark fluid inside, ran from a large blue machine to a patch of tape at his waist. The IV attached to the back of his right hand and some other tube sucked at the inside of his left elbow. It looked like only his eyes, ears and mouth weren't connected to something. The pump in the blue machine whirred softly. I recognized the pinging sound of a heart monitor. The rest was incomprehensible. A couple of chairs stood by the bed, but I didn't sit down. I might have turned around and left if Lou hadn't been holding my hand.

He looked past me, to Louise, and goddamn if he didn't smile. "Thank you," he said to her. Then the smile went away, and he looked at me, searching my face, noticing everything about me, from the sax in my hands to the cut of my hair. He gathered his strength to talk. His voice came out strong, normal, but it cost him plenty to move his arms or turn his head. "I'm glad you came, Ethan."

"What are you dying of?" I said. "How long will it take? I have lunch plans."

He winced. "Ethan, there's something I have to tell you."

"I don't want to hear it."

Louise murmured something placatory, but I waved her off. "I came here. Now I'm going. That's more than you deserved."

"I know you think I was a shitty father," he said.

"Shut up," I explained. "You don't know anything, *anything!*"

He proceeded to prove me wrong. "Jackson Gartner," he said, as if that were meaningful, and he began humming.

I wanted to shut it out, but I couldn't. Without trying, without really wanting to, I listened. It only took five notes for me to recognize it: The summer of my eleventh year. The first soul song I'd ever heard clearly. Jackie's death the next day. The song I'd been trying to get right for twenty-five years. The song I'd been working on just this morning. There was no way Dad could know it, yet he echoed it note for note through the first verse, bringing Jackie back to life for a moment—the quicksilver smile, the twinkling eyes, the honey taste of his lips brushing mine in the most private and holy moment I'd ever experienced.

"Mother of God," I whispered. "You heard it, too." I sank into a chair. Louise didn't sit, but she stood behind me, gently massaged my shoulders. My hands trembled. I pulled out a cigarette, fumbled with the lighter, then saw the no-smoking sign and paused.

"Go ahead," said Dad. "I'm not on oxygen today."

I lit the cigarette, filled my lungs with bitter smoke, and exhaled through clenched teeth. After two or three puffs, my jaw muscles relaxed and my hands steadied down. His eyes never left my face.

"Is that what you wanted to tell me?" I asked. "That you can hear what I hear?"

"No, I can't. I overheard you singing it to yourself once. I've never been able to forget it. I knew it was Jack's song. I recognized it, recognized *him*. I knew, back then, what you were, what you could do."

"Why bring it up now?"

"To get you to listen."

Whumph. Why not a two-by-four instead? "I'm listening," I said at last. "What do you want?"

"A chance to explain. Forgiveness, maybe."

"Fuck you."

"Don't smartass me, Ethan. I'm still your father."

"Right. You hump my mother one night and that gets you eternal respect and filial duty? Sorry, it doesn't work that way. The only things you get from screwing are social diseases and the opportunity to pay child support. Which, by the way, Mom said you never did. Fatherhood takes more of an investment."

"Ethan," Lou said, her voice very soft, but she stopped. I don't know what she would have said next, or if I would have been able to listen.

Goddamn if my father didn't try to slap me. He didn't have the strength for it. He fell back, exhausted, and spent several minutes working on his breathing. I smoked and glared at him, privately wondering if my smoke bothered him, and if I'd smoke more or less if I knew the answer.

"What's wrong with you, anyway?" I asked at last.

I didn't think he would answer. He lay there with his eyes closed, panting. The veins in his arms stood out, purple against his pale, papery skin. "Cancer," he said, finally. "They opened me for exploratory surgery last week, and closed me right back up again. My organs are failing, one after the other." He pointed to the blue machine, the one with the pump. "That one cleans my blood for me. They have another one to breathe for me when my lungs stop. Thank God I haven't needed it yet. I don't want it and have signed the papers: 'No heroic measures' and 'Do not resuscitate,' in big red letters on my chart. But you can never trust doctors. They'll declare me incompetent, double-sign the chart, and intubate anyway. I can't imagine why, except that's what they do. Even if they could fix my liver, lungs, kidneys, pancreas, and colon, my heart is giving out. No transplants for someone in my condition. Why put a viable organ inside a body filled with mets? I've already had two bypasses, and the breathing problem comes from congestive heart failure."

"I'm sorry," said Lou when it became obvious I would remain silent. Thank God for her just then. I reached up, found her hands on my shoulder, and pulled her around to sit beside me while I digested what he'd said.

Multi-organ system failure pending. Dialysis already on board. Pleural and cardiac damage. "Mets"—metastases—the original cancer spawning malignancies in distant organs. Dr. Phillips had been optimistic. Given what I saw, Dad had a day, maybe only hours left. And he'd signed a DNR but didn't trust the doctors to withhold the ventilator. Why tell me that? Wait . . . "I'm your next-of-kin now that Mom's gone. You want me to co-sign your DNR? Hand me the form and a pen."

"Fuck you," he said pleasantly. For just a second, his echo of my profanity was funny, and we shared the joke. It only lasted that one second before I remembered how much I hated him. I tried to force myself to overcome that, but the best I could manage was a sincerely faked fake sincerity that we both knew was a lie. Lou nudged me, so I did the things people do in these situations.

"Does it hurt much?" I asked, half-hoping the answer

was *yes.*

"Not anymore," he said. "I'm so full of drugs that I can hardly tell whether I'm asleep or awake most of the time."

"Morphine in the drip? You seem pretty awake to me."

"I don't know. I don't care. I don't think so. They put special shots in my IV when it's really bad, other shots for normal days. When they give me the shots, I drift off and nap. Then I wake up and the only thing I want is another shot. Every now and then they dissolve something under my tongue. I'm not sure if it's for the nausea or the pain. I'm just a husk, waiting to expire."

I sat there in silence until I finished my cigarette. There was no ashtray, so I crushed the butt with my heel. "Why did you *really* want to see me, Dad? It can't be for forgiveness. You don't deserve that, and you know you won't get it. So it's something else. Do you need money? If you do—"

He interrupted me, not by talking, but with a look I suddenly remembered fearing in my childhood. The look still had its old power. I shut up and waited.

"This body is worn out, eaten alive from the inside. Money isn't the problem. More of it wouldn't help. I want something else from you. I want you to listen. I want to explain. Ethan . . . I've always loved you. I want you to know why—"

My anger boiled over. "Dad, I'm sorry, but you *left.* You skipped out. I was eleven. Just a kid. Hell, I needed you, and you weren't there. And now you want me to listen to this shit? It's too late, Dad. Years too late. If you cared about me—about Mom and me—you would have stayed. Christ! Don't you believe in commitment? Were you thinking that some kind of death-bed confession would make up for all the years that you weren't around when I needed you?" I stood up, shouted at him. He lay with his eyes closed, a pained expression on his face, taking it in. "You *hurt* me, Dad. You hurt Mom, too. And if you think I'm going to forgive you now, you're wrong. Don't you get it? I hated you. I still hate you. You're a no-good fuck-up. Sweet Jesus, you *deserted* us! Deserted me. There's no excuse. There's *nothing* you can say to make up for that."

I ran out of steam and stopped. Tears leaked from under his shut eyelids, but he made no effort to wipe them away.

Finally, his voice husky, he said, "I deserved that."

"Damn right, you son of a bitch."

I felt a tremendous sense of relief. I don't think I'd realized how much resentment I felt until I gave it voice. I'd been saving it up for a long, long time. I wanted to hurt him back, wanted to make him admit his mistakes, wanted to make him eat dirt for the pain he'd given me. And I *had* hurt him. He had no comeback, no defense against my anger. I should have felt victorious, but the satisfaction was hollow. I began to feel guilty for bullying a sick old man.

He opened his eyes again and asked softly, "Are you through?"

I shrugged and sat down. "If you want to explain, go ahead."

"Evelyn Gartner."

Jackie's mom? Is that who he meant? He said it and then stopped, as if those two words constituted an explanation. I raised an eyebrow. "Come again?"

"Evelyn Gartner. You rememb—"

"Your bridge and pinochle partner. Mom's best friend, until you ruined that relationship for them. And, um, oh, yeah, Mrs. Gartner was my best friend's mother. His *mother*—the only other person in the world allowed to call him by his baby name. I think I recall something about them. I'm not sure. Isn't Jackie the one who died? He was only a friend, anyway, the one I lost twenty-five years ago. The one whose song you hummed to get my attention. Why would I remember any of *that*? Nope, the name's a complete and fucking blank. You had my attention, but you're rapidly losing it. What *about* her?"

His eyes didn't flash with anger as I'd hoped. He just looked at me evenly until I ran down.

"I thought you'd already gotten that out of your system," he said at last.

"The first performance seemed to require an encore."

"Can we drop the sarcasm? Yes, she was my bridge partner. Yes, she was your mother's best friend for years. But she wasn't *just* my bridge partner."

A coughing spasm left him too weak to continue. Lou quietly got up and rearranged his pillows, then resumed her seat beside me. While we waited for him to catch his breath, I filled in the rest of the tawdry story without his help. It was so obvious now, and so depressingly common it didn't rate any death-bed confessional time. "An affair?" I said. "How sordid of you. I suppose that's why you laughed so much that summer. You were happy while destroying two marriages. You were *happy*. What an asshole. A commonplace piece of shit pretending it doesn't stink. Well, it does. You failed as a father and as a husband. You failed as a human being. Even your last confession is pathetic. Well, *non ego te absolvo*. I don't forgive you for Mom. I don't forgive you for me. I hope the affair was worth it. Have a nice death."

I stood and would have left, even with Lou plucking at my shirt and urging me to calm down, but then something suddenly clicked—slid into place neatly—and all the disparate pieces of that fateful summer fit together. It made sense by gestalt—the things unsaid, or half-said; the looks; the inner silence I never penetrated; the dark harmonies in Jackie's soul song. A song I'd heard but not been able to understand until this moment. I sank wearily back into the chair.

"Ah, shit. Jackie knew about it."

He nodded. Louise gasped.

"And that's why he killed himself. Congratulations, shithead; you emotionally tortured my best friend into suicide."

"He didn't kill himself, Ethan."

"I know what everyone says, but Jackie would never *play* with a gun. He shot himself deliberately. He *planned* it. He nearly told me about it. I wish he had—maybe I could have stopped him. It wasn't an accident. I wish it was, but I've never believed that story, and I don't believe it now. He killed himself, and now I know why. Because of *you*. Because you couldn't keep your dick in your boxers, and he found out. He was too—"

My father waved a hand weakly and gave me that look, so I stopped, trapped by childhood conditioning, and waited for him to speak. I'm not sure what I would have said next anyway. Jackie was too—what? Too pure, too good, too proud? No, that was sheer romanticization. He had just been a kid whose emotions overruled his reason, and he had killed himself to escape my father's essential rot. I ran out of patience. "Well, what then? What could you possibly add to make things worse?

"It wasn't suicide, Ethan. And it wasn't an accident, either. I have never told anyone about this."

The hairs on the back of my neck rose. Lou's hand found mine and clung fiercely. I found my voice again, without knowing how long I'd been silent. "You still haven't told anyone anything, fuckface. If it wasn't an accident, and wasn't suicide, then what?" His implication was clear, but too horrific to take seriously. But he was serious, and I knew it. After the first shock, a deadly calm washed through me, making my voice frigid, my posture stiff. "Say the words, Dad. You have to say the words."

He nodded, and closed his eyes. "I killed him." Three short

words, barely above the level of a whisper. The iciness in my veins seemed to spread to my mind. I'd known what he would say, but actually hearing it? I knew instantly that it was truth. Time slowed to a crawl, and my vision narrowed to a tunnel. I found myself staring at his fingernails above the coverlet as the three words dropped heavily across my life, each a string being plucked. Playing a melody that could never have been predicted, but, once heard, became inevitable. The missing notes from Jackie's soul song. Beside me, Lou shuddered as she took in his admission, and her hand became a claw in my grip. I smoothed out her fingers until they lay flat on my thigh, and covered them with my own.

"Okay," I said, still filled with the deadly calm that allowed my heart to beat, my vocal cords to work. "Okay. I believe you. But why, Dad? *Why?*"

Eyes still closed, voice still soft, he explained. "Because he saw us. The Gartners were very religious, at least a lot more than we were. Your friend was convinced I'd trapped his mother into a mortal sin."

Fuck religion. I didn't buy it. "Mortal sins" were just words he'd heard in catechism class, not some life-wrecking realities that actually mattered. "You son of a bitch!" I yelled, my icy calm dissolving into anger. "So what? So he saw you. So fucking what?"

"He was always around," my father continued as if I hadn't spoken. "Always around, but always with you. So we didn't think—didn't guess—that he might show up while you and your mother were at the store." He shrugged briefly. "We thought it was safe, and then he was there, staring at us, just staring." He sighed and squeezed his eyes even more tightly closed, forcing himself to finish the narrative. "We tried to talk to him, convince him it didn't mean anything, not really. It was adult stuff he was too young to understand, that's all. Evelyn was so worried he might think it was his fault. After all the talking, I think the only thing he retained was that he mustn't tell."

I sat there, trying to absorb the information. I didn't know whether to be angry or sad. I didn't feel anything, really, except numbness. In a way, I guess I still didn't believe him. "So what?" I said in lieu of anything else. "He never told. Your stupid little secret was safe."

Now my father opened his eyes, met my gaze levelly. "He would have. I had so many talks with him that summer, trying to justify myself mainly, but also trying to convince him. I thought I was winning him over, but I failed. The best I could do was put off the execution date. As time went on, he became more stubborn, and eventually gave me an ultimatum: Either I would tell, or he would. No middle ground, no more room for persuasion or evasion."

"So you killed him? *Really?* You're a lying sack of shit. I don't believe a word you say. Either the drugs are fucking with your memory, or you're making it all up just to hurt me for some sick, twisted reason I hope I never understand."

He didn't reply, but he didn't drop his eyes, either. "Okay," I said at last, my tone brisk. I made a show of standing up, pretending to wash my hands. I met Lou's eyes briefly. She saw the coldness in me and looked away. But she stood beside me anyway, and breathed, "Ethan, don't."

I was beyond her reach. "This has been an entertaining little reunion," I told my father. "We should have done it years ago. Thanks for fucking with my head one last time. Enjoy losing your mind as easily as you lost your family. I'll be going now."

Lou and I were at the door when he rasped, "The cops were

right, it *was* an accident."

"Jesus fucking Christ," I bellowed. "Give it up already. You're not making sense." Louise and I held hands and stared at him in disbelief.

Dad went on, relentlessly. "He was going to tell the priest. All our talks had been for nothing. He was determined, with that sanctimonious piety of his, to right the wrong, stop the sinning. I told him to shut up. I told him terrible things could happen if he told. He didn't back down. He. . . ." Dad fluttered one hand, looking for words— "He got upset. He wasn't rational. He said he had to tell. I got angry, and decided that if words were useless, maybe I could scare him into silence. A beating he would never forget. I only meant to scare him; I even planned it out. I waited until he was alone. I didn't even mean to use a gun, but it was right there in the study when I went by, and I thought it would frighten him more if I took it with me. So I did. I didn't mean to shoot. I didn't even check to see if it was loaded. I held it against his head and yelled at him. But he started crying and screaming. He tried to pull my hand away from his head. The gun went off. I put it in his hand and ran home to wash all my clothes. They found him that way, the gun in his hand, powder burns on his fingers, and a hole where his head used to be. No one ever found out the truth. I waited a bit so it wouldn't look suspicious, then I left."

His eyes grew into twin pools of anguish. He spread his hands. "I couldn't stay, not after that. And you were still there, walking like a zombie, reminding me every day of what I'd done. The affair wasn't as secret as we'd hoped, anyway. It was too much for all of us when everything came out. It's not like I meant to hurt the boy. It wouldn't have done any good for me to confess. I just ran, and I never stopped running. Not until now, today. I had to tell you."

I felt the icy calm return. I knew what I had to do. I gave the sax to Louise and pushed her gently into one of the chairs. She raised her eyebrows in question. I turned back to the thing in the bed. "I'm going to kill you, Dad."

He nodded. "I hoped you would." He gestured at the machinery. "It can't be worse than all this. And I'm tired, boy. Tired of all of it. Tired of the running, the hiding, the lying. Tired of life."

I reached for the tubes that entered his abdomen under the tape, planning to yank them out. I didn't think about the consequences for myself. I didn't think about the alarms that would no doubt go off.

He lifted a hand. His eyes clawed at my face. "Ethan, before you do that, promise me something."

"What?"

"Play Jackie's song. He was a good boy, and the world deserves to know him the way you did."

I nodded. "I will." I could do it now. After twenty-five years, I finally understood the dark harmonies that kept intruding. I'd heard it fully back then, when I was too young to understand. And in later years, when I would have understood, I kept rejecting those parts of the song. No longer. The bitter would marry the sweet, and the whole would become something greater than the parts. I knew it. I could hear it already—strong, dear God, strong and terrible from the first note to the last.

The heart monitor pinged softly, steadily. The other machines hummed. They could keep him alive for a while yet. I wondered if it would be a worse punishment for him to continue living, knowing that someone else knew his secret. But no, I couldn't excuse his actions, couldn't bring myself to forgive. "See you in hell, Dad," I said.

Louise stood up, put her hand over mine. "If you pull that tube," she said, "we'll do it together."

"No. Look away and have no part of it. This is murder, Lou."

"Is that what it sounds like to you?"

What an odd thing to ask. What else could it be? I wasn't self-indulgent enough to pretend it was justice. "What would you call it?"

"That doesn't matter," she said. "What does it *sound like* to you?" She pressed the saxophone into my hands. "What do you *hear?*"

The tune I'd been hearing in the car came back to me. I realized that the walls of the room thrummed with it even now, and I hadn't been listening. I looked at my father and slowly brought the sax to my lips.

The melody started off small, a little boy. As it grew it turned dark. Vulture wings beat at me, drove the melody into odd moments of pain. Here, a glimpse of solitude; there the isolation one feels in a crowd. No difference. A rush of notes fluttered up the scale, screaming out the essential quandary of being alive, of being human, of being ineffectual, of knowing your utter worthlessness. Love became a sour thing, tainted, ruined by a yearning for the unattainable. The sax bleated and moaned, wept for the purity that might have been. A series of low, pulsing notes kept recurring, shame and anger, like a backbeat, driving everything else. And odd moments, almost free from guilt, almost free from regret, light, sweet, piercing, like rays of sunlight across a dark room, notes that mingled with the mounting horror and gave it definition.

The melody grew into adolescence and the bright moments grew fewer. Mordant fear, mingled with resentment, throbbed through the sax, brought tears to my eyes as I played, for I recognized the tune at last.

It was a soul song, certainly, but not my father's, not Jackie's. It was mine. I couldn't have done anything more terrible to him than to let him hear it. The anguish, the years of longing, the anger, beat on him like waves of accusation.

"You shaped me," said the music, "but I reject you." The intensity picked up, driven to a frenzy of notes—high, sharp, piercing. I threw it at him, pummeled him with it, slapped his face with it. "Look what you have done," the music screamed. "Look who you are." The sax squealed out the searing white-hot guilt, the vampiric nature of my gift, my soul. "Look at who I am!"

Raw and unfinished, ugly and fierce, it was nevertheless mine. I owned it, and I owned up to it. Denial and resentment could carry me only so far. I went on from there, grew beyond my father's part in my soul song, left him behind like a dark nightmare. I could finally let him go. The song turned a corner, leaving the hatred behind. I wrestled with the melody until it rang true, until no trace of the grim memories remained. Lou and Scotty started to shine through my song, and it was stronger for their presence. They were part of it, part of me—an essential melodic sequence that made my song whole. Now the notes blew wild, directly from my soul.

Out of the chaotic melody something new emerged. Something powerful, something proud, something capable of going on. The sax soared in triumph. I pushed the limits of the instrument and blew past them. The melody was free and clear now, and it was mine. By God, it was mine.

I let the final notes fade away. Lou's eyes shone. My father lay crying quietly in the bed. The heart monitor missed a beat, warbled, then set up a steady chirping. A buzzer sounded off in the distance. A minute later, the room swarmed with starched white uniforms. Twenty minutes after that, they pulled the sheet over his face. Lou and I left together, and stayed together, leaving my father and his dead secrets behind us.

"Jackie" hit the stores not quite a year later, a few weeks before Louise gave birth to our second son. It topped the charts, of course, but I only cared that I'd finally been able to lay my friend to rest. Once his song stopped monopolizing my brain, I started listening more intently than ever before. I listened to Lou, and learned her soul song, not because she was dying, but because she was living the hell out of her life, enriching everyone who heard even the barest hint of her song.

I didn't need the training wheels anymore. I didn't need grief or loss to call forth soul songs. I heard them everywhere I went, from every person I met. They pounded over me, overwhelming at first, then eventually just part of me, the natural culmination of the wild talent with which I'd been born. For a few people, those who'd become lost, or who were trapped in grief, I sang their soul songs to them. They wept with recognition and acceptance, and, who knows, maybe a few of them found healing.

I listened to our new child's squalling and began to pick out the notes that would define his life. But I listened to my own song most of all, marveling at the harmonies that were only possible now that I'd let the bitterness go. I was amazed that I could love myself, too, and that my song, while complete, wasn't done yet. There were untold key changes, transitions and new stanzas yet to come before the finale arrived.

And when the finale does arrive? I'll sing it, of course, and it will be a solo, as all last songs must be. I wondered idly if I should arrange to have it recorded, but then realized I'm too busy *living* my life to worry about a concert I wouldn't have to perform for decades. The future could take care of itself, as could, at last, the past.

ON THE TRAIN TO OXFORD

I took the train back to Oxford after a day at the British Museum in London, my head full of history, my feet glad to be resting. The clatter and clack of the wheels bumping over the ties provided an omnipresent throb that only accentuated my fatigue. I let the vibrations of the train lull me to sleep.

Every now and then, the train would stop, let off some passengers, admit others. It woke me every time, but I would drift away again as soon as the doors sighed closed. Since it was the end of the day, and most of the passengers were commuters, more got off than on, and the once-crowded compartment incrementally emptied its load into London's northwest suburbs.

At some point after dark, with more than half the trip left to go, I opened my eyes to find a boy sitting across from me, on the bench facing mine. Only a dozen other passengers remained in our compartment. I wondered if he'd been there all along, revealed now only because the crowd had thinned, or if he had boarded or maybe just changed seats at a recent stop.

He stared rigidly out the window into the blackness of the night. He might have been counting the occasional lights that streaked past. He clutched a shabby leather briefcase tightly, as though afraid someone would try to steal it from him. From the top corner of the briefcase half a sock protruded, white against the brown leather, flapping forlornly with the swaying of the train. His face was resolute, his gaze unwavering from the invisible landscape outside. He seemed too young to be traveling alone at night, but I didn't know what was normal for the British. His trousers were some kind of fuzzy purple corduroy, and he wore an unzipped white windbreaker over his blue button-down shirt. I wondered how he could stand wearing a jacket in this humidity. Even with the compartment's windows gaping, I felt stifled by the never-quite-rain that the British simply call overcast.

The other passengers were sullen and mostly quiet. I sat up, rummaged under the bench, and hauled up my rucksack. The boy flinched when I moved, then relaxed when I did nothing more threatening than pull out a paperback and flip it open. He jumped at every cough from the other passengers, was startled by the crackle of a newspaper being smoothed open. On occasion, he scanned the rest of the compartment, flicked his eyes rapidly past mine, then returned his attention to the window. I became convinced he was too young to be riding alone, and pretended to read so he wouldn't know I was watching him. He had brown hair, thin features, green eyes, and a missing bicuspid. I guessed he was around nine or ten years old. Except for checking over his shoulder, his only motions were an occasional blink of an eye or the slow clench of a nail-bitten hand on his briefcase.

One by one, as each successive station appeared from the gloom, the other passengers abandoned the train for the sticky warmth of the summer evening. At length, only the boy and I were left, rushing on into the night together. The silence between us was overwhelming, an inchoate brooding of unspoken questions, mute answers. His skin was clear with the near-translucency of youth, and I could pick out the pulse in his neck. His heart was racing, his breathing shallow and rapid. He was so obviously being brave and trying to be unobtrusive about it.

Finally, I couldn't stand it any longer. I closed the paperback and stuffed it back into my rucksack.

"You're running away, aren't you?" I asked.

The boy glanced up at me, wary, his green eyes registering surprise and fright for a moment, then going flat and unreadable.

"You're not English," he said softly, perhaps accusingly. His voice had that breathy quality only pre-adolescents seem to manage, a mode of phonation in which more air escapes the vocal folds than is necessary to produce words.

I tested the Oxford accent I'd been cultivating for months: "That's not an answer. Are you running away?"

He snorted. "American."

I spread my hands. "Guilty."

He looked away again, his hands grappling with his briefcase as though it were a live thing he was trying to hold down. He spoke to the window, not me. "I only sat here because you were asleep," he said.

"I'm awake now, and you're still sitting here."

"Okay, I'll move then," he said, standing up.

"Wait! How did you know I was American?"

The unexpected question captured his curiosity, made him pause, made him actually meet my eyes for a full second. His affect remained impenetrable as he explained, "Away. You said running *away*. It's running off, scarpering, or doing a runner."

I laughed gently, trying to put him at ease. "I'll remember that," I said, resuming my native Chicago timbre and cadence. "Would you like to hear my fake Yorkshire accent? It sounds like Irish to most people. Don't ask me how."

He snorted again, still standing half-turned toward the aisle. "Don't bother." Yet I'd derailed his instinct to flight with my pitiful humor. I think he decided I wasn't dangerous, being American and likely well-meaning, but stupid. He sat down again, clutching his briefcase, tugging at a trouser leg. We were on the long haul now, with no more stops until we reached Oxford.

"Look," I said after it was clear he wouldn't continue the conversation without help. "I'm a stranger. You'll probably never see me again. So why don't you tell me why you're running away, um, off? It can't hurt."

He didn't say anything for a long time, so long that I thought maybe I'd been wrong about him. Maybe he took this train every night. Maybe he was going to visit his grandmother or something. But then, in a very small voice, he said, "How did you know I was running off?"

I reached over and flipped the corner of the sock with my forefinger and smiled at him, though, of course, that wasn't how I had known. He guiltily stuffed the sock inside the case and smiled back at me, hesitantly at first, then ruefully genuine. It was enough to start him talking.

His name was Kevin; he was ten years old. He didn't have any money left, didn't even know where the train was headed. He lived just a few blocks from Paddington station in downtown London, and had climbed on the first outbound train in an effort to escape. In the gloom and noise of the train, we seemed to be in a private world, and it was easy for him to talk, easy for me to listen. I won't repeat much of what he said —he yielded his story under the rose, as it were, in confidence. It suffices to say only that I learned about his family, his friends, his schoolmates, and his unhappiness. He talked for a long time, with only sympathetic nods from me needed for permission to continue.

With the unconscious self-absorption of a child, sure that his problems were the hub of world concern, he laid out his life, never asking my name, nor indeed asking any questions, save one. Wistfully, after a longish pause when he'd finally run down, he said, "Why do people have to fight all the time?"

I didn't have a good answer to this, but I told him that it's normal for people to get caught up in the moment, say things they didn't mean. Normal to forget that words could hurt. People fought when they were frustrated or angry, but were usually sorry about it afterward.

I saw no bruises, no signs of abuse. His ability to open up to me, to be so vulnerable, meant that he was loved at home. He suffered no essential penury of spirit, no deep-seated damage. Whatever fighting he referred to, it was ordinary family strife. I got the sense that maybe his father shouted after a few too many pints, but Kevin had said everything he cared to say. I granted him the grace of not asking for more.

I talked for a while longer, though, telling him about my own childhood, and how I'd never understood anything, either. I hadn't tried leaving home, but I'd been sure for several of my teen years that I must have been adopted, because I couldn't *possibly* be related to the others in my family. I told him that understanding came from experience, and that experience took time, but that it would get easier as he finished growing up. I told him about the tremendous power of practicing forgiveness, the sacred importance of being generous with his time, his love, and his life. I wondered a bit, listening to my own words, if I were preaching to myself or to him. It probably didn't matter. There was a void to be filled, and I filled it.

He listened with a hungry expression, eager to be reassured, eager to give up his rebellion now that he'd surrendered to the kindness of a stranger. I merged my talk into the standard lecture about the dangers for a youngster traveling alone, and he agreed to return home. He didn't need much persuasion, for he was bravely blinking back tears the whole time. I wanted to touch him, to ruffle his hair or put my hand on his shoulder, but I think what he needed most was just to have someone *listen*, to take him seriously. We rode the train in silence then, and I carefully failed to notice his tears.

When we arrived at Oxford, the muggy fog finally turned to a light rain. We crossed to the other side of the station, and I waited with him on the platform for the next train heading to Paddington. The water beaded on Kevin's windbreaker, trickled down my collar, and it cooled off enough that he pulled up the zipper. When the train showed up, I got a quiet word in with the conductor, then shook Kevin's hand, paid his fare, and sent him home. I had suggested accompanying him, but he insisted it wasn't necessary. He didn't wave or offer thanks, but he did say good-bye, and his eyes said everything else. He would be okay.

I stood in the drizzle watching until the lights of the train were long out of sight, then walked the half-mile to my rented room at the university. I hoped I'd made a difference, but I knew that I'd made a friend, even though I would never see him again.

It is such a strange and terrible world, the world of boys trying to become men. A boy stands within an emotional fortress and gazes out on the encroaching chaos with fierce independence and tremulous pride. Yet a single blow can topple those carefully constructed battlements. There are so many unwritten and unspoken rules which must be learned and obeyed, so many conflicting urges and desires to experience and to understand.

Yet each time the castle ramparts are breached and repaired, we build the walls thicker and base them on a more solid foundation. Thus do we refute entropy and become more as time goes on, rather than less.

He never did tell me why he was running off, not the details. That was something private, part of his battle between pride and shame, part of his battle to understand, part of his battle to forgive, and part of his battle to stand bravely on his own.

His fortress, like every boy's, was bricked with agony and mortared with fear, built privately, stealthily, in the darkness of a bedroom at night.

PRIOR PUBLICATIONS

Eight of the stories in this collection have been previously published, some in substantially different form. The remaining ten stories appear for the first time here.

"Waiting for Grampa to Die"

    – *Midnight Zoo* magazine, v2n3, 1992.

"Extraction"

    – (print) *Galaxy* magazine, Second Series, v01n03, 1994.

    – (audio) *Galaxy Audio Project #4*, read by Catherine Oxenberg, 1995.

"Miracle at Devil's Crick"

    – *Witch Fantastic*, DAW Books, 1995.

"Dying He Dreams, Dreaming He Dies"

    – *Between the Darkness and the Fire, Darkfire* Volume I, Wildside Press, 1998.

"Snowball's Chance" – writing as Lawrence Fitzgerald

– *The Age of Wonders,* The *Darkfire* Anthologies, Volume III, SFF Net, 2000.

"They Went Up" – writing as Lawrence Fitzgerald

– *Bones of the World, Darkfire* Volume IV, SFF Net, 2001. (Nominated for the 2000 Best Short Fiction award by *Gaylactic Spectrum* Awards. Selected by PFLAG's Austin Texas chapter for their Our Voice award.)

"Rite of Passage" – writing as Lawrence Fitzgerald

– *Beyond the Last Star*, *Darkfire* Volume V, SFF Net, 2002.

"Out of Memory" – writing as Brian Springer

– *Beyond the Last Star*, *Darkfire* Volume V, SFF Net, 2002.

ABOUT THE AUTHOR

Jeffry Dwight is an author, editor, musician, pencil artist, *quondam* poet, programmer, and father of two sons. He was born in Illinois, and currently lives in the suburbs of Dallas, Texas. In 2014, he received the *Kevin O'Donnell, Jr. Service to SFWA Award* from the Science Fiction & Fantasy Writers of America. Of himself, Dwight says, "I hate writing, but love having written."

In addition to short fiction and a book of poetry, he has authored or co-authored multiple textbooks on programming and Internet technologies. Before that, he worked in social services among developmentally disabled and abused/neglected children and adults. All of these experiences inform his storytelling.

Dwight is a self-taught singer-songwriter who plays keyboards, guitars, drums, and several other instruments. His style covers ballads, jazz, and 70's-like soft rock. His songs are available on YouTube, Amazon, Spotify, Pandora, iTunes, Apple Music, and other services. You may listen for free on YouTube, or purchase the albums in MP3 format from Amazon.

Dwight is currently working on *All the Shades of Grey*, the first volume of The Sundering Saga, a science fantasy trilogy due out soon. His brief book of poetry, *Phantas*, is available from Amazon and other venues.

Explore more creative works by Jeffry Dwight:

Amazon Author Website: https://amzn.to/3y7UznI

Music on Amazon:
    All Jeffry Dwight results: https://amzn.to/3rAeOYM
    All Jeffry Dwight Album results: https://amzn.to/3rxUI16

Albums:
    Changes: https://amzn.to/3iJuuov
    In My Right Brain: https://amzn.to/3rvRZp0
    Vintage: https://amzn.to/3kSBRMN

YouTube Channel:

YouTube Links:
    Changes: https://bit.ly/2V7L8G3
    In My Right Brain: https://bit.ly/3y6IkYl
    Vintage: https://bit.ly/3kSE09L